A
HERO
FOR
ANTONIA

A
HERO
FOR
ANTONIA

Elisabeth Kidd

Walker and Company
New York

Copyright © 1986 by Linda Triegel

First published in the United States of America
in 1986 by the Walker Publishing Company, Inc.

Published simultaneously in Canada by John Wiley & Sons
Canada, Limited, Rexdale, Ontario.

Library of Congress Cataloging-in-Publication Data

Kidd, Elisabeth.
  A hero for Antonia.

  I. Title.
PS3561.I327H47   1986   813'.54   85-31517
ISBN 0-8027-0877-3

Printed in the United States of America

10 9 8 7 6 5 4 3 2 1

For Lee—at last

=== 1 ===

ANTONIA FAIRFAX STARED dreamily out of her bedroom window on the west front of Wyckham, from which a fine prospect presented itself even at this early hour of a January morning. Pockets of mist lingered among the leafless beeches at the edge of the home wood, and a lacy film of frost decorated the sloping lawn, which was dotted with slender poplars. But Miss Fairfax was oblivious to the lure of the natural beauty around her.

The immediate cause of her abstraction was the letter which fluttered between her slender fingers and at which she glanced frequently, as if to assure herself that the words she had already committed to memory were really there and not merely written on her imagination.

My dear Antonia, it has been too long a time . . .

It had been, indeed, six years since Antonia had last seen Charles Kenyon. It pleased her to think that Charles's consciousness that the end of their separation was in sight had prompted him to write such an uncharacteristically impulsive letter—so unlike his others, which might have been published in the *Morning Post* for all the world to read.

Your beauty is engraved on my memory. . . .

That passage did cause Antonia's cheeks to colour a little. Really, he should not write such things—it was most improper! Worse, it set down in black and white what could no longer be true in reality. Antonia snatched up the looking glass she had resorted to when she read the letter through the first time, peering into it for signs of the ravages of age, but even she could find none to pretend to laugh away when the inevitable mannerly coolness came into Charles's eyes.

At five-and-twenty, Antonia's clear complexion and candid blue eyes were those of a girl. To be sure, her nose was uncompromisingly straight rather than sweetly retroussé, and she was unfashionably rounded of figure. But her careless curls were a rich guinea-gold, her much mended but gaily coloured dressing gown was undeniably becoming, and her generous mouth was invariably curved into a warm smile. She looked like no one's notion of a maiden aunt of advancing years—certainly not her own.

My father tells me how well you have managed Wyckham since your brother's tragic death, and I confess I seized upon that as a reason for your coming to London with Isabel. Surely you will not deny yourself a well-deserved holiday. . . .

A holiday? Oddly enough, she had felt no desire to leave Wyckham for some time now. It had been difficult at first, to be sure, but she was proud of her management of the estate left to her charge on Anthony's death three years before. The ladies in residence there were now quite adept at their little economies, and so practised in the harmless lies they told themselves to prove how little their straitened circumstances mattered to them that they finally had become very cosy in their illusions.

This very morning, Antonia was comfortably ensconced on a velvet sofa facing a warm fire, before which a large grey cat was dozing peacefully. A portable breakfast table arranged before her held a steaming pot of coffee, a half-eaten dish of apple compote and cream, and several varieties of cakes and preserves. There was also, crowding out all the rest, a large ledger opened to a lengthy column of figures, which she had been re-adding in an effort to come up with a more agreeable total. To be sure, a surplus of eighty pounds for the last quarter was nothing to be sneezed at in view of the losses of preceding years, but Antonia's conscience did not permit her to crow about it either. Rather, she sighed, folded up her letter, and regarded the sleeping cat with an unkind eye.

"Wake up, Balthazar! It is too bad of you to sleep when the price of hens is so shockingly low—and everything else appears to be going up! Perhaps we ought to raise partridges instead? Not that anyone would buy them when it is so much more entertaining to shoot them oneself."

Balthazar blinked sleepily and expressed a lamentable lack of interest in the price of livestock.

"Yes, well, I was not raised to a life of cheese-paring and chipped china, either, but I do not shut my eyes to it!"

Antonia reached out to stroke her favourite cat and thought for a moment how pleasant it must feel to be as unconcerned as he was about the source of his next dish of cream. She looked down again at her paisley dressing gown and could not help noticing that the fall of lace at the sleeves was decidedly shabby and no longer very white. She sighed again, and wondered if Charles harboured any desire to indulge her with lace and cream teas.

Your brother would not have expected such a sacrifice as for you to bury yourself in the country, Charles's letter had gone on, as if having once begun, he was determined to marshal every possible argument to further an end Antonia had no wish to dispute. *And of course, little Isabel must have a companion—I dare not say chaperone, for that sounds far too drab to describe Isabel's lovely young aunt—as well as her godfather Kenyon to sponsor her debut. . . .*

It had been Anthony's ambition to give his daughter Isabel a dazzling season, but now it had fallen to Charles's father, Philip, to carry out the old plan. Anthony had been a kind and loving father, but his death—which had occurred unexpectedly but characteristically in an accident when he was leading the field on the turbulent first day of the Quorn—had left his affairs in much the same disorder as his dressing room. It soon became apparent that for all his charm, Tony had possessed no head for business. Neither, for that matter, had his sister, Antonia, who had been raised by doting parents to be equally charming and even more decorative and to conceal her native intelligence behind a lovely countenance and an infectious laugh—to be praised, indeed, for the very frivolousness of her existence.

It was true that she had welcomed the task of repairing their fortunes mainly as a palliative to her grief over her beloved Tony, but later, when her mind had been activated by the challenge of running the estate, she found quite simply that she enjoyed it. She loved her home, and thrived equally on the quiet of her sunny, many-windowed room and on her long rides over the square fields and exhilarating slopes of the country near Wyckham. And if occasionally she felt a stab of regret for the life she might have lived had her family not been what it was, she never regretted her loyalty to them.

Antonia's younger brother, Carey—as charmingly self-centered as the rest of the Fairfax brood—had gone off to the wars well before Anthony's death with a commission in the most decorative regiment he could find. The life of a young lieutenant of hussars in Wellington's Peninsular

Army had suited him to a fare-thee-well, and on his few brief leaves home since, he had declared his complete confidence in his sister's ability to keep the ancestral acres from passing into the hands of their creditors. He had then gone away again as merrily as he had come, to keep his memory alive at home through the cheerful, rambling letters, which had not changed a whit since the first of them arrived from Lisbon nearly six years before.

 . . . *La Belle France, indeed!* the lieutenant had recently complained, disposing thus cavalierly of the British army's entry, after five years of bitter fighting in the Peninsula, into France. *Nothing but Rain & more Rain, & just for the novelty a little more Rain. Old Duoro's tetchy in the damp, & he don't like to sit still. Cadoux says it's his Lumbago & there's no help for it. We do not advance because of the Rain, nor may we retreat, Spain by now having been washed into the Sea. . . .*

A scarcely audible knock on her bedroom door caused Antonia to look up and wonder if she had really heard it, but before she was able to decide on this point, the door opened and her niece, Isabel, entered, wearing a frown of concentration and holding her place in the book she carried by keeping a finger inserted between the pages.

There would have been no doubt in any stranger's mind, upon beholding these two ladies for the first time, that they were related, but beyond the indefinable bond of kinship, there was little resemblance between them. While the elder reminded one forcibly of a luxuriant, full-blown rose, the schoolgirl who carefully pushed the door closed behind her was a pale bud—possibly the lovelier of the two, but that was not yet apparent. Her hair was very fair, but worn in a severe knot on the back of her head. She had a shapely small pink mouth and large grey-blue eyes framed by delicate, well-formed brows. But the gold-rimmed spectacles which concealed them, the neat but plain kerseymere gown which did little to fill out her rather too-slender figure, and a slight air of other-worldliness all combined to obscure her natural beauty.

Antonia transferred her coffee cup to her left hand in order to kiss Isabel's cheek and bid her an affectionate good morning.

"You are looking very pretty today," she said, as she invariably did in an effort to encourage Isabel to think a little more about her natural attributes than those she had cultivated by dint of much reading in Wyckham's otherwise little-used library. Just as invariably, Isabel thanked

4

her, smoothed her hair perfunctorily, and pushed Balthazar aside to make a place for herself on the sofa.

"And how is your mama this morning?" Antonia went on. This question, too, was a ritual, and Isabel did not have to consider her reply.

"Much as usual," she said, replacing her finger in her book with a ribbon she picked up from Antonia's dressing table. "She complains of draughts."

Antonia sighed. "I should think she would rather complain of the lack of air, for I vow we have hung no less than three sets of draperies in her room and one can no longer even see the windows, much less feel any hint of a draught from them."

Isabel's mother, Maria Fairfax, was a self-proclaimed invalid, having proclaimed herself such on the day following her husband's funeral and subsequently taken to her room, from which no one had yet seen her emerge. Since, despite Maria's lamentations, her health appeared to be in no way adversely affected by this unnatural seclusion, and since her small circle of friends was perfectly willing to come to her—bearing all the gossip and glacéed bonbons she could possibly desire—the family had gone along with the widow's eccentricity. Indeed, Antonia frequently thanked Providence that Maria was not to be stumbled on in other parts of the house. At least she required very little extra care or expense and seemed perfectly content with her self-proscribed lot.

"She also complains of the bed linen," Isabel reported. "She put her foot through a sheet last night."

Antonia could not help but laugh. "Oh, dear! And I suppose she will insist that it was one of ours, instead of those dreadfully musty things out of her own trousseau. But never mind. I can with all modesty boast of sufficient improvement in the accounts this quarter to at least purchase new linens. I trust you are properly impressed by my diligence?"

Isabel expressed herself transported with delight at this heartening news and even asked Antonia to explain how it had come about, but her aunt assured her that she would find the penny-farthing details excessively tedious. As if to emphasise this point, she closed the ledger she had been purusing and replaced it on the shelf. Balthazar climbed up on it to resume his oft-interrupted nap.

"What are you reading, love?" Antonia asked, since Isabel offered no opening by which she might approach the subject of Charles's letter.

"Mrs Hannah More's *Practical Piety*," Isabel replied, sinking Antonia's heart to her slippers. It was a long leap from the fervent Mrs More to the fashionable round of a London season.

"Oh, dear—is that all you could find to amuse you? Or have you come to the end of Papa's library at last?"

"Oh, no—in fact, Imogen lent it to me. She knew Mrs More, she says, in her tragedy-writing days. Mrs More's, that is."

"Remind me to have a word with Imogen about her acquaintance," Antonia said, none too charitably inclined toward her best friend just at that moment. But recalled to her engagement to meet Imogen in Melton Mowbray that afternoon and bring her back to take dinner at Wyckham, she let the subject drop and rose to change into her grey merino walking dress. Isabel watched critically as, dissatisfied with their effects, Antonia then discarded one shawl after another; none suited the grey. At last she settled on a lace fichu that had the merit of softening the severe lines of the gown. She then stared reflectively into the mirror until Isabel broke the silence.

"I like your hair done in that fashion," she remarked. "Is it one of Esme's creations?"

"Yes, she claims it is the very latest mode—in Leicestershire, at any rate."

She turned back to Isabel then and, abandoning any notion of presenting her case cautiously, blurted it out. "Isabel, should you like to go to London in the spring? You know that your godfather, Mr Kenyon, has been saying forever that he would sponsor you when the time came, and today I have had a letter from Charles—that is, written by Charles at your Uncle Philip's request—inviting us both. And it seems such a good time to go, for although he is perfectly able to frank such an undertaking, we do have that little extra money—or at least, our credit has been restored—so that we need not be too much of a burden on him and can indulge in some lovely new clothes as well."

She came to a slightly breathless halt and looked to see how Isabel would take this suggestion, but her niece only lowered her eyes and said, "I thought you were going to spend it on new bed linen."

Antonia mentally apostrophised herself for her loose tongue, but laughed and sat down on the sofa again to hug Isabel. "There—you see how sadly frivolous I am still! I would *much* rather buy us both new bonnets and sleep in darned and redarned sheets. But the point is, love, that we both need a little change, and we should seize the opportunity. Don't you agree?"

When Isabel said nothing, Antonia cast out the lures she had previously prepared as most likely to appeal to her serious-minded niece. "Think of the museums we might visit," she coaxed her, "and the concerts and plays we might attend! Should you not like to see the great Edmund Kean perform Shakespeare?"

Isabel replied that her curiosity to see Mr Kean was outweighed by her suspicion that he could not be half so wonderful as everyone said he was, but she did confess to a desire to visit Dr Johnson's house and to gaze upon Lord Elgin's famous marbles.

Antonia wondered momentarily if there might not be more stages necessary to this persuasion than she had anticipated, but she put on a bright smile and exclaimed, "And why should you not see them! I daresay they will be most enlightening."

Isabel smiled serenely, in a way she had that made Antonia feel herself particularly superficial, and said, "What about you, Antonia? I have often thought that you must miss all the gaiety and excitement of the season, hidden away here in our quiet little life."

"Well, perhaps I do—a little," Antonia said, snatching at any straw to convince Isabel of the delights she would be missing. "There is something for every taste in London—indeed, you must remember Dr Johnson's maxim that says if a man is tired of London, he is tired of life."

"A lofty recommendation. Have you any other such in your pocket, Antonia—for future arguments?"

Antonia saw that Isabel was teasing her, and felt even more as if she were the younger and sillier of the two—not that Isabel had ever been silly, but Antonia occasionally wished that she had provided a more uplifting example. But then Isabel surprised her by leaving off her teasing and saying, with perfect composure, "You need not try so hard to cajole me, Antonia. I know why you would like us to go to London, and I am perfectly willing to try."

"Try what, darling?"

"To find a rich husband, of course. I know that one of us must do so in order to provide for the others and to bring Wyckham back to its former prosperity, and I do not mind, Antonia, truly. At least, I shall not mind if he is not old or unkind or . . . unintelligent."

Antonia's first coherent thought on hearing this remarkable statement—delivered so calmly!—was that far from being a bad example to Isabel, she must inadvertently have provided all too potent a one. What else but her aunt's folly could have persuaded this innocent child that such a sacrifice was necessary on her part?

"But, Isabel!"

"No, you need not try to persuade me, either, that such a marriage is not for me. I have thought about it and decided that it will suit me quite well to be married to a gentleman who will expect of me only that I run his household well—for I am well capable of that, you know—and who will otherwise allow me to do as I please. I understand that most fashionable marriages are just such arrangements, with none of the muddled emotions that accompany romantic love to interfere, and that seems to me a most sensible way to go about it."

This effectively removed Antonia's remaining powers of speech, so that she did not even reply to Isabel's calm "Good morning" as she went off to continue her daily round in, no doubt, the same eminently practical spirit in which she had delivered her modest proposal. Her bemused aunt sat down on her sofa again for a moment to collect her wits.

"Well!" she exclaimed to herself finally. "What is one to make of that?" She stood up and addressed the question to Balthazar, but he had no answer either. "Then I shall have to consult with Imogen. Thank heaven she has more sense than any of us foolish females here!"

Antonia gathered up her cloak and muff and set off in a spirit quite as determined as Isabel's. However, she had no sooner descended the stairs into the front hall than she was confronted by a further setback in the person of her formidable housekeeper, Mrs Medwin, who stood firmly in her path with her black brows knitted in concern and her thin lips set in disapproving lines. She was listening to something being said to her by the butler, but Belding spoke so low that Antonia was unable to overhear any of it.

"Good morning!" she said cheerfully, breaking into the tête-à-tête. "I see by your long faces that some new disaster has befallen the household since last evening. I wonder what it could be?"

Belding, whose lugubrious mien would have been alarming if it had not been habitual, was accustomed to his young mistress's unorthodox sense of humour and took no offence at her interpretation of what he considered the proper demeanour for a family retainer of his age and dignity.

"Pardon me, Miss Antonia, but I desired merely to enquire what wine you wish to have served with dinner this evening?"

Antonia assured him that he himself was the best judge of that, and that she would leave the matter entirely in his hands.

"However, I know that Mrs Curtiz is very partial to the Madeira my brother laid down in her honour. We will have some of that after dinner, I think. Will you be so good as to bring up a bottle, Belding?"

"Yes, Miss Antonia."

Her butler bowed stiffly and took his leave, and Antonia turned to Mrs Medwin. Given the floor, the housekeeper launched into a lengthy catalogue of the tribulations she had overcome since rising that morning. Antonia listened attentively, standing erect with her head slightly bowed and her hands folded in her skirt, an attitude which Mrs Medwin took as encouragement to emphasise the weight of every word she uttered, but which in fact concealed Miss Fairfax's lamentable tendency to smile at her housekeeper's earnest catechism. Mrs Medwin had no small number of words to expend on the treachery of a new housemaid, who had broken one of the Sèvres teacups, thereby disrupting the entire set (the maid being infinitely more replaceable), as well as sundry other deficiencies in other members of the household staff. These she concluded with a recital of the inexcusable (but unspecified) sorties by Cook into Mrs Medwin's area of jurisdiction, with the result that Mrs Driscoll had grossly neglected her own duties and, in short, there was no fish course for dinner.

Antonia attempted to relieve her housekeeper's gloom by expressing a joking reluctance to drive all the way home from Melton Mowbray with fresh fish in a very small gig, but Mrs Medwin was not to be so easily diverted by her mistress's cajoling tongue as was Belding, and Antonia finished with a solemn promise to have one of the bailiff's sons go out and catch their dinner.

"As for the teacups—oh, good morning, Baskcomb!"

This last was directed at the groom, who had come into the house at that moment in search of her, carrying his hat in his hands and bringing with him an unmistakeable odour of stables. Mrs Medwin sniffed conspicuously and Antonia hastened to remove her from the scene.

"Thank you, Mrs Medwin, that will be all. Pray do not take Betsy any further to task over the breakage. It is of no significance. Baskcomb, have you the gig ready? Thank you!"

She smiled at the groom, not because she was any more partial than Mrs Medwin to horsey odours in her front hall, but because she liked Baskcomb and would have been sorry to think he dared not venture into her house at all.

Baskcomb's broad, weatherbeaten face broke into a wide grin, and, still holding his hat to his belt, he followed her outside. It was a bright, crisp day, the first break in a long, cold winter that would yet freeze the Thames at London and bring hardship upon the rest of the country. But Baskcomb was an optimist after his mistress's heart.

"Fine day, Miss Antonia, if I may say so!"

"It is indeed, Baskcomb. We are fortunate to have such weather this time of year. Do you think it will hold?"

"Ay, I'd give it another fortnight," the groom replied large-mindedly, helping Antonia into the gig and handing her the ribbons. "You would not wish me to go with you, Miss? Dolly here has been cooped up for a week, and she's feeling a mite skittish this morning."

"Dolly and I understand each other perfectly, Baskcomb, but thank you all the same."

Baskcomb, accustomed to Miss Fairfax's habit of jauntering about the countryside in no company but her own, made no further attempt to intrude himself, and wagged his head paternally as she drove away.

Dolly set off at a brisk pace, but she had not yet reached the edge of the park surrounding Wyckham when Antonia perceived a horseman coming through the gate in her direction. She recognized her bailiff, Ned Fletcher, and brought Dolly to a halt. Ned was in the act of closing the gate behind him when he heard the gig and looked around.

"Good morning, Miss Fairfax!" he called to her.

"Good morning, Ned."

She was occupied for a moment in quieting Dolly, who was clearly disappointed at being checked before she had got into her stride. Ned rode up to the gig and had a quiet word in Dolly's ear, which seemed to appease her. Ned Fletcher was a tall, angular man, who sat his horse with an awkwardness that belied his considerable equestrian ability. He took off his black slouch hat when he addressed Antonia, revealing dark features and a lopsided, wry smile, which lengthened as they conversed.

She sighed feelingly and said, "It seems I am not to escape so easily after all."

Ned raised a sympathetic brow. "Mrs Medwin, I suppose. Or was it Mrs Driscoll this time?"

"Both!" said Antonia vehemently. "*And* Belding!"

"You bring it on yourself," Ned reminded her. "You *will* retain all these faithful servants and you *will* pay their wages before you think of spending anything on yourself—and they know it!"

He smiled, but Antonia saw the truth of this. "I am reminded of how, as a child, I was used to burrow into the bedclothes on winter mornings. Working free of my loyal household staff is rather like working one's way free of those layers of quilting, which are warm and comforting, but suffocating when one most desires to get away!"

She favoured him with a summary of the morning's trials, and ended by saying, "I am charged with asking you if one of the boys will catch some fish for our dinner."

"Jamie will do it. He's been longing for an outing, and in this mild weather, it won't hurt him."

"Is he quite recovered from his mumps?"

"Oh, yes. Having spread them generously amongst the other five children, he found he had no further use for them himself. Where are you escaping to?"

"Melton Mowbray. But I am not escaping—I have some errands to perform there."

"How is it you go alone?"

"I am to meet Imogen Curtiz and to bring her back to dinner." As Ned was still eyeing her disapprovingly, she felt obliged to point out that there would not have been room for a third party in the gig.

"You have a perfectly serviceable—if admittedly outmoded—barouche."

"But had all the proprieties been observed, you would not be enjoying this splendid opportunity to give me a scold!"

He laughed and disclaimed any intention to do such a thing, as well as of having any errands of his own which she might execute for him in the village, and they parted both in better spirits.

Antonia reflected as she drove away that Ned was the principal reason for the ease with which Wyckham was now being run, and therefore also for her own contentment there. She had the duties to her tenants which Anthony, especially during the hunting season, had often neglected—she must visit the Hatchers, who had a new baby, and take some broth to old Silas, now she thought of it—but these tasks were not oppressive. Even if, as Charles had reminded her, she had not taken so much as a holiday jaunt to Nottingham for over a year, nor been to London since her coming-out, she had not missed these dissipations, nor even thought much about them until she had recently begun to consider how to provide Isabel with a few similar delights. But then Isabel—practical, unromantic little Isabel—had announced her intention to throw herself away on a *mariage de convenance,* and her shocked aunt could not help wondering where she had gone wrong.

She should have married; that was it. She should have behaved like a proper lady, thrown away her foolish dreams, and made a respectable marriage herself, so that she would now be in a position to foster Isabel's dreams—for she must have them, as all seventeen-year-old girls did. Proper ladies of five-and-twenty, on the other hand, were expected to have forgotten such youthful follies.

But of course, Antonia had never intended to marry anyone but Charles Kenyon. Indeed, she had gone off to London for her first season secretly betrothed to him—secretly because she had promised Anthony not to make up her mind too quickly and felt the heavy guilt of having already done so, and because, more important, Charles had agreed with Tony. But she knew that she could never give her heart to anyone but her childhood hero.

When, at ten years of age, Antonia had been thrown from her pony, Charles had picked her up and carried her all the way home. When she was twelve, he had taught her to play backgammon and cribbage and loo and all the other games she had imagined to be very grown-up and fashionable. By fourteen, when Charles had just come of age and had reached his full, impressive six feet of height, he had seemed to her, with his blond hair and smiling blue eyes, the model for every Galahad she had ever read about, and she had worshipped him. At sixteen, she herself blossomed suddenly into a sunny beauty who, however attractive now to other men, was still loyal to her dream, so that when she was eighteen and Anthony packed her off to London to see if she could not do better for herself than the son of a middling-prosperous neighbouring squire, she went simply to get it over with. She became, quite unintentionally, the belle of the season—beautiful, vivacious, and—best of all from the point of view of all the confirmed young bachelors—not in the least concerned about making a suitable match.

However, it was scarcely a month before Charles came to London to investigate the discrepancy between the number of Antonia's admirers and their lack of serious intentions, and Antonia, on an impulse prompted as much by the pleasure of seeing a familiar face as by the passion she had thus far contrived to maintain within decorous bounds, flung herself joyfully into his arms. Unfortunately, she chose to do this in the middle of Vauxhall Gardens, in sight of a number of fascinated spectators who had already been enjoying the sight of Miss Fairfax and three of her admirers dangling their bare feet in a fountain along the Italian Walk, and who lost no time in spreading the tale, to Charles's acute embarrassment.

Since there was no shrugging off the incident, Antonia embroidered upon it in an attempt to persuade Charles into announcing their engagement or, better still, eloping to the border immediately. But Charles kept his head, remembered that he was a gentleman even if his impetuous beloved had proved herself no lady, and escorted Antonia back to Wyckham, where she was to wait for the nine days' wonder she had inadvertently stirred up to die down again. Anthony rang a half-hearted peal over her. Maria could not look at her sister-in-law for weeks afterward without hartshorn-and-water at hand to lessen her palpitations. Charles returned to London on the business Antonia's escapade had caused him to neglect. The engagement was not broken, but somehow no more was said about it.

The scandal did indeed die down quickly, but Antonia remained quietly at home for a year, while Isabel, her intelligence outstripping even her tutor Imogen Curtiz's broad knowledge, began her systematic absorption of the entire Wyckham library, and Carey, as impulsive in his way as Antonia was in hers, got himself sent down from Cambridge and was boarding a transport ship to Portugal with scarcely a break in stride.

Then the year stretched into two, and three, and four. Antonia had other offers during this period, which she declined—after some practise— deftly and with growing amusement. Mr Trent had gone down on his plump knees to beg her to allow a ray of sunshine into his life; she had laughed and suggested he would do better to take a turn in the garden. Mr Romney, not knowing how to take no for an answer, proposed for the second time in a month, vowing that he could never love another, upon which Antonia forestalled a third declaration by confessing regretfully that she did not think she could say the same for herself.

She joked to Imogen Curtiz about her swains, knowing that they offered for her for no more powerful reason than that she was pretty and of an old, if unpredictable, family. It did not pain her to turn them down when they compared so unfavourably with her first love, who Antonia was certain would send for her as soon as he had made the fortune he was well on his way to achieving in the carting business he had established in London. She learned to be patient.

Then Anthony died, and she threw herself into the challenge of running the estate, losing herself in the predictable daily round of household affairs and the pleasure of watching Isabel grow up in her charge. Maria was a less pleasurable charge, but Antonia soon discovered that keeping her in tea and cinnamon toast and lending-library comforts dimmed her sister-in-law's resentment at Antonia's authority to a degree that made cohabitation between them tolerable if not precisely cosy.

After a time, she succeeded, too, if not in forgetting Charles Kenyon, at least in pushing him to the back of her mind, where he was easier to overlook behind her myriad daily concerns. His letters came regularly, if infrequently, but Antonia learned to wait for a quiet moment to read them instead of tearing them open the instant they arrived. Once, in her worshipful stage, she and Charles had been walking in a deserted lane, and he had picked a wild rose for her. She had kept it pressed in a volume of poetry for years, until one day she had taken it out and was surprised to find it no more than a bit of potpourri, no longer resembling a living thing. She threw it into the fire.

And now, Antonia could not help thinking, all this un-Fairfax-like patience would reap its reward. She had no doubt that, her advanced age notwithstanding, she was a more eligible connexion for a man like Charles Kenyon now than she had been in her giddy youth. She had proved her ability to manage a large household, had established a reputation for generosity to her dependents and graciousness to her neighbours, and had kept—she hoped—a pleasant disposition. She hoped she could still look up to Charles, but she knew she need no longer feel unworthy of his regard.

A vision of Charles's pleased surprise when they met again came into Antonia's mind, and she smiled at it. But then the accompanying vision of her own smugness at her inevitable conquest caused her to scold herself aloud, "Well, you needn't puff yourself up so!"

Dolly looked back at her enquiringly, and Antonia could not help laughing. "Oh, get along, you silly animal! You were the one in need of fresh air and exercise."

Dolly obligingly quickened her gait and carried Antonia into the tree-lined lane that ran for some distance along the border between Wyckham and Windeshiem, the neighbouring Kenyon estate and Charles's boyhood home. It was colder there, where the sunlight did not penetrate the close-knit grey branches overhead. But coming out of the lane again, Antonia could see in the distance to her left the massive stone walls of Windeshiem Hall rising behind tall cedar trees.

It was a large building and normally appeared more forbidding than welcoming, but today the sun was at such a height as to reach the narrow windows of the Long Gallery, which reflected back the light and gave the old stone an unexpected brightness and charm. Antonia smiled, for that was how she always saw Windeshiem, which was almost as dear to her as her own home, even at that time when she had nearly lost hope of ever becoming mistress of it. It was satisfying, too, to see it unchanged despite the changing seasons, ever springlike even in the deepest winter cold.

Her brief pensive mood was banished, and she began to sing to herself. Dolly trotted placidly on, over the road that she, too, knew well from old memories.

= 2 =

BENEATH THE WORLDLY veneer of the patrons of Melton Mowbray's most fashionable Lounge and Lending Library beat an unextinguishable country curiosity. This was the finest and most renowned hunting country in England, and it was true that had the great Beau Brummell himself appeared there (as he had once frequently done), he would have caused scarcely a ripple of comment amongst persons so accustomed to the glories and fripperies of fashion. Yet it was also true that, like the bored habitués of White's Club and Almack's Assembly Rooms, Melton's residents were, from whatever motive, ever alert to anything or anyone of a truly original style.

Thus the man who now stood in the light of the bow window of the Lending Library, cursorily examining a volume of poetry, was being secretly stared at by a variety of persons all affecting a sublime indifference to his presence. Mr Wakefield, an impressionable young man aspiring to the Corinthian set, looked him over and detected beneath the multicaped driving coat the unmistakeable cut of a coat (blue, very fashionable) by Weston over a veritable jewel of a waistcoat (watered silk, silver buttons) and a pair of modish buff-coloured pantaloons; the boots were by Hoby, and a beaver hat by Baxter restrained black curls that looked to be unaccustomed to discipline of any kind, but which Mr Wakefield took of be of a style with which he was as yet simply unacquainted.

Miss Amelia Pritchard, peeping out from behind her mama's ample form, had almost decided on a place for the gentleman in the novel she had obtained from these very shelves the week before (when she came with her friend Miss Nutley and *not* her mama), for he was darkly handsome and enigmatic enough to have come undiluted from the pen of

Mrs Radcliffe herself. Nevertheless, one could not deny—or could do so only reluctantly—that there was a decided air of—well, of *propriety* about him. And he was quite old, really—five-and-thirty if he was a day! It was such a pity.

The gentleman looked up at that moment, revealing under heavy black brows a pair of startlingly grey eyes. Miss Pritchard blushed and hoped she had not been observed staring so rudely at him. But Colonel Fairchild, standing near her, started, squinted, and apostrophised himself for an old fool. It was impossible, of course, for such a young man to have been there, but something about the stranger—bless him if the colonel was not struck by the oddest notion that he was young again himself and watching campfires flicker in an Indian twilight. It was very strange, to be sure!

Viscount Kedrington obligingly lowered his head, so as not to spoil the sport of the quizzers, thereby concealing from them a decided quiver in the corner of his otherwise rather harsh mouth. He was doing his best to play propriety, but Miss Pritchard would have been amazed to learn how unnatural he felt even to be standing still. In fact, he came close to oversetting himself when, upon picking up another book, he opened it to Chapter One and read: *It is a truth universally acknowledged, that a single man in possession of a good fortune must be in want of a wife. . . .*

Good God! The viscount glanced over the shop for the clerk, determined to purchase this piece of impertinence on the spot, but the clerk, in order to allow prospective buyers to consider their purchases at leisure, had beat a tactful retreat. Kedrington turned back to his book and read on in fascination for a few pages until, distracted by the sound of a departure (Miss Pritchard being dragged out of the shop by her determined mama), he pulled a watch out of his waistcoat pocket, consulted it, frowned, and looked out of the window into the street.

He was to have met Philip Kenyon here quite half an hour earlier— perhaps Kedrington had misunderstood the direction? Oh, no—there he was. And not alone. Mr Kenyon was approaching at a leisurely pace with an unexpected but—considering the gentleman's roving eye—entirely plausible excuse for his tardiness on his arm. She wore a fur-lined cloak with a hood that framed a radiant face and cheeks rosy from the brisk air of the street. She carried a large fur muff which, when Kenyon whispered something into her ear, she raised to her face to smother a bubble of laughter.

Lord Kedrington, who had of late become something of a connoisseur of feminine beauty, considered this particular lady to be a remarkable specimen, but he was not prepared for the enchanting effect of her laughter—more like the gentle cooing of a dove than any human noise—which drifted into the shop when Mr Kenyon opened the door. It ceased abruptly, however, when the lady saw the viscount, and he realised that he had been staring at her. He recovered himself, removed his hat, and made a stiff bow.

Mr Kenyon, a handsome, grey-haired gentleman who walked with a cane and an air of casual elegance, either did not see or chose to disregard the expression on the viscount's face.

"Ah, Duncan—there you are!" he exclaimed blithely. "I beg your pardon for keeping you waiting, I'm sure, but I was delayed by the happy accident of meeting this lady across the way. My dear, may I present to you the Viscount Kedrington? Our neighbour, sir, and my adopted niece—Miss Antonia Fairfax."

Miss Fairfax had pushed back her hood and stood smiling candidly up at Kedrington, who now saw that she was not the remarkably pretty girl he had first thought her, but a lovely woman with not a missish air about her. When his hesitation became pronounced, she held out her hand to him and cocked her head to one side enquiringly.

"Your servant, ma'am!" He took her hand, but rather than letting it go after the customary cursory examination, he held onto it as a thought occurred to him. "Fairfax? Ah, yes . . . "

"Should we know each other, sir? Uncle Philip tells me you are but lately returned from many years in Spain. I cannot imagine that my reputation—such as it may be—can have reached so far!"

"No, no!" he protested, abruptly letting go her hand when he recalled where he had in fact heard the name. "I was once acquainted with a certain George Fairfax, but he lived in Hertfordshire."

Miss Fairfax replied gravely that she had to her knowledge no kin in that part of the country, which failed to surprise Kedrington, who had made George up out of whole cloth.

"Duncan here will be stopping at Windeshiem for a time," Mr Kenyon informed Miss Fairfax, retrieving her unclaimed hand and tucking it into his arm once more. "Came to look the old place over—"

A barely perceptible movement on Kedrington's part halted Mr Kenyon in midstride and nudged him into another conversational path. "Told him he'd have to take potluck with us," Mr Kenyon went on, "but he don't mind that. To be sure, when he told me he'd meet me here, I thought he must be bored already—not being any entertainment at home *but* reading nowadays. What's wanting at this time of year is a cosy little dinner party somewhere. Isn't that so, m'dear?"

Miss Fairfax declined to acknowledge this broad hint, but looked as if she were hard put to keep a sober face. The viscount came to her rescue, enquiring of Mr Kenyon if he had read Mr Scott's latest poem, and if he thought it was up to his *Lady of the Lake.* Mr Kenyon disclaimed any literary opinion at all, but he was not lax in taking a hint. Admitting to an unfortunate ability—acquired in his impressionable youth—to read, he took himself off to the other side of the shop to examine, over the edge of a book held upside-down in his hand, the trim figure of a lady in a blue riding habit.

A gleam of amusement lightened the viscount's grey eyes and lingered in spite of his resumption of what he imagined to be an air of refinement, but when he turned back to Miss Fairfax, she lowered her own eyes demurely, and they discussed *Rokeby* in civil terms. Miss Fairfax regretted that such craftsmen as Mr Scott should be eclipsed by so-called geniuses such as Lord Byron.

"That is the inevitable result of fashionable crazes," Kedrington said. "When we left town, *The Corsair* was all the rage."

Miss Fairfax declared herself disinclined to read Lord Byron's latest, being quite sated with Turkish tales and Athenian maids. "I am convinced that Lord Byron desires nothing more than to create an aura of mystery about himself. I daresay he is in reality quite ordinary. But I beg your pardon—perhaps he is a friend of yours?"

"Merely an acquaintance," the viscount said noncommittally. "He has few friends. I should assure you, however, that whatever his faults, Lord Byron can scarcely be called ordinary!"

"Then you will not tell him I said so, will you?" Miss Fairfax begged of him. Indicating the volume which the viscount still clutched in the same hand that held his modish hat, she advised him, "I should purchase that novel, if I were you. It is quite out of the common way. The author is most adept at depressing pretension and showing up for precisely what they are worth such persons as—for example—wear town fashions in the country, deliberately to cast the local gentry into the shade."

Kedrington glared down at her, but she only enquired sweetly, "Grossly uncivil, don't you agree?" and precipitated the viscount—whom she had rightly perceived to be maintaining only the most precarious hold on propriety—into abandoning it altogether. Their eyes caught, and both laughed aloud. Mr Kenyon overheard them and turned his head in their direction. Kedrington had only time to whisper, "Lives Lady Disdain, Miss Fairfax?" before he rejoined them, demanding to know the joke.

"No jest, sir," said the lady. "Merely the novelty of such as Lord Kedrington in these benighted parts. We are not much addicted to London manners here."

"Pooh, nonsense!" Mr Kenyon protested. "It is not so very long ago that you yourself decreed those manners, my dear. Surely you have not forgotten when all London was at your feet?"

"I sincerely hope London has forgotten it! And if the lure of the metropolis is sufficient to keep you from home so frequently, Uncle Philip, I have reason enough to take exception to it."

Mr Kenyon smiled fondly at her. "But I only go to visit Charles, you know—when he can bear to have me underfoot. When not—why, I go somewhere else!"

Kedrington thought a shadow briefly darkened Miss Fairfax's blue eyes, but she replied lightly, "Why, yes! You are as likely to be flitting off to examine some race horse in Ireland, or a new variety of gas lamp in Bristol."

Kenyon chuckled modestly. "I'm too old to change my ways now, m'dear, however ramshackle they may be, and too old to be posting all the way here whenever Pomfret writes that such-and-such a cottage has fallen into disrepair, or to ask if I think eight sheep to the acre is too many or if we should lease out more pasturage, when half the time I haven't the least notion what he's talking about."

Miss Fairfax looked as if she could well believe this, but not being so tactless as to say so, she made no remark. Lord Kedrington paid for his book, and all three left the shop.

"We shall escort Miss Fairfax on her way," Mr Kenyon announced. "It would not be kind of us to abandon her to the ogling of every demi-beau in town!"

Lord Kedrington acquiesced with suitable gravity, but Miss Fairfax protested that she was quite accustomed to walk out alone.

"I shall be perfectly safe, I assure you, sirs! Melton is still a country town, where a lady may go about unchaperoned with no fear of being molested by gentlemen with . . . London manners!"

Mr Kenyon kept her hand imprisoned in his, however, and she made no further demur when the gentlemen accompanied her down the South Parade. It was soon apparent—much to Miss Fairfax's gratification and Lord Kedrington's chagrin—that the object of attention on the street was to be not the young lady but the fashionable gentleman. Several heads turned to watch him, and although he continued to make polite conversation, the viscount expected too much of Miss Fairfax if he believed that she would imitate his sublime disregard of a bold damsel dressed in a sable-trimmed redingote, who passed them with an appraising look and a flirtatious smile. Antonia looked back after the lady, smiling benignly in return. The viscount, caught in midsentence, sputtered to its end and protested, "Miss Fairfax, you are shameless!"

Miss Fairfax was all innocence. "I, sir?"

"Do not play the ingenue with me, madam! I know what you are about."

"But I should have imagined that to be just your style, my lord."

Curiosity compelled him to ask, "Is that how you fancy my style, Miss Fairfax?"

"Oh, I did not mean that I fancied your style at all, sir!" she replied unblushingly.

"Kenyon!" his lordship appealed in desperation. "Tell me where it is that we are escorting this lady to! We appear to be running out of village."

Having left the South Parade and the church behind, they were in fact walking down a street of cottages, at the end of which stood a small brick house with a trellissed porch. They stopped in front of it, and Miss Fairfax thanked the gentlemen for their escort. Mr Kenyon insisted that this must not be the last time they met during his sojourn in Leicestershire, and she obliged this latest hint by inviting both gentlemen to dinner at Wyckham the next day, an invitation which was quickly accepted. The gentlemen then turned back toward the village, having like Miss Fairfax left their equipage at The George, and the lady pulled at the knocker of her friend's door.

It was Imogen Curtiz's custom to open her own door, since she indulged in no servants other than a housemaid who frequently found herself with nothing to do, but Antonia's summons was answered with an alacrity which caused her to suspect that Imogen had observed her approach from behind the lace-curtained front windows. Her suspicions were confirmed when her friend opened the door, kissed Antonia on the cheek, and rather absently invited her to enter, all the while keeping a sharp lookout on the street from the corner of her eye. But presently she closed the door and devoted her attention fully to her guest.

"Come in and have some tea, my love—let me take your cloak—I have a new concoction for you to try. It has a little Darjeeling, a little dried lemon peel, a pinch of—"

"Imogen, you must not reveal all your secrets."

"Oh, my child, I have no secrets from you!" said the older woman, shepherding Antonia into a sunny alcove in the rear of the house, overlooking a small garden. She seated herself at the tea table opposite Antonia, and for a few minutes addressed to her some trifling remarks upon the weather, the state of her azalea bushes, and a shipment of tea which had unaccountably gone astray in the post.

Imogen Curtiz was a handsome woman in her early fifties. Her dark hair was streaked dramatically with grey, and she had magnificent large black eyes and a long aristocratic nose. She was rather thin—having passed through several of her late husband's illnesses with him—but she carried herself regally and reveled in a reputation for unconventionality of dress and manner. She had once appeared at one of the Fairfaxes' parties in Arab costume, giving Maria palpitations but delighting everyone else.

Today, however—there being no one to shock—she was dressed simply in a grey gown that came up to her throat in a line of small black buttons and ended with a double ruff of pointed lace. She held herself militarily erect, while gracefully pouring tea from a Chinese porcelain pot.

"But do not keep me on tenterhooks!" she admonished Antonia. "Tell me who that was who accompanied you here."

"Why, Imogen, surely you are well acquainted with Mr Kenyon," Antonia teased her.

"Oh—Philip!" Imogen exclaimed, dismissing their mutual friend with a wave of one beringed hand. "You know perfectly well I meant the other one."

"He is Viscount Kedrington."

Imogen's eyes and brows flew up. "Kedrington? Oh, surely not! No, it can't be—Desmond must be dead these fifteen years or more. This must be the—let me see—the sixth viscount? What is his name? I thought he was out of the country."

"I regret I did not ask for particulars."

"No matter. But tell me what he said to you."

Antonia did not appear to recall the interview in any detail, but she did dredge out of her fickle memory the viscount's Christian name and that he had a well-developed literary instinct. Imogen stared at her, as if this was the last thing she would have expected to hear.

"Well!" she said at last. "This Duncan is every bit as attractive as his father was, but no one would ever have accused Desmond of having a literary notion in his head—nor a grain of imagination, for that matter. My dear, you should have heard the—I suppose you may call it a suggestion—he made to me once! I laughed in his face. A remarkably effective means of ridding myself of him, but not the best thing for his pride. Don't you want that cake, Antonia? Would you rather have some bread and butter?"

"Thank you, no. Just another cup of tea, if you please."

Mrs. Curtiz eyed her speculatively. "You don't eat enough, my girl. I have some fruit and cheese, if that will tempt you."

"No, ma'am, I assure you—"

Imogen rose and crossed the room to a shaded window to the side of the garden. "When you begin to call me *ma'am,* I know you are about to turn obstinate," she said, raising the sash. She reached out and plucked two apples and a York cheese from a ledge immediately outside, where they had been keeping cool, and set these down in front of Antonia. "There, now! If you do not eat at least half of that, I shall not finish my story."

Antonia smiled. "That, my friend, is blackmail pure and simple!"

"I thought you would not be able to resist my terms."

Antonia obediently picked up her knife and began to pare an apple. "But really, Imogen, I have only the most academic interest in the family history of the—the—oh, very well! Tell me, if you must. What is the family name?"

"Heywood," said Mrs. Curtiz, making herself comfortable again. "On his mother's side, the Coverleys were Irish aristocrats of some sort—it doesn't signify. Cecily was one of the celebrated Coverley sisters, renowned beauties in their day and both heiresses. Cecily was the frail one, but she had a will of iron. To give Desmond his due, he was never afraid of her—too buffle-headed to think he should be, I suppose. At any rate, when they knew Cecily would have no more children, he spent less and less time at home. She outlived him, nevertheless, so I should not be surprised to find her son taking after her rather than that fool of a father."

She paused to see that Antonia was making satisfactory inroads on the cheese, and went on. "Desmond died, as I recall, the same year the boy came of age, so that he came into his title, his fortune, and his majority all at one stroke. Many a young man in that position would have squandered everything in a few years, but Cecily persuaded him to enter diplomatic service, and he was posted to the West Indies. Mind you, he may have sown his wild oats there—I remember some stories about a Creole countess—and he was transferred rather more abruptly than diplomatically to Spain a few years after that. I don't know what happened to him there. I heard nothing more until today."

"Is he, as was said of Byron, 'mad, bad, and dangerous to know'?"

"Oh, not so bad as all that," Imogen said, adding slyly, "If you are thinking of him for Isabel, I daresay he is perfectly eligible. He does not look to me to be a seducer—or even a hardened flirt—although if he remains single for a few more years, he may well become one."

Antonia suspected that this process was probably more advanced than her friend supposed, but she said only, "How many Coverley sisters were there?"

"Only two. The other is Duncan's Aunt Hester. There's an aunt on the Heywood side as well, but I am not acquainted with her."

"Why, Imogen, how disappointing! We are counting on you to know *everyone,* or how shall we make a success in London?"

The equanimity with which this remark was delivered did not deceive

Mrs Curtiz for an instant. She set her cup on her saucer with a clatter that made Antonia wince, and demanded, "Are you telling me that you have decided to go to London after all? Did you and Philip devise this scheme between you just this morning?"

"No, Isabel decided it," Antonia said. She hesitated for a moment, then looked at her friend enquiringly. "She has determined to marry someone of fortune in order to recover our own, and she believes that London is the most likely place to find such a someone."

There was a brief silence before Imogen said, "How very practical of her, to be sure."

Antonia protested, "But, Imogen! How could she say such a thing? I'm sure I never indicated that we were in such straits, nor—even if we were—that it was Isabel's responsibility to get us out of them! I do not understand how she can have conceived such a notion!"

Imogen smiled in what Antonia thought was a deplorably indulgent way, as if she were an ignorant child. "You must remember, my dear, that you and Isabel are two different people. Isabel has always had the levelest head of any of you Fairfaxes—although I must concede that this notion carries practicality to an extreme."

"It most certainly does! Really, Imogen, I did not know where to look when she said it, I was so taken aback."

"On the other hand," the older woman went on, as if she had not heard this outburst, "there is some merit in it. After all, what could be better for all of you, Isabel included?"

"Anything but selling herself to the highest bidder! It would be better if I married myself, than that."

"How would your marriage solve anything?"

Antonia hesitated. The idea had taken hold of her mind the moment she read Charles's letter that morning, but she saw now that she had given it little real consideration, and she could now make only the most obvious reply.

"Isabel would not then feel so . . . so pressed to take on this supposed responsibility of hers," she said. "As a married lady, I could sponsor her debut and she could then take the time to choose among her multitude of suitors the man she would be most comfortable spending her life with."

"Why should you suppose that Isabel will not decide against making a sacrifice of herself as soon as she meets someone with a face handsomer than his purse—or for that matter, that she could not love a rich man?"

"I daresay she could, but—well, it seems so . . . so cold-blooded to think of fortune first and love a poor second."

"Most people do think that way. I'm sure even I weighed all the advantages before I married Edmund, for all that I was past hope and past thirty when I met him. And here you are contemplating the same for yourself. You will forgive me, my dear, if I point out that your bringing the matter up at all strikes one as calculation every bit as cold-blooded as Isabel's."

Antonia glanced at her friend, who was regarding her fixedly if not critically. Imogen—who never criticised or condemned—had never opposed her attachment to Charles Kenyon, but Antonia had never felt quite comfortable discussing him with her either. She had always supposed this to be due to Imogen's assertedly unromantic outlook on life. However fond Antonia might be of her, she resisted pouring out her heart on those things dearest to her, for fear of meeting with, if not scorn, then that kind of amused sympathy guaranteed to take the blush off the rosiest illusion. But even more daunting was Antonia's suspicion that Imogen was right about her motives. Easing Isabel's passage into society seemed a noble goal, but to commit one marriage of convenience to prevent another presented, even to her own mind, a lowering picture of herself as a designing female of the worst kind.

There was nothing for it but to put Charles out of her calculations— and back into her fancies, where he belonged. Antonia shrugged lightly, and the smile that was never long out of her eyes began to form again.

"What a poor creature you make me out to be, Imogen! Very well—I give you my word not to interfere with whatever course Isabel may choose for herself. I can only hope that whatever it may be, she will not be handicapped by her eccentric relations. Do you suppose London will believe that I have settled down to maiden-aunthood, or will it watch for me to fall into some new scrape? Or, worse still, for Isabel to do so?"

"You Fairfaxes have never cared for what strangers think of you, as I need not remind you. Witness your perfect willingness to walk out with me! I should like, by the by, to meet this Lord Kedrington. Will you introduce me to him?"

"With the greatest pleasure. I should like your opinion. To that very end, I have invited him and Uncle Philip to dinner at Wyckham tomorrow. I naturally hoped to include you in the party, if you care to pack your things to stop over tonight."

Imogen rose with alacrity. "I shall do so this instant. Shall my dress be conformable or outré?"

"I rather think Lord Kedrington expects the worst."

"Then I shall endeavour not to disappoint him."

— 3 —

THE COMPANY AT Windeshiem consisted solely of its lord and master, Mr Philip Kenyon, and his guests, the Viscount Kedrington and Mr Octavian Gary, the viscount's secretary. Furthermore, as Mr Kenyon had been a widower for ten years, and possessed for longer than that of a peripatetic tendency that kept him away from home more often than it led him to it, it had been some time since as many as three persons had occupied the house at once, so that there was no more than a skeleton staff available to wait on them and no entertainment in the ordinary sense of the word at all. The viscount was so well accustomed to hardship, however, and young Mr Gary possessed of so adaptable a nature, that neither gave any thought to their situation until milord's valet saw fit to make certain lugubrious observations.

"That will do, Milford," his employer admonished him after a number of these complaints had been aired. The viscount was stretched out in a wing chair in the library, whence he and Mr Gary had retired with a bottle of brandy and half an hour to themselves. "Had I foreseen that you would prove yourself so ill-bred as to criticise the hospitality afforded you, I would have left you in Brook Street—or better still, sent you to Haverhill, where you would not be marked in the surrounding gloom."

"I beg your pardon, my lord. I meant no disrespect to Mr Kenyon. But it is undeniable that the fireplace in my lord's chamber smokes, and there is a decided draught coming in the north window."

"Milford, have you ever slept in a cave in Spain?"

"No, my lord."

"You should try it, Milford. Once having done so, you would find any other accommodation princely by comparison."

"Yes, my lord," said Milford, unconvinced.

Kedrington shrugged and gave it up. "Go and see to procuring some shaving water hot enough to suit your notions of my consequence. We are invited to dine this evening."

"Yes, my lord. Shall I lay out the grey superfine or the dark blue?"

"Oh God, I don't care!" muttered the viscount, sinking deeper into his chair. But as the valet opened the door to depart, he sat up again abruptly.

"Milford!"

"My lord?"

"The grey, I think. And the striped waistcoat—the narrow stripes."

When Milford, with a satisfied smile, had taken his leave, Mr Gary—who had listened to this exchange with growing amusement—smiled and revealed a quiet charm that his pale, rather solemn face lacked in repose.

"He has you well trained, I see."

Kedrington grinned ruefully. "Well, that's what I hired him for—although when Wellington recommended him to me, I didn't realise I was to be saddled with one of his insoluble disciplinary problems."

"He knows his business."

"Who, Duoro? Oh, Milford—yes, he does. I know some of my habits drive him to professional distraction—I must permit him to shave me tonight to make up for my boorishness just now—but we are learning to compromise. I now sleep with the windows only *half* open."

Mr Gary laughed, and Kedrington joined in. It was not often that Octavian indulged in such easy laughter, and the viscount liked to encourage him when he did. The youngest sibling of the large and impecunious family of a clergyman of the Methodist persuasion, the young man had been raised in circumstances which might have been expected to foster a gloomy outlook on life. However, while Octavian's demeanour was that of an only child who had adopted the sobriety of his elders—the next brothers in line having left home when he was scarcely out of leading strings—there was mixed with this a gentle sense of humour.

This quality was no surprise to Kedrington, who was friendly with Octavian's scapegrace brother Neil and who, on the strength of Neil's awed description of his youngest brother's mental prowess, had offered Octavian a post as his secretary. Octavian had accepted without hesitation, all too aware of the drain on the family finances that his continuing presence at home represented. To be sure, Neil stood to inherit a modest competence—if he behaved himself—from his childless Uncle Junius, but there was no counting on his spending it on anyone but himself. So Octavian jumped at his unexpected good fortune, and moved into the viscount's Brook Street house determined to prove to his exacting father that he, too, could make his way in the world.

Fortunately, since he had given no consideration to whether he would find employment in Kedrington's household congenial, this proved to be a matter of no consideration. After only a year, Octavian was not yet entirely at ease with the viscount's alarmingly egalitarian treatment of his staff, but he had come not only to respect him but to like him as well. He had even learned to parry deftly the sharp conversational thrusts Kedrington made in his direction.

"He's right, you know," Octavian said in response to Milford's fulminations. "The place is so cold that by the time I've reached my room—and I have more than once lost my way in this rabbit warren—I'm half-frozen. Surely you don't really mean to buy Windeshiem?"

Kedrington, who only a few days before had made up his mind not to do so, now unaccountably leapt to the estate's defence.

"I can have the doors and windows tightened," he said consideringly, "and the chimneys swept. I'd almost certainly take out several walls. In fact, I'd enjoy renovating the place. Windeshiem's far sounder and not nearly so prone to damp—whatever you may think tonight—as that mausoleum of mine in Surrey. I don't wonder my father rarely went near it, and even Mother spent most of her time in town. She wouldn't even die there, but went to my Aunt Julia's to do it."

He paused and stared reminiscently into his brandy, watching the firelight reflected in its ruby depths. Octavian waited patiently.

"No," Kedrington said, taking a sip of brandy and stretching his long legs toward the fire—which, since Philip Kenyon was a careless but never an ungenerous host, was a warm one—"there's nothing wrong with Windeshiem that can't be attributed to simple neglect, and that's easily remedied. The situation is right, and the best rooms face to the south. When the windows are cleaned and the shrubbery cut back, there will be light enough. And Kenyon is asking very little for the place, considering."

"Need you consider that?"

"No, not really. My mother was an excellent manager, and I could live on the income of what she rescued from my father for the rest of my life. That is, if Milford and my man of business—not to mention my aunts!— don't put me in Queer Street first."

He gave a short burst of laughter and confessed, "Do you know, I'm actually beginning to enjoy spending money on fripperies? I remember that Neil once told me I had the makings of a dandy, but as I was dressed at the time in a sheepskin coat, a pair of leather breeches I'd tanned myself, and boots I'd pulled off a dead Frenchman, I took him to be roasting me!"

Octavian chuckled. He had not seen his brother Neil since his last brief leave from the army, and he pressed Kedrington for anecdotes which lost nothing in the retelling, and which occupied the two men for nearly an hour. Only when Philip Kenyon came in to remind them that they must leave for Wyckham shortly did Kedrington recall something he had meant to tell Octavian earlier.

"Are you perfectly certain," Octavian asked for the third time, "that it is all right for me to accompany you? The ladies are not acquainted with me, after all."

"I assure you, you would have received a personal invitation had I been beforehand enough to mention your presence here to Miss Fairfax yesterday. However, I confess to having been in something of a muddle at the time. Which reminds me of what I wanted to say to you. Miss Fairfax has a brother in the army. I knew him briefly in Spain, but I don't want her to know that. The fact is, I once rescued him and two of his disreputable friends from a scrape in one of the lower taverns in Salamanca—where none of us was supposed to be at the time—and I wouldn't care to have to explain any of our actions in detail."

"Nor to be thought a hero," said Octavian, who was aware of some of the details of Kedrington's activities behind the scene of Wellington's campaigns in the Peninsula.

"It wasn't very heroic. Neither I nor the several other persons involved acted very nobly, even if it all turned out well enough in the end. Also, there would be the devil of a kick-up in the press!"

"I shall maintain a discreet silence," Mr Gary solemnly promised.

"You may allow yourself to indulge in polite conversation. It should not be difficult. I neglected to mention that the younger Miss Fairfax is—by Kenyon's account, at least—even lovelier than her aunt.

"Although frankly," the viscount added, ascending the broad oak staircase to their rooms, "I doubt that anyone could be."

Kedrington sank into reflexion during the brief drive to Wyckham, a circumstance scarcely noted by their host, who kept up a rambling commentary on the beauties of the countryside. Mr Gary kept his own counsel.

Even the viscount's secretary was not privy to all of his employer's plans for the future. The truth was that Kedrington had only recently come to the sobering conclusion that he was too old for further adventures. God knew, he had had enough of them to satisfy ten other men, but it was not until an unexpected squall had driven him back to England that he knew he could not go on indefinitely living at the edge of death; he had to draw back and seek firmer ground. He had almost forgotten what security and comfort were when he set tentative foot ashore at Weymouth two years before, but Fate pushed him inland. He walked to Dorchester, where he learned from a family friend of his mother's illness. Then he borrowed a horse and set out for Berkshire—and never turned back.

Cecily died a few months later, but long before that her son had made up his mind to stay at home. Half-joking, he asked his Aunts Julia and Hester for their help in reestablishing himself in society, and the ladies instantly took up this *carte blanche,* outlining a plan of campaign designed to put him, by the coming season, as much at his ease in the haut ton of London as any man could wish to be. Within a few months, Kedrington's path was prepared by his becoming a member of Brook's and Watier's Clubs and resuming his acquaintance with the Regent and a contingent of lesser royalty. He had been approved by Mr Brummell, who presented him to three of the patronesses of Almack's. He had established his credit at Tattersall's and Newmarket, redecorated his house in Brook Street, purchased a box at the opera, and sat for his portrait by Mr Lawrence.

"Good Lord, *why?*" Neil Gary had demanded by letter, when apprised of these accomplishments. His friend was hard put to explain it to him.

He could not, in good conscience, put forward the attractions of fashionable life as a reason, for these were false goals even to him, and he knew only too well how Neil would laugh when he saw that his friend was not yet broken of such habits as rising at first light in all weathers to go for a long ride before breakfast, and eating all his meals, in Julia's acerbic opinion, "like a farmer—all appetite and no taste." He was not, at first glance, a very promising candidate for entrance into Society, but he had made up his mind to settle down into a quiet life in his native land, and since he had no desire to do so in the guise of an eccentric recluse, he determined to make himself agreeable to the people he would be obliged to live with.

In this, he thought cynically, he had succeeded more through the size of his fortune than his personal attributes. In self-defence, he had developed a manner of merely raising his quizzing glass to quell a threatening mushroom, and a fund of equivocal remarks and unblushing bouncers to answer upstarts who would not be quelled by a look.

It was partly to escape the quizzers that he had fled to Leicestershire. It was true enough, however, that he wanted to buy another house and dispose of the one in Surrey, so that when he met Philip Kenyon in London, he accepted his invitation to spend a week in the country with him. Even Hester had approved of the scheme, concluding by her peculiar process of reasoning that, in spite of the pronounced lack of interest shown by her uncooperative nephew in the many young ladies she had put him in the way of meeting, he must still be considering matrimony. Why else would he want a home of his own?

Why, indeed? Kedrington wondered. Devil take it, he *had* intended to marry! He had expected that to be the simplest of matters. There were any number of females of an acceptable age and social position to choose from, and he had had leisure to study them all.

But in spite of their differing shapes and sizes, they all looked alike to him. None of them resembled the women he had become familiar with during his sojourn abroad—few of those being either eligible or acceptable—and he did not know what these gently reared specimens expected of him, nor what he might expect of them. He had been long enough in the world not to look for the sudden, at-a-glance knowledge of the rightness of a connexion that the novels called "falling in love," and he was well aware that his private vision of himself, in armour on a white horse, would arouse no more than a smile in the eyes of any damsel of his present acquaintance—none of whom stood in much need of rescue from her cushioned, adventureless life. Accordingly, he had put aside the few romantic notions that still remained to him, and trusted solely to his good judgement to tell him when and to whom to make an offer. But until now, something other than judgement had persisted in preventing him from doing it.

Judgement told him that Antonia Fairfax was a more than eligible *parti,* despite her temporarily straitened circumstances, but that other something that he ought to have outgrown now perversely wished that she were not, so that he might prove himself to her by renouncing rank and fortune to marry her in the face of universal opposition. All of which was, judgement declared, arrant nonsense.

"Duncan? Are you there?"

"Hmmm?"

The viscount sat up and, glancing out of the window of the chaise, saw that they had passed through the park surrounding Wyckham and were approaching the house itself. From behind them, the setting sun cast a rosy glow over the neat brick building and was reflected in the windows and the fanlight over the wide, white-painted door.

"Wool-gathering, sir!" said Mr Kenyon, wagging his finger sagaciously.

Kedrington smiled and apologised. A moment later, they had descended from the chaise, and the butler, presenting his most dignified front, opened the door and assisted in relieving the gentlemen of their outer wear. The viscount thanked him and turned away. Then he caught sight of Antonia Fairfax descending the staircase into the hall, and his breath stopped in his throat.

She was wearing a gown of a deep rose muslin, and her hair was tied simply with a velvet ribbon of the same shade. She came toward her guests with her hands outstretched, a smile on her lips, and a marked twinkle in her eyes.

"Uncle Philip!" she said, passing smoothly over the bemused viscount. "How prodigious elegant you look this evening."

Uncle Philip received a hug and a kiss that made him the envy of his companions, and introduced Mr Gary, who bowed and politely thanked his hostess for allowing him to intrude on the party. Antonia blithely assured him that his presence made the numbers just right and, intrigued by this quiet young man with the gentle eyes, would have gone on to draw him out a bit more, had not Lord Kedrington just at that moment coughed loudly. She looked to him, her brows in alt.

34

"Why, Lord Kedrington, is it not?" she said sweetly. "How obliging of you to come, sir."

"Obliging of you to ask me, Miss Fairfax," he responded with commendable calm.

She had to laugh at that. "I regret that my sister-in-law is indisposed and will not be joining us," she said, putting one hand into Mr Kenyon's and laying the other lightly on Mr Gary's arm. "But will you come in and meet my niece?"

Lord Kedrington followed meekly behind as she led the two gentlemen into the parlour. Miss Fairfax began to put a question to Mr Gary, but just at that moment Mr Gary forgot his manners and started involuntarily forward, becoming oblivious to his hostess the instant he set eyes on Isabel, who was seated on a sofa with Mrs Curtiz, a piece of needlepoint she had been working on her lap. She had left off her spectacles, which gave her face even more of an open, ingenuous look than it usually wore, and her hair was worked into an intricate knot on the top of her head. Her simple gown was nearly new—it having until now been relegated to a trunk as too frivolous for daily wear—and its pale blue colour emphasised her large, luminous eyes. When she raised them and caught Mr Gary's stare, she blushed in confusion—thus completing Octavian's fall from grace.

Antonia, fascinated by this rent in Isabel's normally unruffled composure, glanced from the young lady to the young gentleman and back again consideringly.

"Fickle!" said Kedrington, shaking his head and moving up to take the place next to Antonia which had been vacated by Octavian. Antonia disregarded this manoeuvre and, rapidly thinking how to make use of the unexpected Mr Gary, made Mrs Curtiz and her niece known to Lord Kedrington; said she believed they were too well acquainted with Mr Kenyon to need to be reminded of it; and, at last, presented Isabel and Mr Gary to each other in the most offhand way possible, upon which Mr Gary snapped out of his trance and made a civil bow. Isabel, however, returned only a stiff nod before turning back to her godfather. Antonia felt a distinct itch to box her ears. Apparently, Isabel was losing no time in her scheme to marry a fortune, and a mere secretary—no matter how handsome or personable he might be—had no part in it. Antonia wondered if the foolish child would attempt to insinuate herself with the viscount instead!

But Mrs Curtiz, dressed in a reassuringly orthodox gown of green watered silk, had claimed the viscount's attention, holding her hand out to him and saying briskly, "We must treat one another as old friends, you know! I was acquainted with your father when you were still a schoolboy."

Kedrington gave her an understanding look. "Indeed! I trust we may become better friends because of it." She took his meaning, accepted his smile, and went on to enquire more easily after the rest of his family.

It was only a few minutes before dinner was announced—Antonia explaining that at Wyckham guests were welcome to linger afterward, but that they were never kept waiting for their dinners—and they were soon sitting down to an excellent meal consisting of two full courses and numerous side dishes and featuring a roast duckling stuffed with spiced apples. Mrs Driscoll was in her element catering to a dinner party such as had not been held at Wyckham for years, and Mr Kenyon gratified her further by declaring to Antonia—who passed the compliment along later—that the dinner was comparable to the finest he had ever eaten.

"Every bit as good as White's, eh, Kedrington?"

"My dear sir, to compare this repast to the boiled fowl and oyster sauce that White's persists in inflicting on its members is not only doing it an injustice, but insulting Miss Fairfax's excellent cook as well. One may as well dine in an army mess as patronize White's kitchens."

Antonia smiled. "You need not come so vehemently to our defence, my lord. Mr Kenyon's tastes are well known to be deplorable."

"Unfair!" protested her Uncle Philip. "Erratic, perhaps—but deplorable?"

As this merry dispute threatened to develop into a war, the viscount intervened to invite Mr Kenyon to dine with him at Watier's when he was next in town.

"Have you been to London, Miss Isabel?" Mr Gary enquired softly, leaning a little toward her.

Isabel leaned a little in the other direction, but was obliged to reply. "I am not *out* yet, sir. But I believe that this spring . . . that is, if Mr Kenyon wishes it . . . "

She glanced appealingly at her godfather, who exclaimed, "Most assuredly I do! Never think, my dear, that because I do not spend so much time here with you as I would like, that I cease to be your loving godfather! We will all of us have a delightful time of it in London this season, I assure you."

"All?" murmured the viscount. Antonia, however, was intent on dissecting a raspberry tartlet.

Aloud, Kedrington said to Isabel that he was happy she would be in town to enliven his own debut.

"You see, I have been away from England for some years—first in Jamaica and then in Spain, where, as you may imagine, Society is not precisely as we know it here. But when my mother died last year, it fell upon my unlucky aunts to present me to the ton this season. I fear they are in for a trying time of it."

Isabel stared at him. "I beg your pardon, sir, but I never imagined that gentlemen were obliged to go through . . . that is . . . "

"Yes, it *is* a trial," the viscount said with a sigh, adding slyly, "which is why it is particularly helpful to have the support of one's friends—and one's aunts."

"Oh, yes, that will make everything so much easier! Antonia has been to London and will be able to tell me how to go on, and Imogen is acquainted with absolutely everyone we shall wish to meet."

Fortunately for Antonia, who wondered if Lord Kedrington would ever prove to be as useful an acquaintance as he was already an exasperating one, Mrs Curtiz intervened to say that it did not matter whom she knew, for it was plain that Isabel had only to show herself in the Metropolis and all the ton would be clamouring to make her acquaintance. Mr Gary was swift to agree to this, upon which Isabel blushed and moved the conversation away from herself by asking the viscount how he would choose amongst the various dinner parties, routs, and balls offered to him, for she had been given to understand that having to attend some event every night—even several in the same night—could lead to one's being prostrated with fatigue long before the season ended.

The solicitous tone with which Isabel asked the question caused Antonia to realise with a shock why Isabel had not, in fact, attempted to "insinuate herself" in the viscount's favour. It seemed that in Isabel's seventeen-year-old eyes, Kedrington was far too stricken in years—incapable, indeed, of doddering along to more than one modest evening entertainment at a time!—even to be considered as a prospective suitor. Antonia was torn between relief that Isabel did have some principles and a renewed awareness of the width of the eight-year gap between herself and her niece. But mainly she was amused at the notion of the obviously virile Kedrington in a grandfatherly role.

This last seemed to have occurred to his lordship as well, for an incipient smile played over his harsh features, giving Antonia a fleeting picture of what he must have looked like at Isabel's age. But he was twice that now, and while Antonia had to be grateful that Isabel had recognised the fact, even if her aunt had not, she had an impulse to take her to task for her unintended discourtesy. But Kedrington caught Antonia's eye just then, and smiled, so that she knew he was more amused than offended, and he answered Isabel's question by saying that no sensible person would wish to be seen *everywhere,* for then people might come to expect to see them *anywhere,* which did no one's credit any good.

Presently the company repaired to the drawing room, Antonia saying that the second principle of hospitality at Wyckham was that ladies and gentlemen were not separated merely to allow the former to enjoy a comfortable prose and the latter their cigars and port. Anthony Fairfax had never seen any reason that a sufficiently large drawing room should not accommodate both interests, and the elder Miss Fairfax poured wine for the gentlemen in expert fashion.

She then recommended to Mrs Curtiz that she give the viscount a tour of the portrait gallery; carefully placed Isabel within Mr Gary's line of vision; and drew Isabel's doting godfather off to inspect a marble mantelpiece recently unearthed from a storage shed and added to the decor. However, Imogen promptly upset this little manoeuvre by beginning the tour with a portrait of Maria Fairfax in her wedding gown, which hung over the mantel in question, causing Kedrington to turn his eyes in that direction. With a change in the conversation, the rest of him followed. He pursued Antonia steadily around the room and toward the windows, where, she having exhausted her schemes to avoid a tête-à-tête with him, he caught her behind a large bowl of hothouse flowers and well out of earshot of the others.

"Why, Lord Kedrington," she said, assuming the offensive, "how persistent you are! I thought we had quite worn you down."

"If either you or your niece makes any further reference to my advanced state of decrepitude, Miss Fairfax, I shall expire on your carpet and leave you the unenviable task of removing my emaciated remains to the churchyard."

He made this remark in so absurdly petulant a tone that Antonia gave way to a smile. "I do beg your pardon, my lord, but I assure you, Isabel's . . . ah, reference . . . was as much a shock to me as it was to you!"

"Pray do not mention it to her," he said, dropping his affronted pose. "She never meant it in any but the most innocent way and would only be mortified to have any ulterior motive ascribed to her."

"You are very perceptive," she remarked, a little surprised to find him so.

But he gracefully forestalled any gratitude she might have expressed by saying, "I am sorry not to meet your sister-in-law this evening. I trust her indisposition is not a serious one?"

"It is serious in the sense of chronic, but the indisposition is mainly for effect," Antonia told him. When he looked puzzled, she explained, "Maria has chosen to make herself more interesting by pretending to be an invalid. We have found it kinder to allow her this little eccentricity than to try to dissuade her from it."

She hoped that her voice did not reflect her reluctance to mention Maria at all, but Kedrington appeared to find nothing amiss, merely noting by the way that he had an elderly relation who was much the same.

"She will not accompany you to London, then?"

"Good heavens, no! She will be delighted to have the run of the house—figuratively speaking, of course—and no one to censure her behaviour or screen her guests when we are away."

"Do you do so?"

"Not at all. But it pleases Maria to believe I do."

There was a pause before he said, "How is it that your younger brother did not sell out at the time of your elder brother's death?"

"There was no immediate need for him to do so. Anthony had named me to the temporary charge of Wyckham, with power of attorney. I expect he was taking into account Carey's great eagerness to join up. He knew that he would not come back if it could be prevented."

"Army-mad."

"Yes." She laughed ruefully, saying, "Oh, dear, what a set of irresponsible characters you must think us! I suppose it is too much to expect of you to believe that, despite our overrated charm, we Fairfaxes also enjoy a wide reputation for loyalty and kind intentions?"

She glanced up, hoping for an understanding smile, but the look he gave her, while not unsympathetic, unsettled rather than reassured her.

"I can believe it of *one* Fairfax," he said. "Especially the charm."

Unexpectedly shaken by this offhand tribute, she turned her head away from the warm glow in his dark eyes. It had not, until just that moment, occurred to her that he was flirting with her, and the notion that he was merely beguiling the tedium of a winter visit to the country by teasing her into indiscreet conversation unaccountably sank her spirits. But then it also occurred to her that she might enjoy such a harmless flirtation as much as he; indeed, what else had they been engaged in since the moment they met? The thought of Charles need not deter her from such a pleasant, but meaningless, pastime.

As if sensing her momentary discomfort, he said, more easily, "What I am attempting to ascertain, in my clumsy way, is whether I may look forward to the day your responsibilities here are at an end and you may visit London more frequently."

"Are you looking for a third sponsor for your coming-out, my lord? Are two aunts not sufficient? Isabel has but one, poor child."

"Isabel has many other advantages which I have not. But I meant, fair aunt, that *you* deserve another opportunity to dazzle London."

"I do not think, even if I would, that I could do so," she said. "I was on the town quite long enough to make an undesirable reputation for myself amongst the very persons you have been so careful to cultivate. Indeed, I once had the effrontery to cut the Duke of Cumberland! It is quite a distinction."

"Well for you that it was not Prinny himself. Whatever possessed you to do such a thing?"

"He looked at me in a way that was not precisely . . . that was not what might have led me to believe him a gentleman, much less a royal one."

"Do you always act on your scruples?"

She smiled. "Say, on my impulse, rather. But as I had no position to maintain, I was free to do so. He could scarcely have blighted my career."

Kedrington regarded her quizzically, and she realised that he had not been informed of the means by which she had ended her own career. Not wishing to become the cause of his enlightenment, she did not enlarge on her remark.

"Remind me not to be seen in your company," he said lightly. "I have no wish to have *my* career blighted."

She smiled in spite of herself and thanked him sincerely for his courtesy to Isabel at dinner. "You put her quite at her ease, you know, by comparing—however implausibly!—your situation to her own."

"I see nothing implausible about it. I assure you, I am as much a commodity as any damsel on the marriage mart, and must be every bit as careful to maintain my eligibility."

"Have you 'an intent to turn husband,' sir?"

Recognizing her source, he responded, " 'Will you have me, lady?' "

" 'Why, no, my lord, unless I might have another for working days. Your Grace is too costly to wear every day.' "

"Touché! I had forgotten the rest of that passage."

"Then you should not have set out on the beginning of it."

"Why *have* you never married, my Beatrice?"

She disregarded his use of the possessive. "Because unlike yourself, my lord, I do not care to be treated as a . . . a commodity."

"So I observe. Yet you have no scruples about subjecting Isabel to such treatment?"

"Isabel does not believe—that is, I do not expect Isabel to adhere to my views in everything," she replied in a tone that rang unconvincingly in her ears. "Isabel has a generous and loving nature, but she is not, as you may guess, much given to frivolous pursuits. She will gain more confidence in herself by making new friends of relative strangers, in London."

"She does not look to me to stand in awe of strangers."

Antonia did not doubt that the viscount referred to Mr Gary, who was standing beside Isabel by the bookcase, where they searched the shelves for a particular volume. Isabel kept her eyes resolutely on the search, and when she saw what she wanted on the top shelf, Octavian reached up easily to extract it. He opened the book and handed it to her, at the same time moving closer to whisper something in her ear. Isabel laughed, colouring prettily at the same time. Antonia could not help wondering if her blush was natural or if her niece was becoming a more skillful flirt than she had ever suspected her capable of being.

"And she blushes most artfully," his lordship remarked.

This uncomfortably acute observation succeeded in bringing Antonia's attention back to her companion, but she contrived to say only, "I fear it is too much to expect of you that you *not* remark such a thing, my lord!"

"Do you never blush, Antonia?"

"I am no longer seventeen, my lord," she replied.

"But still very green in some ways, I think."

She took no offence at this. "Perhaps. If I am, it is because I have seen what it means to be what is called world-wise and choose not to impose such wisdom on myself."

He was subdued. "That is the first explanation of your disgust of what you are pleased to call 'London manners' that makes sense to me. I fear I have been attributing it to an unrequited love affair or some such thing. Accept my apologies."

Antonia felt the blushes to which she had proclaimed herself immune rise to her cheeks, but at that moment the tea tray was brought in and she was saved from having to accept an apology for an entirely justified assumption on the viscount's part. But then Mr Kenyon was soliciting Isabel to play for them at the pianoforte, and Isabel was protesting that Mrs Curtiz was much the finer artist. Finally, Mrs Curtiz agreed to play only if Isabel then performed on the balalaika.

This prospect aroused genuine interest. Mrs Curtiz explained that she had brought the instrument back from Russia years ago and lately presented it to Isabel as the only one of the Fairfaxes capable of appreciating it. This was no less than justice. Isabel played with total concentration and a lack of self-consciousness which told Antonia she must have been mistaken in seeing any artifice in her niece's earlier behaviour. The applause that followed several melodies was each time more genuine than the last, and Lord Kedrington informed Miss Fairfax that she need have no fear that Isabel would not be a success, "for anything so exotic is all the crack now, and you may be sure that no other young lady will have even a notion of what a balalaika is."

The evening ended at a late hour, by which all the company had arrived at such a lack of formality with one another that Lord Kedrington's taking Miss Fairfax's hands in his own upon parting went quite unnoticed.

"Promise me something," he said, disregarding her attempts to withdraw her hands. She looked up into his eyes and saw again the intent look that occasionally crept into them.

"What is it?"

"That if there is any service I may perform for you in London, you will not hesitate to call on me for it."

She smiled. "Thank you, my lord. You are very kind."

"I shall hold you to it, you know—and with perfectly selfish motives!"

Her smile turned into a gurgling laugh, and he went out into the night with the sound of it in his ears.

— 4 —

THE DINNER AT Wyckham was soon followed by an invitation to partake of a light nuncheon—this being all, Mr Kenyon regretted, that was available under present circumstances—at Windeshiem. And, now he came to think of it, why did Antonia and Isabel not stay the afternoon, just as they were used to do as children? Antonia knew the house as well as her own and would not refuse to serve as hostess to his guests—and a much more charming companion than a helpless old man could aspire to be.

Antonia informed Mrs Curtiz in confidence, if not in moderation, of what she thought of her Uncle Philip's sly manners.

"But we shall have to go, for Isabel is determined to do so. I could wish that her determination did not so resemble that of a martyr on the way to the stake, but I have hopes that Mr Gary's charms will succeed in putting her more at ease—and that his scruples will prevent her being swept off her feet by them."

The two ladies were waiting in the hallway at Wyckham for the third to join them. Imogen pointed her walking stick at Antonia and said, "I wonder that you are willing to risk the limits of Mr Gary's charm."

Antonia sighed. "I do not see that I have any choice. I admit to a partiality on my own part to the young man, and I *did* say that I wish Isabel will not marry only for money; but at the same time I cannot help wishing that he were not *quite* so ineligible with regard to fortune. I fear that makes me sound a hypocrite—or worse, an opportunist, for taking advantage of Mr Gary to show Isabel how to go on, without allowing him the advantage of being the first to enjoy the fruits of her increased sophistication."

Imogen let her mull over these disquieting considerations before saying,

"If you imagine that she may succumb to Lord Kedrington's charms instead, I should disillusion you on that head immediately."

"I never imagined any such thing!" Antonia replied in a lofty tone that kindled a spark in Imogen's eye. "Kedrington is far too old for Isabel. But I do not see why he cannot make himself useful. He offered to do so."

"Did he, indeed!" exclaimed her friend. "That does put another light on . . . ah, matters."

Antonia glanced at Imogen as she pulled on her gloves and buttoned them, but the older woman merely remarked that Antonia had a small hole in the righthand glove which ought to be mended before it became any larger, and by the time Antonia had gone for another pair, and Isabel had joined them—rather breathlessly for the unaccustomed effort of having to consider her choice of clothing—she had forgotten the conversation.

The ride to Windeshiem was a short one, and since the ladies were well wrapped in furs and muffs, it was accomplished in an open carriage. They had scarcely passed the edge of the park bordering Wyckham when the stone walls of Windeshiem Hall rose to view behind their screen of cedars. The road crossed the stream that separated the two estates, then turned into the long drive leading up to the hall, where a warm welcome awaited the visitors.

The party spent the morning in a tour of the house, Isabel and Octavian Gary in the lead and Mrs Curtiz and Mr Kenyon following sedately behind Antonia and Lord Kedrington. Antonia kept a sharp eye on Isabel, who responded to Mr Gary's cheerful conversation with a coquetry that appeared so natural to her as to give her concerned aunt pause. At the same time, Antonia was not unaware of her escort. His lordship looked very much at home in nankeen breeches and a hunting jacket, with a Barcelona handkerchief knotted carelessly around his neck.

They picked their way around furniture shrouded in holland covers, and Antonia was several times obliged to brush dust from her sleeve. She thought it a pity that the house looked so sadly neglected, but as they walked along the narrow passageway called the Long Gallery, she remarked, "I have always liked this passage. As children, we were used to race one another madly down the length of it, but when I grew up . . ."

She paused and looked up at the high, narrow windows along one wall, through whose leaded panes a faint, rosy light penetrated. "Later, I sometimes sat here for hours on end, reading or only looking up through those windows at the sky. I felt like an ancient alchemist or a mediaeval scholar, or a nun in her cell. There is such a wonderful peace here."

They paused and heard only the click of Octavian's footsteps on the tiled floor far ahead of them.

Kedrington's expression was inscrutable, and he said only, "Miss Fairfax, I suspect you are a romantic at heart after all."

She made a helpless gesture at her own fancies. "Oh, no—merely too indolent to seek greater excitement. Come! We must go ahead or they will be wondering what has become of us."

During their nuncheon, the conversation stayed strictly within the bounds of the prosaic, but Antonia felt herself no less at ease for it. She talked more than she normally would have done about Windeshiem, and thus also about Wyckham and her experiences as its mistress, about her land and her tenants, and her bailiff and the price of hens. Kedrington listened to her much as Ned would have done, respecting her knowledge and her opinions, and asking questions which were intelligent, but which revealed an ignorance, resulting from his long absence, of conditions in England in recent years.

They moved into the library, Mr Kenyon with his pipe and Mrs Curtiz with a glass of tea. Octavian and Isabel set up a small table with a backgammon board, from which Isabel placed herself at a cautious distance, keeping the board within her limited vision but not so far away that Octavian might think her standoffish. Antonia, who alone knew the reason behind this manoeuvre, smiled when the puzzled Mr Gary leaned forward to be closer to the girl.

"Maidenly modesty?" whispered the viscount into her ear. Antonia shook her head, but did not explain Isabel's behaviour. Indeed, she did not entirely understand it herself and was unsure whether her own wishes were obscuring her perception of what was, in reality, occurring. To all appearances, Octavian behaved more as a brother than a suitor toward Isabel, and she seemed to accept him as such. But Antonia was uncertain whether this was clever strategy on Octavian's part or whether she was reading too much into his behaviour. Her niece's motives were becoming entirely inscrutable to her. She sighed.

"Shall we walk in the garden?" Kedrington asked, breaking into her reverie. The day had begun dully after a cold night, and they had seated themselves before the long French windows to watch as it brightened. Antonia wondered how long he had been regarding her rather than the view, but when she turned to him, his face was unreadable. Perhaps he was only restless at being indoors in fine weather.

"You forget the proprieties, sir!" she scolded him.

"What? Oh, I suppose you mean we must have a duenna. Gothic, but still required in this civilised society of ours." He stood up and addressed his host with a counterfeit heartiness. "Kenyon! Shall we take a tour of the garden?"

"Thank you, no," Mr Kenyon declined civilly, placing his feet firmly upon an ottoman so as to preclude his being asked a second time.

"Perhaps the children would like to go," Mrs Curtiz suggested, but Octavian declined vigourously, if with false bravado.

"Can't you see I've almost beat her?"

"Ha!" said Isabel, whose concentration was not so easily distracted, and knocked off one of Octavian's pieces.

"Must I recruit Milford?" demanded the viscount querulously.

"Good God, no!" Octavian protested, immediately thereafter apologising to the dice for raising his voice in their presence. "You know he isn't fit to live with for days after exposure to fresh air—confound it!"

Isabel held out her hand for the dice, which Octavian reluctantly handed over. The viscount saw that it was useless to address either of them further.

"Why don't you take two horses from the stables," Mr Kenyon suggested, as if equine companionship were all that was required. "Antonia will show you all the paths."

Kedrington accepted this solution as the best he would get, leaving the company before the offer could be withdrawn again. "Can you ride in that?" he asked Antonia of her carefully chosen morning ensemble.

"Mrs. Walker—the housekeeper—was used to keep some things here for us to ramble about in. I daresay they are still here somewhere, if you do not mind appearing abroad with a positive frump."

"I don't expect we shall be observed."

"Dear me! Don't remind Uncle Philip of that."

Antonia excused herself and reappeared after a short time in an old, but undeniably becoming, dark blue riding habit. Kedrington exercised his self-control in declining to comment on it, confining himself to admiring the ribbon trim on her hat, and they were off.

The horses were as eager to be loose as their riders. The overnight cold had frozen the ground hard, and they began with a quick gallop across country, almost to the edge of the estate. The crisp air was exhilarating, and Antonia's cheeks were flushed with the pleasure of the first such good ride she had enjoyed in weeks. Kedrington looked as if he did it every day.

They halted for a moment on the ridge looking toward Wyckham and an expanse of rolling country. The viscount's eyes narrowed as they swept the horizon with a keenness that most observers would not have granted it. He reminded Antonia just then of her brother, who had told her that in Spain survival often depended on keeping the eyes in the back of his head open. He had also said that attending to what *might* happen rather that to what *was* happening was a difficult habit to break.

"You look as if you are expecting to be ambushed," she said.

Kedrington smiled. "By you, fair one?"

She was anticipating this line of attack today and met his opening volley with a broadside of her own.

"Is it true that you were betrothed to a Creole countess?" she asked in a tone of detached enquiry.

He threw back his head and laughed. "Good God! Wherever did you hear that?"

"Is it not true, then?"

He leaned over to stroke the neck of his horse, which had begun cropping the sparse grass around them, but he did not turn away quickly enough to conceal the unmistakeable glint of mischief in his eye.

"She wasn't a countess," he said.

Antonia had a suspicion that she ought not to pursue the subject, but could not help asking, "What happened to her?"

"She sailed away with a Barbary pirate."

"Wretch!" she exclaimed, choking. "How shall I know what to believe of you?"

"My heart, don't you recognise a Banbury tale when you hear one?"

"You mean it is all a hum?"

"Entirely!" he confessed cheerfully. "Believe me, if I had been the subject of half so many true stories as apocryphal that fly about after me, I should have been dead of exhaustion years ago."

"Well, I don't know what was so implausible about that one. Although it is quite true that people will believe what it suits them to believe. I once said—quite in jest—that I painted my face with honey and crushed rosemary to aid my complexion, and before I knew how it had come about, this absurdity had become all the crack. Some ladies even claimed it helped them! I soon denied I had anything to do with promoting such nonsense, however, and I do not understand how you can allow such much more likely tales to be spread about yourself. Do your aunts believe them?"

"Julia does not credit them, but I sometimes suspect Hester of inventing half of them herself. I believe she thinks they enhance my prospects."

"Nonsense! You must have every matchmaking mama in town encamped on your doorstep as it is."

"I do. That is precisely the end for which Hester strives."

She frowned. "Do you truly wish to have a wife *chosen* for you?"

"Have you an alternative suggestion?"

"No, indeed!" she stumbled, put off by the apparent earnestness of the question. "How should I? I merely wonder that you cannot—that is, *you* must know what you want. Is there no one you . . . you *wish* to offer for?"

"Oh, yes. But she has refused me."

"Who—oh, I take it you are referring to me! But you will have to do better than a Shakespearean aside at a dinner party, you know—I was scarcely attending."

"Very well."

Before she had quite caught up with his thinking, she found her hand being held in his—his horse's reins being carelessly discarded—and herself being addressed forcefully, "My dear Miss Fairfax! Allow me to tell you how very ardently—I beg your pardon, but it is as difficult to be ardent on horseback as at a dinner party—my dear Miss Fairfax, you must know how much I admire you! Will you . . . dare I hope you will consent to be my wife? Blast this animal!"

He let go of her hands to steady his mount, and Antonia, who was torn between amusement and exasperation, finally burst into laughter at his foolishness. "Do you always make your offers so casually?"

"I generally, as I have said, do not make them at all. Do you accept?"

"I do not."

He did not look very disappointed. "I understand that it is usual with young ladies to reject, sometimes two or three times, the addresses of the man they secretly mean to accept, and I am therefore by no means discouraged."

"However do you come to understand anything so idiotish?"

"Why, I have it on the best of authority, Miss Fairfax. That delightful novel you insisted I read tells me it is true, and I must therefore suppose it to be so."

"Well, let me tell you, sir, I have at least as many refusals at my command as you may have offers."

"Excellent! I shall essay my various styles on you. May I?"

"Certainly not."

"You refuse to help me? How am I to know what is the proper thing to say when such time should come that I meet the young woman I shall—er, *wish* to offer for?"

"You cannot expect me to choose a wife for you!"

"Why not?"

"Why, it is the same as . . . as picking out another man's home for him!" she said, "Would you send Mr Gary to purchase a house on your behalf?"

"I trust his judgement."

"Oh! Oh—thank you."

A wicked gleam came into his eye. "But the fact is, I asked you to help me choose the words, not the woman. Believe me, I am quite capable of making that choice myself."

"I am sure I may hope so!" she said, indignant at being again drawn into the same trap. But then she had to laugh at her own slow-wittedness. Really, it had been much too long since she had engaged in a verbal sparring match with so quick an opponent! It occurred to her that this was the one thing she had missed from her life in London—the opportunity to exchange both nonsense and earnest conversation with someone intelligent enough to follow her nimblest thoughts and to make verbal leaps of his own that challenged her mind to follow.

"Tell me, Antonia," he said then, with another of those quicksilver shifts that so disconcerted her, "what are you going to do with yourself

50

when your brother grows up at last and comes home to take his proper place as head of the family? Will you continue here as you have been?"

She considered several defiant retorts, but she had always been all too aware that she was mistress of Wyckham only by virtue of Carey's absence. The inheritance was his. When he married—as he was bound to do, for he was not such a shuttlecock as he made out to be—and brought a new mistress to Wyckham, then she must think about . . . what? Begging Carey for a corner of her own to live in, like Cinderella? Or worse, like Maria, living out a half-demented existence? She ended by admitting simply to Kedrington, "I don't know."

He looked intently at her. "Will nothing tempt you willingly to leave Wyckham?"

"No."

"Have you never been tempted?"

She stumbled, but said again, "No," and turned her eyes away. This time he did not pursue his advantage, but instead suggested that they ride toward the stream that bordered that side of the Kenyon property. They did so slowly, following a ridge that gave them a view of the stream to one side and, to the other, a few straggling hedgerows that separated the individual holdings of some tenants, whose cottages were in need of repair. Antonia remarked on it, and Kedrington gave her a quizzical look.

"Do I detect a note of censure, Miss Fairfax?"

"I did not intend it so, but . . . well, I cannot help wishing that Uncle Philip would take a greater interest in Windeshiem. It is not as if he cannot afford to have roofs rethatched and hedges replanted. At any rate, Charles could certainly afford it, but he—"

She stopped then, aware of venturing into conversational waters that might prove too deep, but Kedrington was tactful enough not to press her. Instead he gazed fixedly in the direction of a fringe of bare willow branches that hung over the stream and shivered slightly in the light wind.

"I think you may have a prowler or a poacher," he remarked. "At least, there is some unusual activity in that copse by the brook."

Antonia could see nothing, but as they neared the trees, two boys dropped out of one of the largest of them and ran off across the fields on the far side of the stream.

"Oh, it's only the Fletcher boys. I suppose they did not recognise me, and of course they do not know you."

"Is that sufficient reason to run off like a pair of hedge-thieves? Who are they?"

"The sons of my bailiff. They have the run of both estates, and indeed are often of assistance in one way or another. But they do have a lamentable tendency to get into scrapes. I think it was young George— still home with the mumps today, I fancy—who broke a collarbone on that very tree only last summer. All the boys appear to look upon it as something of a challenge."

They had reached the stream, and the viscount surveyed the tree in question critically. It was a large oak with thickly woven branches, the first of which was fully six feet from the ground, but he declared just the same that it did not look unscalable.

"An expert opinion, sir?"

"Do you doubt me, madam?"

Before she had time to say whether she did or not, he had dismounted and tossed off his cloak. Then, with the speed, dexterity, and utter disregard for grace of a gypsy's monkey being pursued by a very large dog, he jumped for the first available branch, hauled himself over it, and clambered halfway to the top of the oak.

"Is there anything you would like from up here?"

"Yes!" she shouted, laughing. "You! *Down* from there!"

"Your whim is my command."

He descended nearly as rapidly as he had gone up, landing on both feet and rubbing his hands together to clean them. Otherwise, he looked as if he had not moved from where he stood. Even the polish on his topboots remained unviolated.

"You see how simple it is."

"I grant you to be a man of many and varied talents."

"None of which is of any use, nor may be taken seriously."

"I did not say so."

He mounted again. "But you do *not* take me seriously, Miss Fairfax."

"How can I?" she objected feelingly. "Were I to take *you* in all seriousness, how would I judge everything else in my life that I once thought important?"

He looked sharply at her, but lapsed into a silence as unaccountable as his previous ebullience had been, and which was maintained until they turned up the road to the stables. They slowed their horses to a walk up the slope from the road, beyond which lay fields neatly divided by hawthorn hedges and a progression of low hills fading into the horizon. Over them hung a light gauze of mist, pink-tinted where the chill, pallid sun struck it.

Kedrington stopped and leaned forward in his saddle to look at the country—not as an observer this time, but as a man looking on his homeland. Antonia waited patiently.

"Have you ever been to Spain, Antonia?" he asked. "No, a stupid question—of course you have not. But your brother will have told you that it is a bewitching land. It holds one in its spell, but it offers no comfort in return, no gentleness. It is never so soft and green as England is in the spring, or so full of promise even in the dead of winter."

He was silent then, drinking in the view. But after a moment, he said, "We saw ourselves as demi-gods there, or at least as heroes of no mean order, and Spain was a land to match our ambition. But . . . well, one outgrows adventure." He turned to her. "Do you understand what I am attempting to say?"

"I think I do. But I think it is braver of you to come back. It is generally so much more comfortable to go on in one's old, accustomed ways than to make an absolute change, even from a harsh life to an easier one; and then, to make anyone understand what a change it was must be more difficult still."

He smiled. "Yes, that's very true. You said earlier that people believe what they wish to believe; it is also true that they close their eyes to that which they do not understand or cannot sympathise with. Oh, it's true that an occasional boy, mad for a pair of colours, will ask me if I was at Busaco or Ciudad Rodrigo. But it is far more likely that anyone who mentions the subject at all will only skim the surface or, like my Aunt Julia, vocally deplore the unfortunate habits I have acquired in my wanderings. No one wants to know what it was really like. Memories are uncommunicable things."

He reached out to press her hand briefly. "I understand that well enough not to burden you with any more of them!"

Antonia thought, as they turned their horses toward home, that she could understand his feelings. She lacked the life of adventure which gave finality to his sense of peace at coming to the end of it, but it seemed to her that it was not necessary to have been in danger to know how to live—nor deprived of love to know how to love.

She was, nevertheless, a little surprised to find herself wishing that he *had* burdened her with more of his memories.

= 5 =

THE FINE WEATHER held into the middle of the week, allowing for several sight-seeing expeditions into the neighbouring countryside, in order to acquaint the newcomers with the local landmarks. On Friday, with Philip Kenyon as their guide, they rode to Foxton to inspect the famous seven locks in the Grand Union Canal and enjoyed a nuncheon at an inn from which they were able to observe the canal traffic and the complicated exercise of moving it uphill through each of the locks in turn.

On Saturday, in somewhat more sedate style—Antonia and Isabel in Mr Kenyon's landaulet and the gentlemen riding alongside—they visited some of the churches near Wyckham. Isabel took it upon herself to play the guide here and pointed out to Mr Gary—who alone was eager to be shown them—a fine Norman font and some unusual tombs with coloured effigies. Lord Kedrington was content to seat himself in one of the pews and wait for them. He invited Antonia to sit beside him, which she did, contemplating from that vantage point the carved wooden roof decorated with angels holding musical instruments. A silence fell between them, less comfortable than before. Kedrington found himself wondering what was going through her mind—and fearing that he had no part in her thoughts.

"Don't stiffen up, Antonia," he said, as much to catch her attention as to break the mood. "I'm not going to propose to you today."

Startled, she turned her head sharply. He smiled at her and was grateful to see a corresponding twinkle light her eyes.

"Why, when this is the perfect place to do so!" she admonished him. "We are alone—for who else would venture out on a weekday to inspect churches?—and unlikely to be disturbed. *I* certainly would not disturb the peace of such a place by jumping up and running away. So you have a meek, if not precisely willing, audience in me."

"I can only suggest that you focus your attention instead on the attractions your niece has been so diligent as to point out to us."

"Oh, dear! I wonder if I ought to mention to her that gentlemen are not generally impressed by such displays of erudition?"

"Octavian seems to be impressed."

"I daresay he may only be excessively well mannered."

"Perhaps you had rather she did not make an impression on him?"

"If you mean, do I approve of Mr Gary keeping her company, it is not up to me to approve or disapprove. Isabel is quite capable of choosing her own friends."

"If it eases you to know it, Octavian, while the youngest son of a family of modest means, will never want for a means to live comfortably."

She regarded him speculatively, and it struck him that she wanted to confide something to him and could not decide whether to risk it. He held his breath for a moment, but was disappointed when she looked away.

"It is true, you know, that most gentlemen are not fond of bookish females," she said. "I should not care to have Isabel suffer in future for such an easily remedied affliction. I think I will drop her a hint."

"No, don't do that," he advised. "Far from its being a deficit, I count Isabel's enthusiasm one of her greatest charms. It would be too bad if she were to become like so many girls, afraid to open her mouth for fear of saying something intelligent. Isabel will find her future far easier to live with if she has not built it for herself upon deceit and pretending to be what she is not."

Miss Fairfax appeared to consider this. "You are perfectly in the right, of course. It is only that it is so much more difficult for me, being closer to her, to see the matter in such a light."

"I shall make it my business to remind you of it, as the need arises."

She said nothing, but glanced at him sideways, a roguish smile hovering at the corners of her mouth. He went on, "And—naturally—to see that you continue to set her an excellent example."

"Do you imagine, my lord, that I stand in danger of succumbing to the very lures against which I must guard Isabel?"

"I think, fair one, that a surprise attack might rush your defences before you are aware of the danger."

"I have a good eye, my lord. 'I can see a church by daylight.' "

He laughed appreciatively and stood up, holding his hand out to her. "That is precisely how I should prefer to view a church! Shall we await the tourists outside?"

She was agreeable, and they resumed their conversation with a walk around the churchyard, forgetting how long it had been since Isabel and Octavian had wandered away together, until the pair reappeared via the side door, full of the merriment of two children sharing a prank. They regaled Antonia and Lord Kedrington with the tale of the persistent delusion of an old caretaker they had encountered, who was convinced that they had come in search of a cleric to marry them, and who, despite their denials, continued to insist that the vicar was in Oakham and that if they wished to be married, they would have to go there.

"In the end," Mr Gary said, "we were obliged to tell him we would go to Oakham at once, and left him shaking his head over the whimsies of modern youth, none of whom know what they want or what they will do with it when they get it!"

Even Isabel laughed freely over this episode, and Antonia told the viscount on their way home how gratified she was to see that the incident had not thrown her niece into the blushes that would have afflicted any other damsel of her age. "Indeed, I believe you may well be right, and a lack of missishness in Isabel may after all be of benefit to her—at least, it will set her apart from the common run of young ladies."

The same lack in the elder Miss Fairfax was, however, causing Lord Kedrington less satisfaction. He lapsed into contemplative silence on the ride home through the still, wintry afternoon and the empty countryside, over which a leaden sky hung heavily. They passed no living soul, and all that stood out in that melancholy landscape were the lonely spires of parish churches, keenly visible in the remaining light of day. His mood was not lightened by Antonia's observation that Anthony had often been so blue-devilled on such days. When he replied that he had no wish to remind her of her brother, she only laughed and said he could not hope to be exalted much higher than that.

The upshot of these exchanges was that his lordship spent the evening staring morosely into a glass of port until Octavian at last enjoined him, if he could not keep his mind on their chess game, to take himself to bed. But he awoke the following morning in much the same humour. On the pretext of giving his horse some exercise, he rode out to a remote part of the estate, keeping half an eye out for signs of Miss Fairfax, who had informed him that she was accustomed to pass at least one day each week in paying calls on her tenants, but that due to the dissipated life she had been leading of late, she had not attended to this duty for some time. Kedrington entertained little hope, therefore, of calling on her at home, but trusted to their old familiarity to make a chance encounter acceptable.

Old? Good God, had it been less than a week since they met? It did not seem possible. They had already settled into the familiarity of old friends, which was precisely what he did not want and which he attempted—with dulling regularity, it seemed!—to upset with reminders to her that it was not friendship at all that he sought from her. Indeed, the more evidence she presented to him that she did not need his friendship, but accepted it as a kind of unlooked-for luxury in her life—something that made her more comfortable, like a new pair of boots or a warm shawl—the more determined he became to prove himself of genuine value to her. But there was nothing he could do for her in the way of chivalrous deeds, and she would not, it seemed, oblige him by simply falling in love with him.

He had not even a friend's or a brother's advantage of inspiring confidences from her. Antonia had not told him the entire truth about her season in London—this he discovered through Octavian Gary, who had it from heaven knew where—and while such secrecy would have been understandable in a more reticent maiden, it did not fit in with what he thought he knew of Antonia Fairfax. In addition, it gave him her present relationship to Charles Kenyon to puzzle over. Of course, he had not been entirely candid with her, either, not having mentioned the possibility of his purchasing Windesheim and moving to Leicestershire. He was not certain why he had not told her of it. Lord knew, he had bared his soul about everything else, unaware as she seemed to be that he had done so.

Kedrington's horse snorted impatiently and he brought his wandering wits to heel. He urged his mount up a slight rise and rode along it for a time until, looking down, he saw a small cottage set on what must have been the edge of the Fairfax property. Antonia's gig stood in the front yard, but there was no horse between the shafts, indicating that she must have been there for longer than she would ordinarily spend in a visit with a tenant.

Curious, he rode to the cottage and dismounted. No one came out to see who was there, so he led his horse to a shed on one side of the building and saw Antonia's Dolly already stabled there. He knocked on the cottage door, which was opened to him by a large, hulking man with a young face and staring, uncertain eyes. They blinked in confusion and ran quickly over Kedrington's leather coat and breeches, coming to rest on his top-boots, spattered with mud from the yard but still obviously of a quality the man had never before beheld.

Kedrington asked for Miss Fairfax. The man moved backward and waved his hand into the large, low-ceilinged room behind him. There was a huge fire in the grate, but the room had a chill about it, as if the fire had only just been kindled. In one dark corner, Kedrington could see a bed, occupied by a slight feminine form. Beside the bed was a cradle, from which emanated a light raspy breathing. Antonia knelt on the floor beside it, but the light from the door caused her to look up and shade her eyes with her hand.

"Ned?" She stood up. "Oh, Lord Kedrington. What are you doing here?" She sounded as if she scarcely remembered him.

"I beg your pardon," he said. "I saw your gig in the yard—is there something amiss?"

"The baby is ill. I . . . Baskcomb has gone for Ned Fletcher. I thought you were he, and—oh, I don't know what to *do!*" She had at first sounded merely distracted, but at this she put her fist to her mouth in an attempt to keep her concern from the child's mother, who stirred on the bed and reached out a hand to Antonia.

"Only a bit of chill, miss," she insisted in a plaintive voice. "Naught to worry tha'self on."

Antonia smiled weakly at the woman and patted her hand. "Yes, Mrs Hatcher, to be sure it is, but I will wait for Mr Fletcher just the same. He will know what to do."

"Why do you not send for Dr Metcalf?" Kedrington asked. "That is his name, is it not? In Melton?"

"Ned can get here much more quickly, and with six boys of his own, he has as much experience in such things as any physician. He will send Baskcomb or one of his boys for the doctor later, if he is needed."

"What happened?"

"I am not perfectly sure. Henry is mute, you see. Mrs Hatcher says the fire went out after he left this morning—I imagine the door blew open. She was asleep, but the cold woke her and she tried to crawl to the fire—she is not yet recovered from the baby's birth, I fear—and she fainted before she could start the fire again. When I arrived, Henry had just come in for his midday meal and had got the fire going. It is the baby I am concerned for."

Just then the child woke and began to cry and make feeble attempts to cast off the blanket Antonia had carefully wrapped around him. She reached out to pick him up, and cradled him as best she could against her shoulder, but the child continued to whimper. Kedrington watched her and cursed himself for his helplessness, wondering how in all his experience of wounds and illness and emergency surgery he had never encountered anything so simple—and yet so dangerous—as a sick child.

His frustration must have been mirrored in his face, for when a moment later Ned Fletcher opened the door and surveyed the scene, his black eyes lit on Kedrington and something like a sympathetic smile flickered across his angular features. He carried several blankets over his arm and a bottle of something in one hand, which he handed to Antonia while Kedrington retreated into the shadows to watch.

Ned took the child from Antonia, holding him expertly while he felt the small forehead and moved his strong hands over the rest of the tiny body. He then placed him back in the cradle and wrapped another blanket around him, folding the ends over the tiny feet. He turned to Antonia and said, "It is not so bad—do not look so anxious!" Then he sat down on the bed and laid his hand on Mrs Hatcher's forehead.

"How are you today, Susan?" He smiled, but studied her carefully. When Susan admitted to feeling poorly, Ned asked why she had not sent for Mrs Fletcher to help her. "You got up and to your work before you were strong enough, didn't you?"

Susan nodded.

"But you know that Henry can find his own meals—as he has done these twenty years past!—and my Maureen would happily have cared for the baby. Shame on you, Susan!"

Mrs Hatcher smiled weakly and confessed, when Ned confronted her with it, that she could not nurse the baby.

"Do you have any cow's milk in the house?"

"Aye. In the cooler."

Ned turned around. "Miss Fairfax, can you find something to heat a little milk in for young Henry here? And give me that barley water, please—Mrs Hatcher needs it far more than he does." Ned turned again and said to the doorway, "Henry!"

Hatcher came forward eagerly, and Ned told him to fetch more wood to keep the fire going. The mute Henry nodded and stamped out, closing the door carefully behind him. Ned smiled at the gesture and said to Kedrington, "Poor Henry! He's lived alone so long that he's not yet accustomed to have to think about other people. He married Susan only last year, and he's older than I am. Having a wife he adores and a son on top of it is more that he can contend with. I wonder, my lord . . . ?"

"Yes?"

"May I ask you to see Miss Fairfax home?" Ned asked in a confidential whisper. "When she's finished warming the milk? Baskcomb's gone for the doctor and won't be back soon."

"Yes, certainly. That at least is something I can do!"

Ned chuckled. "I can't in all conscience recommend every man to have six children, my lord, but I'm bound to say they have been an education!"

"I've seen some of your brood. They look to be a lively tribe."

"They've not caused you any trouble?"

"Not at all. What about this one, however? How did you know his name is Henry, by the way?"

Ned laughed. "The first one is inevitably named for his father. He's very ill—although we needn't tell Miss Fairfax that just yet—but I believe it is not so much the cold as simple lack of nourishment that ails him. Susan can't nurse him, and I don't suppose he's had enough cow's milk to keep hope alive, much less a newborn child."

"If only the trouble is so easily remedied! I trust you may find all you need here, but I'm certain that Miss Fairfax, and myself in particular, are superfluous. I shall see to her horse, now, if you will convince her that she may leave the Hatchers in your care."

Antonia had found the bottle Mrs Hatcher used to feed the baby, washed it in the water she had previously put on to boil for tea, and filled it with the warmed milk. Mrs Hatcher reached out for it and insisted on giving it to the baby herself. Antonia gave her the child and stood over her, watching as she fed him, until Ned put his hand on her shoulder and said, "I wish you would go home now. There is nothing further to be done until Dr Metcalf comes."

She protested, but he would hear none of it. "Lord Kedrington will see you home. I'll come myself after the doctor's been, and tell you what he says. I'm certain the case is not so desperate as you think."

"Thank you, Ned. I hope not."

Antonia found her cloak, and Ned accompanied her outside, where between them Kedrington and Henry Hatcher had already put Dolly to the gig. Henry then picked up his load of firewood, and Kedrington led his own horse out of the shed as Ned handed Antonia up into the gig.

The drive to Wyckham was accomplished in silence, and Lord Kedrington declined Miss Fairfax's invitation to come into the house for refreshment.

"I think I must make haste if I am to arrive dry-shod at Windeshiem. Our fine weather seems to be coming rapidly to an end."

Antonia looked up at the sky, but replied without interest, "So it would appear. Good-bye, then—and thank you for your assistance."

"I did nothing."

She frowned at the harsh tone of his voice, but he only smiled regretfully and said, "I shall go now. Do not be standing about in the cold." He took her hand and pressed it between his two. The lingering distress in her eyes made him want to say more, but he thought she would not understand.

"Good-bye," he said quickly, and left her.

The storm broke that evening and continued overnight, signalling a return to the cold weather that had plagued the country that winter. By Monday afternoon the wind had eased, but the rain continued, so that Belding was amazed to open the door to a caller who came in dripping water from his heavy frieze cloak and slouch hat and asking to see Miss Fairfax. Belding, ill concealing his fascination at this bizarre costume, relieved him with some trepidation of the cloak, said he would inform the lady of his arrival, and send a maid scurrying for a hairbrush and a towel.

Antonia found her visitor a few minutes later in front of the library fire, and for an instant she did not recognise him. He was wearing a shirt of some rough cloth, open at the neck, over which he had thrown a sheepskin vest of sorts, with no sleeves. His boots were uncharacteristically scuffed, and his dark hair, although recently brushed, shone with damp.

He had brought in with him an unmistakeable aura of the out-of-doors, and Antonia, coming from a small, well-heated room, was a little taken aback at his vitality, as if a wild creature had been let into the house.

"Why, Lord Kedrington! What an intrepid caller you are, to be sure. Are the roads very bad?"

"I rode across country," he said, advancing quickly toward her and taking her hand. "It was quicker and not at all discommoding, so you may spare your kind solicitude."

"I assure you, my solicitude was all for your unfortunate horse!" she said, then gave in to curiosity and asked, "Is that how you dressed in Spain?"

"Only to informal parties," he said, smiling.

As if the words triggered some instinct in her, she waved him toward the sofa and said, "You will, of course, take some tea to warm you."

"Thank you, but I cannot stay long. I merely came to say . . . but tell me first if you have heard anything of the Hatchers?"

She made him sit down, if for no other reason than to reduce the forceful effect of his proximity. "Oh, yes! The baby is much improved. Maureen—Mrs Fletcher, that is—has taken both Susan and the baby into her home, where they may be properly looked after until Susan is well enough to take the child back to the cottage. Little Henry improved immediately when Dr Metcalf found a wet-nurse for him in the village, and a few bowls of Maureen's excellent potato soup will soon put Susan back on her feet. Ned complains loudly about having his two youngest boys sleeping on a trundle bed in their parents' room, but I know he is glad to help."

"You are fortunate to have such a man in your service."

"Yes, he is a great help to me. My brother's first bailiff was not so honest and thought he could cheat an inexperienced woman. I was forced to let him go shortly after Anthony died, but Philip Kenyon happened upon Ned during one of his—Uncle Philip's, I mean—expeditions into the West Country. The poor man was obliged to pack up and move his home and entire family all the way to Leicestershire, but I am very grateful that he did."

She did not know why she was rattling away in this distracted fashion and made herself stop and take a deep breath before asking, with more composure, "What is the other thing you wished to say to me?"

"That I am leaving for London in the morning."

She thought for a moment that she had not heard him, through the sudden ringing in her ears. But he was still speaking.

"Urgent family affairs call me away. I had a letter only this morning from . . . " He said something more that she did not hear. When she realised that he had fallen silent, she looked up, confused.

"I'm . . . I am sorry to see you leave so soon."

He put his hand under her chin and turned her face up to his. "Are you truly sorry, my heart, or was that only the usual courtesy?"

She hesitated, aware of an impulse to reach out to touch his face in return, to smooth away those harsh lines around his mouth. But then her sense of humour belatedly rescued her from what she felt might have been an irretrievable blunder.

"Indeed, I am excessively sorry!" she assured him, smiling. "Isabel and Mr Gary had organized a rubber of whist for this evening, you will recall, and you were needed to make a fourth. Of course, if Mr Gary goes with you, as I suppose he must, we are quite lost—reduced to our usual two-handed game, in fact. It is too bad of you!"

Accommodating himself to her mood, he accused her of incurable frivolity. "If it is only whist and piquet you want, my enchanting butterfly, you have only—as I have repeatedly told you—to marry me and I promise you an eternal round of dissipation—with my aunts to make us four, playing for penny points."

"It was my impression, sir, that I had made quite clear my intention not to so engage myself."

"Not even for love, Antonia?"

His tone was still light, but his questioning eyes were in earnest, and she fought not to look into them.

"Especially not for love!"

There was a brief, awkward silence before he lifted his brows and levelled a mocking gaze at her. "Take care, madam—I may not ask you again." She gave an exaggerated sigh of relief, but he went on mercilessly, "I *may* find some pliable creature more willing to tolerate my advances."

"I wish you well of her."

"Cruel Lady Disdain! But I have another argument."

"I thought you might."

"Need I remind you of your promise to call on me for whatever aid I may render you in London?"

"I have not forgotten. Isabel, too, is grateful—"

"Spare me Isabel's gratitude! I do what I can because *I* want to do it—for you."

She was disconcerted by the intensity with which he spoke, as if he were afraid of losing something important by having to leave her, even for so short a time.

"Indeed, my lord, you are very kind. I shall not forget, and I—we both—look forward to meeting you again."

He said no more, but took her hands again, and for a moment looked off into the distance beyond her right shoulder while she waited, feeling in his hands the effort he was making at self-control. At last, he relaxed perceptibly and smiled, saying, "I don't know why I prejudice my own cause with every word I utter. Remember only that I wish above all things that we may see each other again very soon."

With that, he raised her palm to his lips and kissed it softly. She knew she ought not to let him do that, but could not bring herself to pull her hand away. She felt it grow warmer under the pressure of his kiss, and all at once a shock of unidentifiable feeling communicated itself from him, through her hand, coursing all through her. She pulled away abruptly then, a blush of breathless confusion rising to her cheeks. Kedrington seemed not to notice, although he did not meet her eyes. Then, saying all that was customary and remembering to express his regrets to Isabel, he took his leave.

When he was gone, Antonia stood alone in the hall, staring at the closed door until she became aware again of normal sensations. It was cold in the hall; she wrapped her shawl tighter around her shoulders but could not stop shivering. She looked around her at the home that had always held the greater part of her happiness within its walls and wondered why it suddenly seemed so empty.

6

IT WAS PHILIP Kenyon, suddenly recalled to his godfatherly duties, who took it cheerfully upon himself to find a suitable house in London which the Misses Fairfax might rent for the season. In February he wrote to them that they might move immediately into a large house in Queen Anne Street, or they might wait until March, when a smaller, better-furnished one in Mount Street would fall vacant, but—discharging that obligation as cheerfully as he had assumed it—he left the choice to the ladies. He would not be in Leicestershire in the near future, having committed himself to an inspection tour of the Sussex Iron Railway, but he had left instructions with his solicitor in London—Antonia would know his direction—to settle the question of the lease for them and to forward the bills for all their expenses to Mr Kenyon. Their loving Uncle Philip hoped to see them very soon and in good health, and oh yes—Lord Kedrington had charged him to ask Antonia if she preferred whist to piquet. Mr Kenyon supposed Antonia knew what he meant.

Antonia would dearly have liked to reply in kind to the viscount's impertinence, but while she was grateful to him for reverting to that easy camaraderie they had enjoyed at the beginning of their acquaintance, she hesitated to initiate a correspondence with him that must at some point recall the disquieting incident on which they had parted.

She had done her best to put that out of her mind, instead conjuring up those comforting images of Charles Kenyon which had hitherto been all she required for happiness. She succeeded thus in restoring her equanimity—at least until the next mention of Kedrington's name, which seemed to crop up far too frequently in the conversation nowadays. She slipped the last page of Mr Kenyon's letter into her pocket and went to consult with Isabel about the rest of it.

"Oh, Antonia, we couldn't possibly go *now,*" asserted that young lady. "Miss Jensen won't finish my satin ball dress or any of the new pelisses for a fortnight, and Madame Labiche said she will have to send to London for the *gros de Naples* for those two bonnets, and . . . oh, there must be a dozen things to do still!"

Antonia was satisfied to have the matter so easily resolved—although she remarked that it seemed a trifle odd that they must send to London to trim the bonnets they were to wear there. Isabel smiled perfunctorily at this attempt at levity and went away to attend to more serious business. Antonia was amused by her niece's attitude of mingled apprehension and determination, and by the feverish activity in which she attempted to overcome the former with a great deal of the latter. She suspected that Isabel was in as much of a mental quandary as she was herself, but she could not question her niece about it without also revealing her own dilemma, and that she was not yet prepared to do. Instead, she concentrated on following Isabel's orders and marvelling at her energy.

She did not in fact know Mr Quigley's direction but, acting on Isabel's sensible suggestion, she speedily obtained it from Pomfret and wrote to the solicitor's offices in the Temple to say that they would take the house in Mount Street. Belding, two footmen, and three housemaids were duly despatched thither a few weeks later, together with Mrs Driscoll, who at the last moment won out over Antonia's notion of hiring a modish French chef for the season by producing an unexpectedly elegant dinner, which included lobster in a sauce whose ingredients Mrs Driscoll triumphantly refused to divulge, and a meringue of so delicate a texture that Isabel declared that no London chef could equal it.

But not until the first week of April was all in order, and even on the very day of their departure, it was only Isabel's abigail, Esme—newly promoted from housemaid—who stood ready in the yard of The George in Melton Mowbray, proud of both her new post and her new bonnet and eager to be off in the handsome hired chaise which awaited them. Everyone else seemed to find any number of excuses sufficient to detain them.

They had been half an hour late in leaving Wyckham, Maria having become suddenly cognizant of that which had been mentioned to her a dozen times a day for a fortnight. She had thereupon announced her intention of coming down to see them all off, and the ladies had waited in the parlour for twenty minutes only to learn that she had changed her mind and they were all obliged to troop up to her bedroom to take an affecting farewell before Maria could forget once again where it was they were going.

At The George, Antonia suddenly realised how long it would be before she saw Ned Fletcher again, and she took him aside to add some remarks to the list of instructions she had already given him. While Ned listened patiently, nodding in agreement, Baskcomb shifted from one foot to the other and wondered if he should walk the horses.

At last, however, they were really on their way. They intended to make a leisurely journey, spending the first night at Huntingdon and a second at Stevanage, leaving them to arrive in London early on the third day without excessive fatigue. This scheme was successfully carried out, but unknown to the travellers, their schedule brought them into London precisely on the day following the arrival of the news from Paris that the remains of the Imperial Army had surrendered, and that the Allies had at last entered the French capital. To be sure, they had been expecting something of that nature from Carey's recent description of what turned out to be the final campaign of the war, near Toulouse.

Gen'l Soult's army seems to be deserting him on all sides, Lieutenant Fairfax had written, *including the Rear, where this Action is referred to as 'Straggling.' Duoro kept old Salt out of Bordeaux handily, 'spite of our Reinforcements not fetching up in time. This looks like Ball is over at last. . . .*

But the Fairfax ladies were unaware of the extent of the jubilation in London, where the continental news was even in ordinary times received with considerably more interest than the neighbouring shires evinced in it; and little suspected that the city would be in a whirl of celebration through the months leading to the official victory festivities the following August.

Isabel was reading aloud from a guidebook as they were crossing a peaceful corner of Finchley Common on the last phase of their journey, when she looked up, blinked through her spectacles, and exclaimed, "Goodness! What was that?"

"It sounded like cannon," Antonia said, mystified.

"I fancy it is the Tower guns," ventured Mrs Curtiz. "The sound seems to be coming from that direction."

Antonia put her head out of the window and called to Baskcomb on the perch, but that country-bred worthy could add nothing to their speculations.

They were soon to be informed, however. The country to the north of the New Road, which ran from Paddington to Islington, was still largely wooded and peaceful, but soon the neat brown and grey brick houses began to come closer together, and to rise to three and four stories. The flagstone pavements and cobbled streets between them narrowed, and from behind archways and down narrow lanes emanated the faint but unmistakeable aromas of stables and kitchens and chimneystacks. South of Oxford Street, foot and horse traffic grew heavier. Pedestrians, sedan-chairs, carts, and carriages slowed their progress, so that the travellers had leisure to admire the luxurious mansions lining Grosvenor Square, with their handsome carved doors and the brightly polished knockers which indicated by their presence that their owners were at home to callers.

Many of these houses were decorated with white bunting and fleurs-de-lis. Flambeaux outside their doors stood ready to be kindled at dusk. Some of the citizens who passed by wore white cockades in their hats, and two or three vehicles were even draped with laurel leaves. A dowager in a purple turban stared rudely at Antonia from a passing barouche, but Antonia's irritation at this insolence evaporated at the sight of two ladies out for a walk. One of them had her hair dressed in an ethereal fashion which Antonia later learned was called *à la Médusa,* and which now caused her to exclaim, "Oh, I like that!"

Mrs Curtiz looked after the passing lady and approved. "Very nice, although hardly suitable for morning. You would look well with it for a dinner party."

Suddenly a sporting phaeton, with an equally sporting young driver in canary-yellow pantaloons, dashed out of South Audley Street at an alarming pace. Baskcomb manoeuvred to avoid the phaeton, but a red-haired young lady on the perch beside the reckless whipster glanced curiously into the chaise as she passed and cried out, "Oh, Ollie—stop! It's Isabel Fairfax! Do *stop,* you stupid boy! Izzy, Izzy—halloo!"

Baskcomb, who had been put to the unenviable choice of running into a fence on his right or a small boy and his nurse emerging from the square on his left, came .gratefully to a halt. The young man on the

69

phaeton backed his horses and Isabel looked out of her window just as the red-haired lady clambered down from her perch with the aid of an agile tiger in pale green livery, who had been clinging to the rear of the phaeton.

The lady was a vivacious little beauty of eighteen, with sparkling green eyes and small, perfect white teeth, which flashed when she laughed (which was frequently). She wore an emerald-green pelisse trimmed with gold braid for a dashing military touch, and carried a huge muff trimmed with a gold tassel. When she had descended from the phaeton, it could be observed that her stature was somewhat less than the average, her figure perhaps more ample than most women found desirable, and her hair a lamentably unfashionable scarlet. But she contrived nonetheless to turn these faults into assets by the simple expedient of flaunting them before the world and daring anyone to criticise her for possessing them.

But Cloris Beecham's greatest asset lay behind the smile and the trilling laugh, in a genuine generosity of heart that made lifelong beaux of all the young men she met, and fast friends of nearly as many young ladies. She had known Isabel Fairfax at the Bath seminary they had both attended for a year before Isabel left from homesickness and Cloris because she had wider worlds to conquer.

Baskcomb had scarcely climbed down from his perch to open the door for Isabel before Cloris was embracing her heartily and demanding to know why her dear Izzy had not written to say she was coming to London.

"Why, I should have planned such *delicious* things for us to do together! All sorts of parties—the theatre, Vauxhall, Astley's—although *that* won't be open until after Easter—and *Almack's!* Izzy, how many ball gowns have you? Oh, not nearly enough, I'll vow! But I know the most *exquisite* modiste in Bruton Street. We shall go everywhere together, dearest, for we do make a *stunning* pair, do we not?"

Cloris rattled on in this italicised manner while Isabel attempted—injecting "Oh, to be sure!" and "How lovely that sounds!" between—to present her friend to her aunt and Mrs Curtiz. This was accomplished at last, Cloris declaring that she had heard wondrous things of Isabel's Aunt Tonia, which made Antonia wince, but she claimed to be happy to meet Miss Beecham as well. Miss Beecham even remembered to introduce—with a wave of her hand in his general direction—"Oh, my brother Oliver." Oliver rose slightly on his perch to manoeuvre a bow, and Isabel took advantage of this check in the flow of his sister's chatter to ask the meaning of the festival decorations in the square.

"Oh, the most famous news!" Cloris exclaimed, on course again. "The *Ogre* is beaten! Yesterday! I mean, the *news* came yesterday. I went out to buy a dozen pair of silk stockings at Grafton House—not that I generally patronize Grafton House, my dear, but they were only twelve shillings the pair—can you *imagine?* But there was Worthing—my steppapa, you know—standing in the middle of the pavement reading from a newspaper and any *number* of old quizzes capering about and waving their canes. I got it out of them what had happened, which was fortunate, for as a rule, Grafton House is *frightfully* crowded in the afternoon, only yesterday no one was there on account of the excitement, and besides the stockings, I purchased ells and *ells* of silks and muslins, for you will see, Izzy dear, that this means there will be ever so many more routs and parties and things this season, and—oh, I'm *so* glad you're here!"

Cloris hugged Isabel again and demanded to know where they were stopping.

"Mount Street! Oh, that *is* splendid! We are here in the square—that pink house in the corner—and so we are practically neighbours!" She then addressed herself to Antonia, as the nominal head of the expedition, to ask prettily if she and Oliver might call the next morning. Upon receiving that lady's smiling consent, she climbed back up into the phaeton and, with a last trill of laughter, was gone.

"Heavens!" said Mrs Curtiz into the deafening silence which reigned inside the chaise upon their parting from the voluble Miss Beecham. "What an exhausting experience!"

At that, all the ladies burst into gay laughter and arrived in Mount Street a few moments later feeling merry as grigs and quite up to taking the town by storm. No sooner had Baskcomb let down the steps of the chaise than they were standing on the pavement waiting for fame to rush up to them. But it was only Belding who did so, rubbing his hands together in the nearest he would ever come to glee, as he called their notice to the various features of their new house and, modestly, to the improvements he himself had installed there.

Antonia was contemplating the graceful folds of the new blue silk curtains covering the front windows when her reflexion in the glass of a tall clock called her attention to the less than graceful folds of her travel-crushed gown. Before any of the ladies was allowed to attend to her appearance, however, they were all obliged to greet the other servants and to hear Mrs Driscoll announce that nuncheon would be served at three o'clock, and dinner—their cook having been thoroughly corrupted by city habits—at eight. Mrs Curtiz received this announcement with equanimity but, taking matters in her own hands, demanded that a pot of tea be sent immediately to their rooms and shepherded the younger ladies upstairs.

Antonia slipped out of her travelling dress and rang for hot water, but when Esme, still in her bonnet, answered the bell, she stopped in the midst of opening the bandbox containing her hairbrushes to laugh.

"Esme! Whatever are you about? Go to your room and take care of your own needs. One of the housemaids will attend me."

"Oh, Miss Antonia!" Esme exclaimed breathlessly. "I just couldn't! I just couldn't sit down."

"Well, you might at least remove your bonnet."

"Oh!" Esme reached up to feel her head. "Oh—yes, ma'am, I'll do it now." She backed out of the door again, but Antonia stopped her to tell her to send one of the other maids up with some hot water.

"And I don't want to see you again this afternoon, Esme."

"Yes, ma'am! I mean, no, ma'am. Oh, dear. . . . "

Antonia sympathised with the abigail's restlessness. She could not sit down either, and paced the room until her trunk was brought up. Then she extracted a comfortable day dress from it and went to drink her tea in the window seat while she contemplated the passing parade. It was a pleasant vantage point, and now she came to look at it, she saw that her room was a very handsome one indeed. She would have to make a point of thanking Belding for the excellent job he had done of preparing the house for them. It now remained only to unpack and settle themselves in to begin their new life.

Antonia contemplated the mountain of baggage that had been brought into her room and thought that at the very least she would be so exhausted by the night that she would sleep quite well in her new surroundings.

However, the parade outside scarcely thinned at all during the night, and Antonia, accustomed to the stillness of the country, woke several times to the cries of the watchman and the rattle of creaky wooden carts over the cobbles; by the next morning, she felt as fatigued as if she had already been in London for weeks.

Cloris Beecham kept her promise to call—not precisely that morning, for her day did not normally begin until well after noon—and spirited Isabel away with her on a shopping expedition. Alone with Mrs Curtiz, who seemed to have suffered no ill effects from her first night in town, Antonia set out soon after Isabel to visit Mr Quigley's offices to sign the lease for the house and to hear from him that neither of the Kenyons was in town at present. Antonia was conscious of both annoyance and a certain relief that she would not be obliged to face Charles until . . . well, at least until she had become more comfortable in her new surroundings than she felt that morning.

In Charles's stead, she received a letter which he had left for her, welcoming her to London and trusting that she would not object to his offering some little hints as to where she might go for such household necessities and so forth as his father might have neglected to provide for her comfort.

For my father, as you know, however kind and generous, is apt to wander from his intentions, went Charles's note, *so that I must make myself responsible for seeing that your new life is as pleasant and homelike as possible. . . .*

"What does he say?" enquired Mrs Curtiz, after they had been some way on their return from the solicitor's office and Antonia still had her eyes fastened on the letter.

"That Layton and Shear's have some excellent poplin at six shillings the yard," was the rather dry reply. A few minutes later, Antonia folded the letter and remarked only, "I wonder if we ought to take a box at Drury Lane? I should very much like to see this Mr Kean who is all the rage, but Isabel may prefer the ballet."

If Mrs Curtiz was deceived by Antonia's bland tone into thinking there was no more to Charles Kenyon's letter than that, she nevertheless confined herself to pointing out that a box at the King's Theatre, where the ballet was given, could cost as much as two thousand guineas for the season. Furthermore, although the Regent himself, the Royal Dukes, and any number of ladies of the highest rank often attended the ballet or the opera, the audience was more usually composed of fops and dandies who made great nuisances of themselves, particularly if one were young and pretty and on clear display in a rented box. If a young lady of quality chose to disregard this rudeness and attend to the performance, it was equally inevitable that she would be labelled an ignorant provincial. On the whole, Imogen thought, the Theatre Royal at Drury Lane might better enjoy their patronage.

They returned to Mount Street after this first venture to find Lord Kedrington's card resting on the hall table; the viscount himself, within twenty-four hours, was to be found resting on a chair in what they had, due to its elegantly gilded wainscoting, dubbed the "gold drawing room."

"Why are you sequestering yourself indoors on such a fine day?" his lordship asked Miss Fairfax, coming directly to the point of his visit.

"Isabel's friend Miss Beecham has taken her for a drive," she said, feeling herself unaccountably on the defensive. He was, after all, behaving precisely as she would have wished.

"That must be a non sequitur," he said.

"Not at all. I only meant that since Clory's brother Oliver is driving, and Clory's governess Miss Blaine is acting as chaperone, there was no necessity for my presence."

"You were never so obtuse in the country, Miss Fairfax. It must be the closed air of your parlour that has turned you so. My point is that you, too, should be out disporting yourself among the gentry."

Antonia gave him a comprehensive look. "Why, when the leaders of fashion come to call on me?"

His lordship was indeed looking very à la mode in pearl-grey pantaloons and a dark grey coat, elegantly simple and set off by a wine-coloured waistcoat. But when Antonia explained that she had not yet purchased any suitable clothing—Miss Jensen's talents having been dedicated exclusively to Isabel's wardrobe—and dared not appear in public before ordering a few new gowns that would not cause his lordship to blush to be seen with her, he abandoned his scolding.

"Alas, Miss Fairfax, I see that you still regard me as a mere fribble of fashion. But perhaps you will allow me to advise you at least on such matters, in which case my first recommendation is that you look in your mirror. It will show you that you are in blooming looks—if somewhat dimmer of wit than usual—and that anyone who appears in your company will be considered to have the most exquisite taste for so doing.

Indeed, I challenge you to see this for yourself by riding in the park with me tomorrow."

Antonia began to decline, protesting that they were not yet settled in and that once they were, the first order of business would be to make plans for Isabel's coming-out ball. Kedrington countered that they would have no acquaintance to invite to the ball if they did not begin cultivating them immediately, and they compromised in the end by agreeing to make a party of the outing—to include Isabel, Mrs Curtiz, and Mr Gary—two days hence, when Antonia's first new gowns were to be delivered.

The viscount took his leave on this conciliatory note, and after she had seen him out, Antonia watched through the window as he sauntered away down the street. She smiled to herself and reflected that, despite Kedrington's often too acute perceptions, she had to be grateful for the interest he took in paving their way in this new adventure. Furthermore, he knew precisely when to cease pressing his advice on her, turning the subject deftly to a jest or his mocking accusations that she did not take him sufficiently seriously. This was no longer true, for she was even more grateful to him for restoring the friendly laughter and ease of mind she had feared left behind at Wyckham. It seemed, however, that Kedrington, too, preferred to go on as they had begun. She only hoped it would continue to be possible.

When Imogen came in later to call her to tea, she found Antonia humming contentedly as she tried on various bonnets she had brought with her. Antonia told her friend about their invitation to drive out with the viscount and confessed that she felt a wish to do something that very evening, new clothes or no.

"I must say, it is very provoking of Uncle Philip to be away just at this moment!" Antonia complained. "There are so few places where ladies alone may be seen without being considered unladylike. Do you think we might take dinner at Grillon's Hotel? It is said to be excessively genteel."

"With the result that no one except persons of excessive gentility would see us there," Imogen said, effectively defeating what little enthusiasm Antonia had for the idea.

However, when Isabel came home, bearing the tale of her day's adventures, Antonia began to perceive that the delicate matter of their social calendar could all too easily be resolved contrary to their most careful calculations.

Isabel had begun the day in a state of acute apprehension, which was not alleviated by Esmé's habit, in which Isabel joined, of running to the window whenever she heard a particularly loud noise in the street. When she was not thus engaged, she was chattering with the servants who had come down from Wyckham before her arrival, until Antonia, to curb her excess energy, pretended to see a stain on Isabel's skirt and advised her to go upstairs and change her gown before Cloris arrived to fetch her. Fortunately, Miss Beecham proved the very person to put Isabel at ease, by assuring her with supreme confidence in the truth of her assertions that nothing could be smoother than the passage of such a pretty, well-mannered, self-possessed young woman as Isabel through the portals of the ton. Isabel thus returned from their outing transformed, at least temporarily, into just such a paragon—although for a few apprehensive moments Antonia had to wonder if Miss Beecham had perhaps not gone too far.

"We went to look at the botanical gardens at Kew," Isabel reported breathlessly to her aunt. "We met a Lord Geoffrey Dane there, who is an acquaintance of Clory's. She had told me he is a *beautiful* young man, as indeed he proved to be, and excessively eligible as well. On our return, we passed Mr Gary in Park Lane. Oh, and Clory invites us to a very informal dinner tomorrow evening to meet Mr and Mrs Worthing—Clory's mama and steppapa, you know."

Antonia's perverse imagination immediately conjured up visions of an entirely *ineligible* Lord Geoffrey, made dispiriting note of the offhandedness of Isabel's mention of Mr Gary, and prodded herself with the nasty suspicion that the Worthings might prove as dull as their name. But she smiled brightly and said only that a small dinner party among friends would be an acceptably modest start to their careers and that she would send an acceptance around to Grosvenor Square immediately.

"Isabel . . . " she began, as her niece started off again to change for dinner.

"Yes?" Isabel turned back, but did not sit down again. Antonia postponed her intended attempt to persuade Isabel to confide in her.

"Shall we add Lord Geoffrey's name to your list of ball guests?"

"Oh, yes, I think so," Isabel said. "I expect we shall see him often before then."

It did not escape Antonia's still-acute notice that there was a decided note of calculation behind this statement. When Isabel had gone, she sighed and hoped—as perversely as ever—that Lord Geoffrey would prove either a paragon or totally impossible.

= 7 =

EVERY DAY AFTER the Fairfaxes' arrival in London brought further glad news from abroad—that Bonaparte's marshals had deserted him, that the French senate had thrown him over for their exiled Bourbon king, and that the Allied sovereigns were resolved upon his abdication. London, which had been living in a disbelieving dream, now woke to the realisation that it was all true. Church bells rang with an extra thanksgiving on Easter Sunday, and a large portion of the population was literally singing and dancing in the streets. Lord Byron, who after the success of *The Corsair* had announced his resolution to leave his mountebank profession forever, promptly broke his vow to compose an ode to his fallen hero, Bonaparte.

The poet's melancholy outlook was shared by very few, however. No one but he was displeased when Bonaparte abdicated at last, but at least one gouty old man who had been living in rustic security in Buckinghamshire was somewhat nonplussed when he learned that the French senate had proclaimed him king. The Comte de Lille—known as Louis *le Désiré* to his admirers and Louis *le Gros* to such as my lord Byron—and his exiled court may well have felt some small annoyance at being made to pack up and begin the long uncomfortable journey back to Paris, but he could scarcely say so when the Prince Regent himself, in all his corpulent finery and accompanied by a troop of the Blues, met him at Stanmore with the intention of escorting him on his ponderous progress to London, where a tumultuous welcome awaited both royal gentlemen.

Crowds of Londoners wearing the white cockade of the House of Bourbon had filled Hyde Park from early morning, supplied with picnic lunches, which they spread out in the sunshine along Rotten Row while they waited for the procession to pass by. It was an excellent opportunity to ogle and remark upon the celebrated beauties and notable horsemen who vied with one another for the admiration of the throng—and the Misses Fairfaxes were not above taking advantage of the opportunity to preen their own fine feathers.

Fully conscious that this would be Isabel's first important public appearance, that morning Antonia had merely taken a quickly appraising glance in the mirror after donning her new morning gown of amber crepe and her villager hat with long amber silk ribbons, before going in to assist Isabel with her toilette. Pausing at the door to her niece's room, however, she could not help smiling at the springlike picture Isabel presented as she placed a charming chip-straw bonnet over her silver-gold hair. Isabel looked up and, returning her smile, observed that Antonia had lost an earbob.

Antonia laughed and felt her earlobe. "Oh, dear—and here I had come to be certain that *you* were ready, which you quite obviously are, while I am going about half-dressed and doubtless looking a positive hoyden!"

Isabel assured her that she looked no such thing, and after many expressions of mutual admiration, in addition to Imogen Curtiz's only slightly more restrained compliments to both young ladies, the three of them went downstairs to meet their escorts not more than five minutes tardily—but with Antonia's earbob forgotten once again—and set off for the day's adventure. Miss Cloris Beecham had declined to join them, declaring unequivocally, "Thank you, no! *I* to be outshone by an old man—*two* old men!—so fat they cannot stand without swaying? No, I shall remain quietly indoors until they have gone away again."

Miss Beecham had, however, agreed to meet them in the park at whichever hour public attention should have left the royal gentlemen to seek a pleasanter focus. The Fairfax party, therefore, consisted only of the three ladies in a newly rented carriage, accompanied by Lord Kedrington and Mr Gary on horseback. Antonia had no doubt, on laying eyes on his lordship, that any attention there was to be had would immediately focus itself on him, who had come arrayed in an unusual but striking ensemble consisting of an ivory-coloured coat, matching pantaloons, and, in place of the prescribed tall beaver hat, a wide-brimmed straw concoction. Antonia had no means of recognising this headgear as the sort common in tropical climates, and she therefore regarded it with a kind of suspicious fascination but was determined not to pander to Kedrington's vanity by enquiring about it.

They made their way first to Grillon's Hotel in Albemarle Street, where the king would be putting up. There, another, more sedate crowd had cleared a passage from the door of the hotel toward the spot where, after an hour's wait—only partially relieved by Kedrington's irreverent account of the new king's petulant reluctance to have his throne back after Bonaparte had sat upon it—they began to hear faint cheers in the distance, which gradually became louder and then nearly deafening as the royal coach neared the hotel.

Then the king was lifted bodily from his vehicle and set down. In the manner of a man far too given to indulgence, he moved toward the hotel, swaying and nodding acknowledgement of the tribute of his admirers. He was escorted to a large chair thoughtfully provided for him, and when he had lowered himself onto it, the Regent, who had been following at a discreet distance, bustled forward and burdened the weary king further with the Order of the Garter, which he buckled with a theatrical flourish around Louis's knee. Then he rose, puffing a little, and made the kind of flowery speech he imagined appealed to the lower orders. The king made a contrastingly simple speech in which he declared that he owed the recovery of his throne solely to the efforts of the British Army on his behalf. On another chorus of cheers from the crowd, he then went into the hotel, the Prince Regent huffing along after him.

The Fairfaxes declared themselves vastly amused by this first part of the day's entertainment, and as soon as there was room to manoeuvre their carriage in the crowded street, they set off for the park to see the commencement of the next act. Their progress was somewhat slow, but enlivened for Antonia and Imogen by recognition of several familiar faces from the past and their exchanged whispered comments on how this or that person had changed, or had not done so a whit. Kedrington's acquaintance was even wider, if seeming to consist mainly of matronly ladies with bashful younger ladies in tow. There was one lady, however, riding alone behind her coachman, who turned her head toward Kedrington as she passed. He appeared to recognise her as well, despite the veil pulled forward over her face, although he gave her only the curtest of bows.

"Not the Creole countess, I take it?" Antonia said.

He looked at her uncomprehendingly, and for an uncomfortable instant she thought she must have gone a step too far in her teasing. But as soon as it had appeared, his frown vanished.

"*She* is not a Creole," he said, smiling.

They had little difficulty locating Miss Beecham in the crush, thanks to the huge pink ostrich plumes in the bonnet she had recently purchased for an extravagant sum for just such a public occasion. Her stylish barouche, containing Cloris and a prim, apprehensive Miss Blaine, had already attracted a retinue of gentlemen escorts, whom the Fairfaxes subsequently discovered to be Oliver Beecham; his best friend, Harley Chatham-Hill; and Clory's "beautiful young man," Lord Geoffrey Dane, heir presumptive to his grand-uncle, the bachelor Earl of Danesmere (who was reported, if not actually known, to be a veritable Croesus) and therefore the new darling of the matchmakers.

Mr Chatham-Hill was an attractive if not striking young man of medium height, characterized chiefly by an expressive pair of light blue eyes. Like Oliver, who was two years his junior and regarded Harley in the light of a brother with whom he might indulge in sparring matches, cock fights, race meetings, mutual insults, and the other masculine pursuits common to boys of their age, Harley did not appear at all disconcerted that Clory was at that very moment engaged in a flirtation with a slender young man with curling chestnut locks. This commotion had an unfortunate tendency to obscure the young man's vision so that he was obliged to toss his head prefatory to any remark he wished to address to Miss Beecham.

It was otherwise with Lord Geoffrey. This fair-haired exquisite had a face and figure which were fortunately so near the ideal of fashion that he was able, after the briefest of toilettes, to be assured of the impeccability of his appearance. Aided by such charms, Lord Geoffrey was able to devote his public self exclusively to his goal of contracting a matrimonial alliance acceptable to his grand-uncle in order to induce the old scratch — that was to say, the old gentleman — to loose his hold on the pursestrings and allow Geoffrey an allowance sufficient to keep him — and his new wife, of course — in the style to which Geoffrey had accustomed himself, to the despair of numerous creditors who were becoming decidedly restless at his nonpayment of their long-standing accounts.

Miss Beecham could not, to more realistic eyes, be quite what the old earl would approve, but Geoffrey had no doubt Clory could win his uncle round, once he made clear to her the advantages of the social position she would occupy as his wife. He only wished that she did not feel obliged to tease him along, as so many young ladies did. It was very tiresome to be continually fending off the onslaught of Miss Beecham's other—that was to say, *former*—beaux, who would wave to her as she passed or catch her up on the path to exchange a few words.

Indeed, Geoffrey was rapidly approaching the edge of his tolerance when he espied a fresh, and infinitely more menacing, threat to his hopes in the person of a dark gentleman on an even darker horse, whom Cloris had now caught sight of. A moment later, however, he perceived that although Miss Beecham was staring at this gentleman, her admiration was directed solely at his hat. The gentleman's attention was directed not toward her at all, but toward one of the ladies in his company, who laughed softly at something he said to her and leaned forward slightly to repeat it to her older companion.

Baskcomb slowed the carriage to a tortoise's pace as they approached the Beecham party, allowing Isabel to wave happily at Cloris. When presented to Lord Kedrington, Miss Beecham smiled dazzlingly and held out a hand, which the viscount, with an amused glint in his grey eyes, took and kissed lightly.

"The pleasure is wholly mine, my lord!" Clory replied to his greeting, with a roguish look in her eyes, which made Lord Geoffrey squirm in his saddle but appeared to have no effect whatever on Kedrington. "May I make you known to my governess, Miss Blaine, my brother Oliver, Mr Chatham-Hill, Mr . . . ah, I beg your pardon, Lord Geoffrey Dane."

Bows were exchanged all around. Miss Blaine, accustomed to being treated as a convenience much like a spare umbrella or a repository for shoes to be mended, stammered slightly when Kedrington shook her hand and asked her kindly how she did. Geoffrey, seizing an opportunity to demonstrate to Miss Beecham that she was not the only fish on his line either, bowed low over Miss Isabel Fairfax's hand and favoured her with one of his most charming smiles, which she returned with one of her own. Mr Gary obligingly made way for Lord Geoffrey and turned politely to Mrs Curtiz, while Mr Chatham-Hill and Mr Beecham, following the path of least resistance, dropped behind.

Miss Beecham enquired of Lord Kedrington how it was that she had not seen him at Almack's last Wednesday.

"No one ever sees me at Almack's, Miss Beecham," he told her. "Pray do not suppose yourself discriminated against."

"I do not suppose it, my lord. But I should not care to be treated with strict *égalité*, either. It would be less than flattering to believe that you regarded me as merely another of your vast acquaintance!"

"I fear I am yet imperfectly instructed—having lived so many years abroad, you understand—in the procedures of polite society," the viscount lied smoothly. "Perhaps you will be good enough to tell me how to go on in future. What must I do?"

"Present yourself at Almack's on Wednesday!" was Miss Beecham's prompt advice.

The viscount bowed. "I shall endeavour to do so, if that is your advice, ma'am."

So saying, he backed his horse away imperceptibly, and Cloris, unaware that she was being dismissed, decided after exchanging some further words with Isabel that it was time she were on her way.

"Oh, there is a *dear* friend of mine by the gate! I must not let her escape. So happy to have met you, my lord—come along, Ollie. Geoffrey, why do not you and Harley take a canter along the row—you look as if you need a run. Frances, do mind my hat! Good-bye, Izzy. Good-bye!"

Miss Fairfax, however appreciative of this latest comic turn, nevertheless watched Clory's departure with little regret. On being first introduced to Miss Beecham's escorts, Antonia had passed them each in mental review as possible suitors for Isabel's hand. Mr Beecham and Mr Chatham-Hill she had quickly dismissed as mere boys who, however engaging they might be, lacked seriousness of purpose toward any adult subject, and marriage was doubtless still a very long way from entering their minds. On the other hand, she could not be sorry that Lord Geoffrey, however eligible he might be, had eyes only for Cloris. Not two minutes of his company revealed him—inadvertently, perhaps—to be entirely without humour, let alone wit. Of course, Isabel was herself of a serious cast of mind and might view the young man in a different light, but Antonia was able to be pleasant to him only because she did not seem likely to be given reason to consider him in the same thought as Isabel.

It was then that Antonia realised that she had been making judgements based entirely on her own preferences. Mr Chatham-Hill was, after all, precisely the right age for her young niece, and Lord Geoffrey might well be happy to marry her under just those conditions—however abhorrent to Antonia—that Isabel had set forth at Wyckham. She glanced at Isabel to see if she had made any note of Lord Geoffrey's departure, but on the way her glance caught Octavian Gary's. He had moved closer to the carriage and was gazing down at Isabel—who was quite unaware of it, being engaged in conversation with Imogen—with a look of fond longing tinged with a melancholy that Antonia immediately interpreted as recognition that his case was hopeless.

Gone suddenly was Antonia's half-hearted resolve to assist Isabel in her marital schemes. Instead, she instantly determined to promote Octavian's cause with all the persuasiveness she could muster, caring not a whit that she was whistling prospective fortunes down the wind. Rather, she smiled at the vision—which came to her logically if prematurely—of Octavian and Isabel as the happy owners of a rose-covered cottage and a pair of bouncing twins.

Thus engaged in reverie, she was unaware of a similar gaze more discreetly directed at her until Lord Kedrington enquired, as Baskcomb turned the carriage into Rotten Row, "Do you waltz, Miss Fairfax?"

"Only on the Serpentine," Miss Fairfax replied instantly. "You, of course—Spain having proved you not to be a demi-god—would be obliged to wear a cork belt."

The viscount gave an involuntary crack of laughter, drawing a surprised glance from Mrs Curtiz, and Antonia's mocking "Hush!" did little to curb his merriment. Presently, however, he was able to say more collectedly, "I had a legitimate reason for asking that question, however, and Miss Beecham has put me in mind of it. Maria Sefton has obliged me by procuring vouchers for Almack's for you and your niece, and of course for Mrs Curtiz. If Isabel is reluctant to attend the assemblies before her formal coming-out, she may postpone her appearance, but I trust *you* will have no such scruples. When is her ball to be, by the way?"

"Why, on the ninth—no, I beg your pardon, the tenth of next month. You will naturally be sent an invitation. But, my lord, you are too kind! Almack's! Indeed, you should not have troubled."

"I assure you, it was no trouble—at any rate, not very much! I should warn you, however, that there is a small condition. You must bear a visit shortly from Lady Sefton—she is one of the patronesses, as you know— who insists upon presenting the cards to you personally, and on the right to look you over, since it appears she did not have that honour when you were last in town."

"I shall naturally be happy to receive her," Antonia replied, recalling that Lady Sefton had not before made any effort to become acquainted with her, and therefore grateful to Kedrington for convincing her, however he may have achieved it, that she had missed something.

"I think you may like her," Kedrington said, seeming to read her thoughts. "She strikes some as being affected, but she has a kind heart. You will do well to befriend her—for Isabel's sake, of course!"

"I thank you for the caution, if that is what it is. And it happens that we have embarked on a course of dancing lessons. The waltz was not yet fashionable when I was last in London, and although Isabel knows the steps, she had not been able to practise them at our country assemblies. Mr Chatham-Hill and Miss Beecham have undertaken to instruct us. Clory is very accomplished."

"An accomplished flirt, I think."

"Oh, undoubtedly. Take care, my lord, lest she set her cap at *you!*"

He smiled. "I do not expect it. At this moment, she is wondering, rather, what sort of a cap to put on her pretty head next."

"I fear you will not be outshone on that score."

"I do my humble best. Which of her entourage does she favour—Dane?"

"No more than any other, I believe. However volatile she may appear, I suspect Cloris knows precisely what she wants. She is no self-deceiver and therefore could never deceive anyone else. One must admire her."

"Indeed, for she *is* singular if that is true. Who was it said, 'The reason so few marriages are happy is that young ladies spend their time in making nets, not in making cages'?"

"It was Swift, and very ungallant it is of you to think of it!"

"I am not generally thought ungallant."

"Then something has gone sadly amiss with you of late, my lord, for you do not live up to your reputation so far as I can perceive!"

"Perhaps you may reform me."

"I have no intention to do any such thing."

"But will you not consider—"

"Thank you, no!"

"How did you know what I was about to say?" he demanded, offended.

"I naturally assumed—"

"Never stoop to assumptions, Miss Fairfax. I might have wished to know the context of that infelicitous quotation, or perhaps merely to enquire if you are attempting to set a new fashion of wearing only one earbob?"

She reached her hand to first one ear, then the other, and snatched the lone ornament off, stuffing it quickly into her muff. "How provoking! I had quite forgot the silly thing, and I trust you will not point its absence out to anyone else. I have no desire to make a further exhibition of myself!"

"An admirable ambition, although not an easily attainable one, you know. Fashion decrees that you shall reap what you have sown—however little you may now desire the harvest."

"Do me the kindness not to throw my past follies in my face, please. What *was* it you wished to know?"

"Whether you will not," the viscount began again, unrepentant, "take pity upon a mere mortal so exposed to the insalubrious influences of bachelor society, and so in need of the uplifting companionship and guidance offered within the noble state of matrimony as I am, and bestow your hand upon him?"

After a moment's struggle with herself, Miss Fairfax replied in a like spirit, "I thank you, sir, for the compliment you pay me in deeming me so creditable an influence upon your life, but I fear it is impossible for me to do otherwise than decline your generous offer."

There was another pause, during which Antonia endeavoured not to look the viscount in the face.

"Well?" he said at last. "How was that?"

"Oh, much better!" she told him, breathlessly.

"Thank you," he replied, gratified. "There is hope for me yet, I perceive."

At that moment, Isabel exclaimed, "Oh, *who* is that?" and Antonia's mirth found release in a smile as she turned to see what her niece was staring at.

They were being followed by a curricle with two gentlemen on the perch, both of whom were clothed, shod, and hatted to the finest degree of elegance, the effect of which was unfortunately lost by reason of their being crowded to either side of the perch by a large, equally well-manicured grey poodle seated between them.

"Alvanley and Poodle Byng!" Kedrington said, leaving little doubt of his opinion of the spectacle these gentlemen presented. "It would be best to avoid an encounter with them, but as I perceive the approach from our other flank of a certain Mrs Ebberley-Mercer, an ambitious gorgon with three hopeful but dismal daughters, I am about to introduce you ladies to a pair of very fashionable, if somewhat eccentric, dandies."

So saying, he lifted one hand slightly to the gentlemen. Lord Alvanley, a good-natured peer whose round face bore a perpetual smile, raised his hat to the ladies and hailed Kedrington cheerily, demanding to be told if the viscount had for a fact been robbed on the Kennington Pike, as he had been told.

"You have the direction wrong, William. It was at Holbourn—the Daffy Club, to be precise, where anyone may be fleeced at the card table. I believe you are not acquainted with these ladies, Byng. Allow me to present them to your notice."

This done, a congenial exchange of conversation ensued among the members of the party, during which Lord Alvanley grew cheerier and Mr Byng ogled the young ladies. Alvanley claimed to remember Antonia very well—causing that lady to wince slightly—informed Isabel that she was the image of her mother at the same age and at her prettiest, and succeeded in slipping in an oar with Mrs Curtiz as well, while Byng's aristocratic canine took a notion to rub shoulders with the viscount.

Miss Fairfax smiled at this spectacle, which Mr Byng took as encouragement to him to engage that lady in a one-sided conversation, consisting mainly of his heavy-handed flattery. She tolerated this frivolity for several minutes before comprehending that Kedrington showed no disposition to come to her rescue. It was some time before she was finally able to extricate herself on her own, but she did so deftly and wasted no time in breaking up the other couples, although she did not succeed in dismissing Lord Alvanley and Mr Byng until they had seen the ladies home.

When the two dandies at last parted from them in Mount Street, Antonia accused Lord Kedrington of deliberately prolonging the interview. He denied any such intent, explaining that he had only wanted to give her the opportunity to "steer her own course," as she had professed herself capable of doing. Imogen, overhearing this, enquired then—much to Antonia's delight—after the progress of his own coming-out.

"I trust, my lord, that you have not been worn down by the exigencies of fashionable life?"

Kedrington smiled appreciatively and assured her that he took care not to allow his dissipations to overcome his judgement, and to drink a glass of warm milk before retiring each night.

"I expect," Antonia added, not about to let him off so easily, "that his lordship must be inundated with nosegays and passionate *billets* from all the young ladies who have become enslaved to his charms."

"I assure you, ma'am, several have gone so far as to offer to throw themselves into the Thames for love of me. I do not understand how you can continue to refuse to join them, although I have informed you that you will be quite out of the mode if you do not do so."

"But I don't know how to swim!" Antonia objected.

"Miss Fairfax, I regret to inform you that you have *no* sensibility!"

In vain did Antonia profess herself ready to perform such offices as to turn pale at his snub, or to go into raptures at his smile, or even to give up gaming and dueling for his sake.

"I draw the line at tearing my hair out, however—particularly after Monsieur Antoine has so carefully arranged it for me!"

Mr Gary, who until now had succeeded, albeit with difficulty, in restraining his mirth, finally gave up the struggle. Kedrington threw up his hands.

"It is apparent that my dazzling career is fast coming to a crashing conclusion. I shall take my leave of you ladies while some shred of illusion still remains to me. Octavian, if you wish to reinstate yourself in my good graces, you will remove that idiotic grin from your face and come along with me to pay a call on my Aunt Hester. You know that I rely on you to tear me away—that is, to remind me of the appropriate moment to take my leave of her. Ladies, we bid you a good day!"

= 8 =

ON THE AFTERNOON following their first exposure to London in the season, the ladies of the Fairfax household and Miss Cloris Beecham—who, for the sake of maintaining her lead in social sophistication, had aroused herself at an unaccustomed hour and hastened to Mount Street after the scantiest of breakfasts—were seated in the gold drawing room engaged in a variety of activities of the sort which could be accomplished with a minimum of concentration.

"Oh, look, Antonia!" exclaimed Isabel, who was seated cross-legged on the window seat and examining through her spectacles the inscriptions on the calling cards that had appeared in great quantities on their hall table that morning. "This one is from an earl!"

"There is also a marquess somewhere in the collection," Antonia said, unimpressed.

"No, he is only the eldest son of a marquess, heir to the title," Mrs Curtiz corrected her, not looking up from the flounce she was mending.

"What a pity there are no available kings or princes," Antonia lamented. "One would think that with all the notables there are in town, there would be at least one to shower Isabel with diamonds."

"Countess Lieven had on a *magnificent* diamond tiara at last week's Carleton House fête," Clory said, helping herself to another slice of the toast which had been sent for on her account. "I saw her go by in her carriage. Imogen says the Princess of Wales wears diamonds as big as *robin's* eggs."

Isabel turned wide-eyed to Mrs Curtiz. "Is that true, Imogen? I've never seen such large ones. Are they beautiful?"

"No, my love, they are cold and unapproachable. Don't blame Caroline for taking what she can get in place of real affection, but you ought rather to have, one day, a medium-size emerald or ruby, I think.

"I had a ruby once," she continued reminiscently. "It was given me by a king. Only a Bedouin king, to be sure, and goodness knows how *he* came by it."

"Will you show it to me?" Isabel asked.

"I wish I were able to do so, my dear, but it was lost a short time afterward when our caravan overturned in a flooded wadi. I never saw the king again, I'm happy to say. I don't know how I should have broken the news to him, poor little man."

Everyone laughed at this except Cloris, who considered it thoughtfully for a moment, concluding, "Well, I daresay *I* should not care for diamonds, either. I'm sure I could be happy with cream teas and muslin sheets and a reliable modiste."

"You are a flighty baggage," Mrs Curtiz scolded her.

Cloris smiled knowingly. "At least, whatever man wins me will get precisely what he bargained for. There will be no surprises on *my* wedding night."

"Cloris!"

"Oh, you know what I mean! Think now—is there anything any of you could tell about me that would surprise anyone? I do as I please, and people accept me or they do not. I do not ask for the moon."

"I expect Lord Geoffrey would give it to you if you did," Antonia suggested slyly.

"Oh, I shall certainly break it off with *him*," Clory informed her. "He is forever offering to do such things, *demanding* to be allowed to prove his devotion to me, although why he thinks going off to missions in foreign climes would prove any such thing, I'm sure I don't know. He is becoming a dreadful bore."

"You *are* cruel," Isabel said in defence of the much-maligned Lord Geoffrey. "I'm sure I am very sorry for him!"

"I tell you what, Isabel Fairfax, *you* are too soft-hearted! Apart from his being heir to that old stickler Danesmere, you must know, his mama is quite *determined* that Geoffrey should marry as soon as possible so that she may have grandchildren to be a comfort to her in her dotage. He is therefore convinced that he is *ripe* for marriage, and failure in his efforts to achieve it only frustrates him the more. I don't know how many ladies he has proposed to already, but don't you be the next, Izzy, for you will in all likelihood be too *sorry* for him to refuse him!"

With that, Cloris rose and licked the last of the strawberry jam from her fingers. "Izzy, dear, would you care to accompany me to Owen's? I have only just this moment remembered that I have some lace on order there, which I may need for my ball gown."

"Do go along," Mrs Curtiz advised before Isabel had the opportunity to say whether she wished to go along or not. "It's a lovely day, and the air will do you good."

"Oh, you and Antonia must come as well," Cloris insisted. "Afterward we may drive by the Pultney Hotel and ogle the Russians."

"A splendid idea! I don't believe I've seen a Grand Duchess before." Mrs Curtiz broke off her thread and folded her mending neatly into her basket. "Antonia, do you not care to join us?"

Antonia had remained in her chair, observing the street outside the window. Cloris eyed her speculatively.

"I met Lord Kedrington on my way here this morning," she remarked offhandedly. "He was coming out of the churchyard down the street—of all the unlikely places—and he promised to be at Lady Sefton's soirée next week. I must say, it was very provoking of him to tell me he never attends Almack's, when in fact he goes all the time—or so Fanny Mercer tells me—but one cannot help but forgive such a wickedly attractive gentleman *anything,* can one?"

Antonia frowned, piqued as much at being misunderstood—she had in fact been wondering if Mr Gary might call before Isabel left the house—as by Clory's references to the viscount. But with that lady's sharp eye on her, she made an effort to smooth her forehead and smile serenely, as befitted a worldy aunt of her years. Unfortunately, Clory had by this time joined Antonia's vigil at the window, and while she was drawing on her gloves and speculating as to who that dumpy woman across the street with the *shrieking* orange pelisse might be, an unfamiliar curricle came into view from around the corner of South Audley Street.

"Oh, look, *there* is a much more attractive sight, indeed. How is it that handsome, broad-shouldered young men like that never drive past *my* window? Oh, but he is not going past at all—he is stopping at this very house! Who in the world . . . ?"

She stopped to stare, with dawning comprehension, at Antonia's rapidly colouring face. "Why, Antonia Fairfax, you sly thing. I do believe you have been found out in a secret *amour!* He must be a secret, for I am sure *I* have never seen him before. Wherever did you find him?"

"That will do, Cloris," interposed Mrs Curtiz, pulling her inexorably away from the window and toward the door, clucking like a mother hen. Cloris said no more, but winked back at Antonia as she went out the door, and Antonia knew she would speedily get to the bottom of the mysterious stranger. Before following her friends out, Isabel bent to kiss her aunt's cheek and whispered, "Don't mind Clory, love. I know how it is."

"Thank you, darling," Antonia said, smiling up at her. "But—I cannot help but think she is right about Lord Geoffrey, Isabel. Do you not agree?"

Isabel did not answer directly, saying only, "Please don't worry about me," before turning away.

This answer had precisely the opposite effect on her aunt, but Isabel was gone before Antonia could press her further. A moment later she could hear, over Isabel's more subdued greetings, Cloris being simply *enchantée* to make Charles Kenyon's acquaintance, and when Charles was at last ushered into the drawing room, Antonia looked up at him with a mingling of delight and apprehension.

He had not changed. If anything, he was more handsome than before. Tall and fair, he wore a pair of grey-and-white-striped pantaloons with a fawn coat that did little to minimise his broad shoulders. His cravat was neatly tied, and of a pale yellow colour that gave his costume a foreign look, at variance with the general impression of solid English respectability. It was this aspect which disconcerted Antonia a little—his stolidness. He looked scarcely the dashing hero her memory had made of him.

But his smile was the same—slow and unexpectedly charming. As Charles came forward, carrying a delicate bouquet of lilies-of-the-valley in his hand, Belding discreetly pulled the door to behind him, and Antonia was aware of a girlish confusion that caused her to take a step backward and look warily up at him. He laughed. He had a pleasant, low laugh that matched the vibrant baritone of his voice, which, as it had always done, sent a chill up Antonia's spine. She had forgotten that voice.

"I have just been introduced to a Miss Beecham," he said, thoughtfully

92

removing some of the awkwardness from the moment by transferring it to himself.

"What you mean to say," Antonia said as she took the lilies from him and concealed her blush in their sweet scent until it had faded somewhat, "is that you have just been *overwhelmed* by a Miss Beecham. Fortunately, she is the only Miss Beecham of our acquaintance, and when you once come to know her, I daresay you will find her perfectly amiable—or at least, diverting!"

"I must bow to your superior knowledge, my dear, but . . . are you quite sure she is an appropriate companion for Isabel?"

"Oh, she is precisely what Isabel needs! Cloris may scarcely be called shy herself, but she has a generous nature and a supremely practical turn of mind which leads her directly to the most appropriate remedy for any affliction—including Isabel's shyness. I must confess, however, that her liveliness frequently makes *me* feel like a grandmother!"

Charles rose readily to the occasion. "Then you cannot have looked into your glass recently, my dear, for you do not look in the least like a grandmother. Indeed, you are more lovely than I remember—no, that is a churlish thing to say! I only meant that I would not have supposed you *could* become lovelier!"

"You have always been very kind, Charles."

"No, no! Nonsense. What I have always been is singularly inept at making pretty speeches. You see, I have even brought you those flowers to speak for me. But it requires no talent for flattery to say that you are beautiful, for it is the simple truth."

Antonia was both surprised and touched by this unexpected but obviously sincere tribute, and she was silent, bereft for the moment of her powers of speech. He raised her hand to his lips, and she felt her fingers tremble involuntarily in his. She tried to withdraw them, but he pressed them tighter for a moment, smiling in a rather abstracted way as he searched her eyes intently.

She lowered her own eyes and, to turn the subject, said, "Would you care for a little refreshment, Charles?"

"I beg you, do not trouble yourself."

"Oh, it is no trouble to *me!*" she replied, quizzing him, and reached for the bell cord behind her. "I have merely to pull the cord—thusly—for my every whim to be granted me. Also, you must give me your opinion of Imogen's latest blend."

He smiled. "I am not a connoisseur, and I cannot imagine that Mrs Curtiz cares a jot for my opinion of her teas, although I will certainly be honoured to sample her new blend. But, come, tell me, Antonia—how is it that you are alone here? Never tell me you have no suitors beating a path to your door, no offers of marriage?"

"Oh, in fact, I have had several!" she replied unsteadily, unable to keep the laughter out of her voice at the memory of Lord Kedrington's experimental offers. Charles, scarcely expecting a literal reply to his *plaisanterie,* raised his brows enquiringly, but Antonia was saved from having to explain the joke to him by Belding's entrance in response to her ring. During the brief pause while she conveyed their pressing need for a pot of tea to her butler, she contrived to pull herself together, so that when she turned back to Charles, her smile was easy and she felt more in command of herself.

"Well, Charles, you are become quite the successful man of business," she said, as she motioned him to be seated.

"Why, yes," he confessed, with a modest pride. "In my small way, I have done quite well. I have just moved the firm's offices to a new building in Long Acre, in fact."

"As well as that?" Antonia exclaimed, then bit her tongue at the unbecoming surprise in her voice. "Uncle Philip tells us you have to do with the continental trade—I take him to mean luxuries such as wines and laces and the like. Now the peace is signed, you must become very prosperous indeed, for all those things which have been in short supply for so many years must now be in great demand. But it is a pity that the *supplying* of such niceties has *demanded* that you spend so much time away from Leicestershire!"

Charles Kenyon had a wide acquaintance among the prominent merchant families of the city of London and was not unknown in the drawing rooms of Mayfair. But while many a shy young lady had hung on his words and gazed worshipfully up at him while he explained the various enterprises which he had built up from a carrier business that had been on its last legs when he bought it, his pride had never been so great that he could deceive himself into believing the interest of these damsels to be in his achievements rather than in the fruits of his success. Any sign of ostentation was foreign to Charles Kenyon's temperament, but he dressed like a gentleman, belonged to the best clubs, and kept only the finest horses in his stables. At thirty-two, he had the demeanour of a much more mature man and an air of having been out in the world long enough to know what was what. He was undeniably, as the mothers of the Lizzies and Jennies and Bellas of Bloomsbury and Islington daily reminded their giddy offspring, as good a catch as any lord.

It had been some time, however, since Charles had encountered the kind of intelligent curiosity that Antonia Fairfax took in all subjects, and especially in those which concerned people she was fond of. But then he recalled that she had always been somewhat precocious, asking questions about matters that most girls took no interest in. He had admired her for that—indeed, for many things. The ignominious end of their brief, long-ago engagement temporarily forgotten, Charles could not now think why he had let so much time pass since their last meeting.

"Yes, I have been fortunate," he told her. "My only regret is that my affairs have kept me so much in London—not that things would have collapsed without me had I taken a short holiday, but . . . well, tell me, Antonia, is your sister—that is, how are they all at Wyckham? Do you hear from Carey? It must have been very trying for you, to be obliged to undertake the affairs of the estate yourself."

"Not at all," Antonia replied, disregarding Charles's reluctance to mention Maria. "Naturally, we have greatly missed having Carey with us, but as for Wyckham—why, you would be amazed, Charles, at how proficient I have become at figures and accounts. Indeed, when Carey returns, I may need to seek a position as clerk with you to keep myself occupied! What would be very trying for me would be to have nothing to do all day."

"Nothing but parties and pretty gowns and the latest mode in hairstyles."

She smiled. "You must think me a sadly frivolous creature, Charles! But I would not deprive Isabel of the pleasures a pretty young girl finds in such fripperies, even at the risk of my becoming one of those managing females everyone despises. It is very difficult, when one has been her own mistress for years and years—"

"Not so many years as that!"

She gave a watery chuckle and spread her hands helplessly. "My dear Charles, you must know that my last birthday was my twenty-fifth!"

"Which is still far too young to be speaking of yourself in terms of years and years."

And indeed, she did feel very young and helpless beside Charles, whose living presence was so much more vital than mere memories. They, having brought her girlhood so quickly back to her, now receded, leaving it in the hands of this strong, familiar stranger. It was not an unpleasant sensation, but it was a new one, and she was not yet certain how to deal with it.

Fortunately, since Charles seemed inclined to pursue the subject, Mrs Curtiz, having decided not to join the shopping expedition after all, had relieved Belding of the tea tray and entered just at that moment with it in hand. Antonia could not help admiring Imogen's sense of timing, but Charles seemed to see no calculation in it and rose to his feet to take the tray from her.

"My dear ma'am! You must not be allowed to—"

"My dear Charles! I am perfectly capable of this little exertion. Do allow me to indulge myself."

She shot a speaking look at Antonia as she set the tray on an inlaid mahogany table. "Not," she went on, "that this represents much of an indulgence. I declare, I have never seen such a meagre repast in this house. Can Cloris have eaten everything? I have sent Belding after some of those macaroons Mrs Driscoll made yesterday. How are you, Charles? How is your father? More to the point, *where* is your father? Do sit down, dear boy."

Looking not unlike a large dog being kept at bay by a very vocal terrier, Charles meekly obeyed. He took a cup of tea, together with instructions on how to sip it so as to savour its flavour to the fullest, and ventured the information that he expected his father within the week.

"That is, I have not had a letter recently, but such was his last intention. I presume he means to abide by it."

"There is no telling," Mrs Curtiz said, implying darkly that Philip Kenyon's intentions were not to be trusted. "Oh, here are the macaroons."

Here was, in fact, Belding with a plate of macaroons, which Imogen rose to relieve him of and Charles, determinedly gallant, leapt to take from her. Antonia promptly joined in the game, admonishing them both to sit down so that she might play her proper role as hostess.

"For I must impress on you, Charles," she said as she offered the macaroons to each of them in turn, "how adept I am becoming at entertaining visitors. We have already had a great many, you know, in addition to which I am obliged to devote myself to such matters as hiring another kitchen maid to assist Mrs Driscoll in her macaroon-making."

"You still have Mrs Driscoll with you, then?" Charles enquired, displaying—or pretending to display—a gratifying memory of life at Wyckham, despite his having had no part of it for so long. Mrs Curtiz raised her eyebrows, but did not voice her enquiry; instead, she sat back with the air of one about to be granted the answer to a long-standing riddle. Antonia shot her a warning look, and then, reassured by Imogen's discreet silence, returned her attention to Charles.

"Indeed, yes. And now that she has escaped the influence of our formidable Mrs Medwin—you remember our housekeeper, of course, Charles?—she has waxed positively jovial and makes nothing of daily expeditions to Covent Garden market for fresh vegetables. She has even been induced—by the neighbours' superior chefs, I daresay—to experiment with dishes *à la française* and exotic sauces that her country-bred soul has heretofore scorned. Even Belding has revealed an unexpectedly intimate knowledge of such corners of London as I had not known to exist but which seem a veritable treasure house of fine wines and cheap candles."

Charles declared himself pleased that matters were so well in train toward making their season a great success. He offered once again to assist in any way he could and enquired if Belding was aware of a certain source for the champagne they would need to lay in for Isabel's ball, and if Mrs Driscoll's foodstuffs could not be acquired at an even better price at such-and-such a vendor's, until presently Charles and Antonia fell into a discussion of the minutiae of household management which cast Mrs Curtiz into the role of silent observer, rather like a witness to a contest between two Billingsgate fishmongers over which of them was the more knowledgeable and resourceful in the pursuit of his trade.

"There was a note from Lady Sefton in this morning's post as well," she interposed suddenly, as if continuing rather than interrupting the flow of conversation. "I daresay that means she and her vouchers for Almack's will be upon us shortly."

"Almack's!" Charles exclaimed, apparently oblivious to any ulterior motive that might lurk behind Imogen's pointed turn of the subject.

"That *is* splendid. I did not know you were acquainted with any of the patronesses."

"We are not, as yet," Antonia was obliged to concede. "We are, rather, fortunate to be acquainted with someone who is and interceded most kindly on our behalf. I do hope you will accompany us when we attend the assembly, Charles."

"Alas, I wish I were able to do so," Charles replied, causing Mrs Curtiz to give him an admiring look for his honesty. "But I understand that persons engaged in commerce have no hope of gaining an entrée to the famous assemblies. I have not cared to humiliate myself by seeking one."

"Surely you might have had your father seek it for you," Antonia suggested. "*He* is scarcely a giant of industry."

Charles did not see the pun, but smiled just the same.

"Shall we at least see you for dinner this evening?" she asked, feeling as if she should apologise to him. "I seem to recall that you are particularly fond of saddle of mutton, which indeed I trust is so, for Mrs Driscoll has managed to procure an especially fine one for this evening."

"Well, well, I must accept your invitation in that case. I shall certainly look forward to it. And I wonder if I may challenge Isabel to a game of backgammon after dinner? I seem to recall now that she was quite a hand at it, as they say."

"She will trounce you soundly, I warn you."

"I trust my pride will sustain the blow," he replied with a smile. "How pretty little Isabel has grown to be, by the way. I remember her as a mere slip of a girl, who adored her aunt and uncle and was quite miserable when they would not play with her, taking refuge in the nearest book!"

"Well, she is still very literary, of course," Antonia conceded. "But she has been very good about—that is, she appears to be enjoying the amusements of the city quite as well as the solitude of the library."

"You are, certainly, hoping that she will make a good match this season. Are there any serious candidates as yet?"

Antonia was somewhat taken aback at this plain speaking, but reminded herself that putting a pretty face on it would not alter the truth of the situation. "Not as yet," she told him. "There is one very pleasant young man who—"

She stopped then, suddenly aware that Charles would not be likely to consider Octavian Gary a "serious candidate."

98

"—who has called several times," she finished, without mentioning a name. She glanced appealingly at Imogen Curtiz, who remarked that there would be sure to be any number of young men at Almack's for Isabel to look over. This led to a discussion of Isabel's social calendar, an inventory of her wardrobe, and a number of recommendations from Charles—who revealed an unexpectedly wide knowledge of current gossip—on whom she might profitably *not* consider. Mrs Curtiz looked as if she expected this latest verbal contest to go on at inconvenient length and rose to excuse herself as soon as Charles took a breath.

"If you children will pardon me, I did promise to meet Isabel and Cloris after they finish at Owen's, and I would not care to let them stand about waiting by themselves for very long."

"Certainly not. Do not let us detain you!" Charles said, rising from his chair as Mrs Curtiz put down her teacup. "But may I not offer you my escort?"

Imogen waved her hand at him to be seated again and told him such a sacrifice would not be required of him. "I am certain it will be much more agreeable for you both to stay here and decide all our fates over the macaroons."

With that, she swept out of the room, leaving Charles gazing thoughtfully after her. At last he said, "I do beg your pardon, Antonia! I had not realised I was becoming so—officious. I fear that the requirements of running a business make me far too prone to giving orders outside the office as well."

"You have done no such thing here," Antonia assured him, hoping she did not appear too quick to deny it. She put out her hand to lay it reassuringly over Charles's. "For my part, I welcome your suggestions most eagerly."

"Thank you, my dear. In that case, I shall take the liberty of offering yet another—even more presumptuous, I fear. Tell me, do you still have the intention of holding Isabel's ball here?"

"Oh, yes. We are already up to our ears in redecoration schemes."

"Excellent! But let me put this to you. I have recently purchased a house in Cavendish Square, you may know. Not the most fashionable of addresses, perhaps, but quite fine enough for . . . ah, a man of business. I had hoped to convince you—and you must not refuse me, Antonia, since I as well as my father stand as Isabel's sponsor—that you will consent to hold the ball there. I have quite a large, well-appointed ballroom, as you shall see for yourself, and several very fine smaller rooms in which card tables may be set up. In short, I should be very pleased to do this for you, my dear."

She smiled, touched more by this last impulsive utterance than by Charles's rehearsed and not entirely unexpected offer of hospitality.

"Anything you may do for Isabel is indeed a favour to me as well, Charles. Thank you; we shall be happy to accept your generous offer. And do please come to dinner this evening—indeed, you will always be welcome in our home."

"Thank you," he said, adding quietly, "I . . . I *am* happy to see you again, Antonia. I trust we may renew our friendship?"

"I am certain we shall."

"Splendid! Well—well, I shall take my leave, then. Do not trouble to see me out. I can find my way."

She saw him to the door just the same, and although he regretted once again that he was unable to attend Almack's with them, he assured her that he would be on hand that evening as well, to approve their finery.

When he had gone, she sat down at her window and gazed thoughtfully out of it at the house across the street, reviewing their meeting. She had not known precisely what to expect of it, but she was a little disconcerted to discover that it was both more and less than she had hoped. Charles's voice, his smile, the touch of his hand were all as she remembered, and his apparent forgiveness of their past estrangement ought to have represented the realisation of a years-old dream. But something else had happened in those years. She could not put a name to it, but it seemed to have to do with those things which had not changed in her—and perhaps not in Charles, either—but which were nevertheless not quite the same.

=9=

Viscount Kedrington was unable to call on the Fairfaxes for several days after their encounter in the park, finding himself required to consult with his solicitor and to compose a number of letters calling for a certain diplomatic tact—at which he was disconcerted to discover he had become somewhat maladroit since his consular days. He also paid several calls at a small house in Half Moon Street, in which his past experience of subterfuge came more handily.

Between these matters of business, he was committed to certain social engagements to which he did not like to draw attention by his absence. He was therefore reduced to sending his secretary—after Octavian had written out the more pressing letters in his neat hand—off to Mount Street to keep his employer's memory alive in that quarter. This duty was no hardship for Octavian, even though the viscount charged him not to overlook Miss Antonia Fairfax in favour of pursuing a more attractive tête-à-tête with Miss Isabel. Kedrington reined in his own impatience and went to visit his aunts in Berkeley Square. He arrived to find a vaguely familiar landaulet standing in the stableyard, but it was not until he had handed his hat and gloves to his aunts' elderly butler that he remembered whose it was.

"Good morning, Webster. Is my aunt receiving?"

"Yes, my lord," he was informed. "Miss Coverley is also in the drawing room. Mr and Mrs Rowland Wilmot and Mr Angus Wilmot arrived twenty minutes ago."

Kedrington hesitated. "Good God, it's Sunday, isn't it?" he enquired rhetorically of the bronze Apollo set on the hall table. "I'd forgotten. However, since I'm here, I must make the best of it, eh, Webster?"

"Yes, my lord," the butler agreed woodenly.

Sundays were customarily set aside for family visits, not because Julia Wilmot possessed any abundance of familial affection, but because she refused to be plagued with unannounced invasions of relatives on any day it suited them to descend upon her. Kedrington being the sole exception to this rule, Miss Hester Coverley was obliged to smuggle into her own home any stray cousin who chanced to call on a weekday. She was not in fact often reduced to such a subterfuge, for although Julia left Coverley House but twice a year, journeying to and from her house in Berkshire, Hester was free to gad about as she pleased, and to pay any number of calls on whomever she pleased—even, indeed, to do so wearing the daring, brightly coloured bonnets she adored but which Julia disapproved in humiliatingly frank terms.

Hester had never lost the vivacity which made the Coverley girls—the other of whom was Kedrington's mother, Cecily—famous in their day, nor the affectionate nature which prevented her from being overwhelmed by Julia's more forceful personality. Julia had been born a Heywood, but succumbed to the Wilmot charm, with which her husband, Gerald, had been blessed in abundance, long enough to give birth to her son Rowland before she began to regret her lapse.

In recent years, Julia had become more vocal in her condemnation of the Wilmot side of the family, and when Kedrington returned from Spain as from the dead, she lost no time in assuring the world that she considered the event nothing short of divine intercession. Kedrington did not share his aunt's strong feelings, however, with the result that his indifference toward any relatives other than his eccentric but personable aunts was generally if erroneously interpreted as malicious. He did nothing to correct this misconception, and being as phlegmatic about it as Julia was outspoken, he unwittingly reinforced it.

It was therefore not to be wondered at that Kedrington took no pains to conceal his distaste when the first sight to greet him as he was ushered into Julia's drawing room was that of his heir—his right arm flung up on the windowpane in a posture of romantic despair, his eyes staring glassily into the square. Angus's spindly frame was clothed in a remarkable ensemble of funereal black, relieved only partially by a grey waistcoat with silver buttons and a white cravat spotted with black. His cousin raised his quizzing glass and surveyed this unorthodox costume with a critical eye.

"Who died?"

Angus, recognizing the Voice of Authority, jumped, sputtered, recalled himself, and said he was dam—dashed if he knew what my lord meant.

The viscount was prevented from telling him by the icy accents of his Aunt Julia, who requested her tiresome grandson to refrain kindly from making a further display of himself and to fetch the viscount a chair. She herself, seated in state upon an elegant rose satin sofa, reached out an imperious hand to her nephew, who smiled, touched his lips lightly to the parchmentlike fingers, and expressed regret that he could not stay very long.

"Nonsense! You scarcely ever come to visit me, Kedrington. The least you can do is to take a glass of sherry with me when you do."

"Unfair, ma'am! Aunt Hester, I appeal to you. Have I neglected you?"

Miss Hester Coverley, with a delicate flutter of her plump hands, declared that indeed no! Her dear Duncan was ever kind and considerate. . . . No one could possibly think . . . Her voice trailed off, leaving, as it usually did, unfinished sentences in its wake.

"Sally Jersey called this morning," Julia said, not hesitating to interrupt. Kedrington was in the act of greeting Angus's mother, a pretty but unanimated woman; and not being so easily quelled as his Aunt Hester, he went on in a leisurely way to shake Rowland Wilmot's hand. As Julia watched with a hint of approval behind her glare, he said conversationally that he had heard Devil's Own had won by two lengths at Newmarket last week.

Wilmot, a good-looking, likeable man with more savoir-faire than he would ever pass on to his lackluster offspring, smiled wryly (well aware that Kedrington knew he had dropped a good many guineas at that race by betting on the horse that came in second), said that it was closer to three lengths, and hoped that my lord had not wasted an afternoon watching the debacle.

"No, Wilmot, I never put money on cattle I cannot control myself. What did Sally want, Julia?"

The grey eyes that matched his own held a smile, but Julia's voice was as dry as the rustle of the old-fashioned petticoats she spread around her on the sofa.

"She wanted to know if it is true that you engaged in espionage in Spain, disguised as a priest."

Kedrington accepted Angus's obedient offer of a chair, and sat down near his aunt, taking her hand at the same time and holding it in his own as he spoke. "Who told her that?"

"You did, apparently."

"Did I? Then it must be true."

"There!" declared Hester feelingly. "Do you not see how awkward it is? I don't know what your poor mama would think if . . . Duncan, dearest, you must not say such things if they are not true!"

"My dear Hester, what has their veracity to say to anything? People expect to hear such things, and have you not above all instructed me to be obliging?"

Hester protested that he must have misunderstood her—for how could he think that untruthfulness obliged anyone?—and looked as if she would burst into tears. Since she frequently fell into this state, however, her nephew was not overly concerned that he had hurt her feelings. He knew very well that his return to England, which had so gratified Julia, had also been something of a honeyfall to Hester. The aura of romance about him—not to mention his value on the marriage mart—added much to her consequence, and although she disclaimed any desire to manage his affairs, both she and Kedrington recognised this little fiction for what it was. The viscount had long since discovered that the energy his aunt thus expended was formidable and, if properly channelled, could be turned to good account. So he allowed her to regret his appalling want of conduct for a little longer, and then promised humbly that he would take care to conduct himself more suitably in future.

"That is all very well," Hester quavered, "but as you have not been about at all for the past fortnight, there is no saying what rumours may not be afloat concerning you."

"I rather think I must count myself fortunate not to have been forgotten in a fortnight's time. But I shall take care not to run the risk again. I am prepared to accept your authority on such matters, Aunt."

Hester looked up from her reticule, in which she had been fumbling for a handkerchief, and stared at her nephew, struggling to accept what seemed to her the inevitable implication of what she had just heard. Kedrington took his own handkerchief out of his pocket and handed it to her. She blew her nose delicately, composed herself, and said, "Dearest, do you . . . Can you possibly mean . . . ?"

"I mean, dearest Aunt Hester, that I regret taking your eminently sensible advice insufficiently to heart, and that I am willing to rectify this inauspicious beginning—shall we say, with an appearance at Almack's on Wednesday?"

"Almack's!" Hester exclaimed, recovering with astonishing speed from her dejection. "But that is a splendid notion! You will cause a sensation, I have no doubt, and once everyone learns that you truly intend to go about more in society, we—you—will be showered with invitations."

Kedrington grimaced. "It seems to me that my hall table is already overflowing with cards and engraved effusions of several sorts. I cannot respond to all of them, Aunt, or I shall have no time left to eat and sleep.

"However," he added, to brighten Hester's crestfallen expression, "if you will be so kind as to assist Octavian in the selection, I will agree to respond to one in ten of the more, ah . . . tolerable propositions offered."

"One in ten?"

"At the most."

Kedrington watched his younger aunt, upon whose pretty plump countenance began to dance visions of the ladies who would swoon with delight at the prospect of the viscount's appearance at one of their functions—and of the power this would give Hester herself as the person through whom petitions for his presence must pass. Since this prospect appeared to have temporarily bereft her of speech, her nephew suggested gently that she might begin as soon as possible.

"Oh, to be sure!" Hester exclaimed. "I shall make up a list this very evening and consult with you in the morning. But do you not think, dearest, that one in ten . . . ?"

"Is a very tidy number, yes. I am certain I may leave it all in your capable hands."

"To be sure, my love. But—"

"Perhaps if you were to begin immediately," the viscount suggested, before Hester could voice what he suspected would be plans of her own to return the hospitality of the ton, "you would not then have to strain your eyes by candlelight this evening."

This suggestion struck Hester forcibly—for she was much troubled by migraine headaches—and she begged to be forgiven if she dashed away. Julia nodded her head, but maintained the ominous silence which she had drawn over herself when Kedrington had first presented his plan for the amusement of the Metropolis in general and of his Aunt Hester in particular.

When the door shortly closed behind Hester, however, Julia embarked upon a stream of small talk consisting of a description of every bloom in the small garden to the rear of the house, in which she was accustomed to take the air each morning, followed by an enumeration of the callers she had received that day and a detailing of the precise relationship to the Heywoods in which each of them stood. All of this was nicely calculated to induce in Rowland Wilmot a boredom that very soon had him shifting restlessly in his chair, and in Fanny an acute consciousness of her own lack of social accomplishments—of which she was well aware, but of which she disliked to be reminded—so that she shortly gratified her husband more than she had in twenty years of marriage by rising during a break thoughtfully provided by Julia in her recital, thanking her hostess for a delightful hour, and adjuring her son to make his bow and come along.

"I believe I'll stay," Angus declared uncooperatively. He had been studying for some minutes the arrangement of his cousin's neckcloth, and only a few seconds more of concentration would, he felt, provide him with the key to its construction. Unfortunately, the viscount chose that moment to turn his head and ruin Angus's perspective. Kedrington atoned for this inconsideration, however, by civilly enquiring if Angus would care to accompany him to Manton's Shooting Gallery on the following Tuesday. Angus, with more acuity than might have been expected of him, rightly understood this to be a Hint and—after accepting his mentor's invitation—removed himself from the room close on the heels of his parents.

Julia sat in silence for a moment, watching her nephew casually flick a bit of lint from his sleeve.

"You are become very autocratic, Duncan," she observed, in the tone of an impartial observer.

"Do you wonder at it? When I am continually assaulted by reminders of my position as head of the family?"

"You need not tell me that I have been the source of most of those reminders," Julia said. "I had hoped, however, to depress certain pretensions in other members of the family rather than to raise you in your own esteem! It is bad enough to be obliged to hear Fanny prate on about The

Family, holding her nose in the air for all the world like a hare sniffing the wind—but actually to add to her consequence by passing the title on to that branch is not even to be considered!"

"But you do consider it."

"I must, if you will not."

"There's no harm in Angus."

Julia sniffed. "Only if an utter lack of will and substance can be called harmless. It is a negative virtue at best, to have no harm in one. But it is the same with all the Wilmots—look at Rowland, all charm and no matter—and Angus is a Wilmot clear through. Even his father speaks of him as if he were a horse, as if blood and bone were all—which in this case they most certainly are not! And you . . . well, for all your talk about there being no harm in Angus, you treat your secretary with more respect."

"You are very harsh, my love. The Heywood strain may come out in Angus's son after all."

Julia winced, but concluded with commendable calm, "I shall not, thank God, be here to discover whether it will or no. Do not force me, Duncan, to remind you how much, much rather I would see a son of yours in the succession before I die."

Julia's voice had lost its acerbity, and she sounded so unlike herself and so much like Duncan's own mother that he was moved to smile and reach out to press her hand.

"If I have disappointed you, my love, I have not done so deliberately."

With a rustle of grey silk, Julia moved to one side and patted the sofa beside her to urge her nephew to sit near her. "Then none of the fair eligibles Hester has thrown in your way has pleased you?"

"They have all pleased me. Some for as long as five minutes."

"What about the Adderley chit?"

"Too short."

"You won't be standing up *all* the time!" Julia snapped, reverting to her caustic self and drawing a crack of laughter from Kedrington, who expressed regret, when he had recovered his gravity, that he was simply not in the petticoat line.

"Nonsense! I have never seen any man so enjoy the effect of his charm upon women as you do. Why else are you now seeking new conquests at Almack's?"

107

"I owe Maria Sefton a favour."

Julia gave him an appraising look, but his expression remained bland. "Well, I won't pretend to know what that means. But you need not try to deceive me, Kedrington, that you are not a thorough romantic at heart. Do you think I do not know that is why you deserted hearth and home to run off and lose yourself in Spain, only to return home to make a friend of the likes of Byron? Heaven knows it was not for any love of conformity. What about the Fairfax girl?" she demanded, suddenly changing her tack.

The viscount stiffened momentarily, but kept the lightness in his voice. "Which one, Aunt Julia?"

"If you must ask that, it doesn't much matter, I suppose. I had hoped that this sudden desire of yours to mingle with the ton meant that you had found at least one member of it worth the trouble. I should not expect you to explain your motives. I can only hope that you have not set your heart on some romantic dream that you can never realise."

Kedrington breathed more easily. He had not known that his aunt was even aware of Antonia Fairfax's existence, and he had an absurd fancy to keep its value to his own from becoming known to anyone but Antonia — particularly since he was in some doubt still about his own course of action regarding her. He had asked himself frequently if he ought to have behaved differently with Antonia at Wyckham; he might have been less obvious in his attentions, since she seemed unready to accept them. On the other hand, she behaved toward him now as if nothing at all had happened between them, so that he sometimes thought it might have been better if he had declared himself to her then and there and not been obliged now to attempt a subtle courtship in the full glare of the public scrutiny he had mercifully been able to forget during his stay in Leicestershire.

He had reckoned, for instance, without Julia's multitude of confidants. It was still considered an honour to take tea with Julia Wilmot, and such diverse personalities as Emily Cowper and the Duke of Clarence often did, to refresh themselves with her astringent opinions on matters which they themselves had not often the courage to express themselves publicly. Julia judged people harshly and at times unjustly, but she was honest and she was discreet. Kedrington was occasionally tempted to confide in Julia about Antonia, for when Julia cared for someone, she was generous and affectionate. Her callers repaid her by keeping her entertained with the latest news and gossip—and exhaustingly informed of the truth behind rumours and the secrets behind the doors she no longer troubled to call at herself.

"Honoré Gaillard also called," she was saying. "I had not seen him for an age. None of the Devereaux but Honoré and Clare ever comes to town—not that Honoré's a blood relation. It's a great pity, but . . . what was I about to say? Oh, yes. He told me he had seen that Neville woman—the one Neil Gary made a cake of himself over—at Osborne's Hotel and couldn't imagine what she was doing there. That was weeks ago, and he hasn't seen her since, but I wonder if I ought to write Henry Neville about it?"

"I shouldn't do that, love," Kedrington said blandly.

Julia, who had been searching her nephew's face in vain for some indication of precisely how much he knew of the regrettable Miss Neville's affairs, was reduced to asking point-blank, "Do you know anything about it?"

"I couldn't say, Aunt."

"You mean you won't," Julia acknowledged. "Hester's right. One may as well wait for the official despatches as try to get anything out of you! Oh, don't poker up, I won't press you any further." She sighed. "But I do wish you wouldn't keep your *amours* so secret."

Kedrington laughed in spite of himself. "That sounds reprehensible, indeed! What of my reputation, Julia? My position? Consider The Family!" He rose with that and took his aunt's hand to kiss it.

Julia smiled. "Stuff! I know very well you have taste enough not to go that course. But where *are* you going?"

"To pay a call."

"On a lady?"

Kedrington smiled oddly. "Yes, on a *lady.*"

"Well, be off with you, then!"

— 10 —

THE FAIRFAXES ARRIVED at Almack's famed assembly rooms the following Wednesday shortly after ten o'clock. A wave of warm, heavily perfumed air swept over them as they entered, causing Mrs Curtiz to wrinkle her nose in distaste. Isabel scarcely noticed the heat and gazed wide-eyed around her, drawing several other pairs of eyes toward her. Dressed in a white gown with very short puffed sleeves trimmed with lace, a gold locket suspended around her throat from a velvet ribbon, Isabel was a sight to refresh the most weary eyes. Antonia, in a scarcely less striking ensemble of cream muslin, wore her own hair in a cluster of artless curls confined by a velvet ribbon that matched the one Isabel was wearing.

Gentlemen in knee breeches and snow-white cravats stood about with young misses in the latest modes or elderly ladies in old-fashioned finery, and drank lemonade from minuscule cups as they waited for the musicians—seated on a little balcony above the heads of the dancers—to strike up the next tune. The Wednesday subscription balls had been got up with the object of introducing the most fashionable new dances from the Continent, but the normal decorum of the proceedings had been scrupulously maintained even in the face of the scandalous waltz, which had passed through Almack's causing scarcely a ripple in the complacency of the seven autocratic patronesses of the club.

Not all of these were present this evening, and the first to make note of the newcomers was Lady Jersey. Passing her hand gracefully over that of the gentleman to whom she had been speaking, in a gesture of dismissal, she turned and, as the Queen of Scots might have walked to the scaffold, crossed the room and approached the Fairfaxes with a marble smile affixed to her lovely pale countenance.

"Miss Fairfax, is it not? How good of you to come. Maria Sefton has been singing your praises, but I see that she has quite understated the case. . . .

"What an enchanting gown, my dear," she added in Isabel's direction. Isabel, handicapped both physically and temperamentally from perceiving the archness in her patroness's expression, smiled disarmingly. Lady Jersey looked her over a little more carefully.

Antonia, discerning in Lady Jersey the sort of person who would wait hopefully for one who had stumbled once to stumble again, warily presented Imogen Curtiz. Lady Sefton joined them, but Lady Jersey assumed the burden of the conversation by the simple expedient of never allowing anyone else to put in a word.

"Ah, my dear Lady Sefton, here are Miss Fairfax and Miss Isabel Fairfax, and Mrs . . . oh, yes, Curtiz, the good friends you so kindly brought to our attention. We must take them in hand and see that they meet everyone, must we not?"

Antonia, half-amused and half-vexed by Lady Jersey's use of the first-person plural, contrived not to catch Mrs oh-yes-Curtiz's eye. The musicians struck up a providential mazurka at that moment, and Lady Sefton deftly separated Isabel from Lady Jersey's voluble clutches and led her off to be introduced to her son, Lord Molyneux, who might be counted on to stand up with her for her first dance without pressing his good fortune.

Lady Jersey resumed her soliloquy, touching upon every subject from Tsar Alexander's impending visit to the sins of a parlourmaid Lady Jersey had been obliged to dismiss the day before and an exquisite hat she had seen at Clarimond's in New Bond Street and which she felt would become Isabel to perfection. All the while she appeared to be absorbed in this small talk, however, her eyes took in every movement of Isabel's on the dance floor.

Antonia supposed that Lady Jersey had taken it into her head to adopt Isabel as her personal protégée and was running over in her mind the names of the bachelors present whom she might profitably present to the little Fairfax. She must be grateful, Antonia further supposed, if this were the case, since Lady Jersey was doubtless considerably more experienced in this sort of thing than Isabel's doting—and not very clear-sighted—aunt. Nevertheless, she had been determined to fulfill her chaperone's duty properly tonight, and it irked her to have the responsibility taken away from her. She was certain that Isabel would not care to have *three* solicitous elders hovering over her, which left Antonia with nothing to do but to make something of this unexpected freedom to enjoy her own evening.

Almost as if to confirm her in this resolution, Lord Kedrington arrived just then and, as he invariably did without having to do anything in particular to achieve it, he made her smile.

His lordship was dressed in a satin coat and knee breeches—there were no exceptions to the rule against pantaloons at Almack's—and escorted a very small, very lively lady in a lavender silk gown with artificial flowers all over it and in her extravagant white curls as well. But no sooner had he divested this lady of her silver-trimmed cloak than his eyes went directly to Antonia's. Lady Jersey's plucked brows went up when Miss Fairfax first looked away, then looked back at him, smiling. Lady Jersey beckoned imperiously to the viscount.

"My dear Kedrington! What an age it's been since we saw each other last. I declare, I feel quite neglected."

"Yes, it's been nearly a week, hasn't it? We met at Lady Holland's soirée, I seem to remember."

"Wretch! Will you never learn the difference between an inconsequential *plaisanterie* and an assault that must be met with all force of arms?"

"Never, apparently. You are acquainted with Miss Coverley, are you not, Sally? She will tell you I am far too literally minded to be perfectly at ease in civilised society. Aunt, may I make known to you Miss Fairfax and Mrs Curtiz?"

Greetings were exchanged all around, and when Lady Jersey peremptorily claimed Lord Kedrington for a dance, Antonia and Imogen were left alone with Miss Coverley, who immediately demanded to have Isabel pointed out to her, and then became, much to Antonia's dismay, quite as voluble as Lady Jersey. The smallest hint of malice, however, was so foreign to Hester Coverley's warm nature that Antonia was willing, even amused, to let her ramble on.

"Oh, my!" she exclaimed artlessly. "Dear Isabel is every bit as pretty as Duncan told me she was! I am convinced she will be the belle of the season, and you, my dear, its fashion leader. So clever of you to set a style of wearing only one earbob; there is Miss Wolfson, you see, wearing only the one diamond, and Mrs Smith-Morehouse with one pearl, however large and gaudy a one it may be. . . .

"Not that there is not always a goodly supply of young ladies in pretty dresses," Hester went on, as Antonia exchanged a resigned look with Mrs Curtiz, "but now the war is over at last, there will be many more young men for you to dazzle, and that, you know, is what makes a girl a belle, to be popular with the young men—and *such* young men—the officers, my dear! My head is always quite turned by the sight of a dress uniform, dear me, yes. . . . Not that there are not also a number of fascinating young men in town at all seasons. . . . I wonder if we may see Byron here tonight? He need not be afraid of encountering Caro Lamb— *she* is in mourning, naturally, since her grandmama, the Duchess of Spencer's, death last month, and does not appear in public. They say she has secluded herself and is writing an exposé of the whole *affaire*. . . . "

"Not another *Bride of Abydos,* I trust," Mrs Curtiz interposed.

Hester's eyes widened. "Oh, heavens, I do hope not! Have you read it? I declare, I never . . . Well, Kedrington says Caroline cannot help what she does, while Byron knows exactly what he is about, although how he can think that bringing out such a tale when his own sister was in the family way—oh dear, what an unfortunate expression that is!" Hester sighed feelingly. "Well, I have always thought that one should strive to be *au courant,* but there are some fashions I cannot admire! I must be older than I thought. . . . "

Antonia laughed and said it was no such thing, which appeared to please Miss Coverley, who then began to point out for Antonia's edification various other personages of note, as well as some of her particular friends. Antonia took a second look at the highly polished beauty who was Sir Henry Mildmay's partner, but who glanced meaningfully at Viscount Kedrington whenever the movement of the dance permitted her to do so. She asked Hester who the beauty might be.

"Oh, that is Mrs Pennell," Hester said with little enthusiasm. "I daresay *Mr* Pennell is somewhere about as well." She turned the subject back to her own acquaintances, most of whom were young people in whom the irrepressible Miss Coverley took an affectionate interest.

"I must introduce you to Miss Thomas, my dear; I am certain you would approve her as a friend for Isabel, and I assure you she would find no rival in that quarter, for Miss Thomas—apart from being of a style quite dissimilar to your niece's—is as good as engaged to Lord Frederick Colby. . . . Oh, and there is my grand-nephew Angus with Miss Mercer. . . . I will introduce you, for he is Kedrington's heir, you know. I have been trying to persuade him to look at Miss Thomas's sister Phoebe for an age now, but I suppose Miss Mercer will do as well, although I cannot care for her complexion, which certainly does not complement Angus's costume."

Since Angus's costume consisted of a pair of snuff-coloured satin breeches and a yellow waistcoat, which caused Miss Mercer's sallow complexion to appear positively murky, Antonia could not help but agree. She could also not help but notice that, the dance having ended, Lord Kedrington showed no inclination to return to her side, but was engaged in earnest talk with Lady Cowper. Then, as Lord Molyneux, ever mindful of his social duties, approached her to solicit a dance, she was unable to discover immediately whether Kedrington was avoiding her or merely being polite to Emily Cowper, and it was some time before their paths crossed again.

Lord Molyneux was properly attentive and did not even mind when Antonia's attention was diverted from what he was saying to watch Isabel, who, having scrupulously declined to waltz, was engaged in conversation with Harley Chatham-Hill. They were joined by Lord Geoffrey Dane, who, although Antonia could not hear their precise words over the music, appeared to be attempting to persuade Isabel to waltz after all. She smiled at him at the same time that she shook her head apologetically, but Harley was less sensitive to his feelings and said something that made Geoffrey throw back his head angrily and take a step toward Harley. Isabel put one hand on each young gentleman's arm and said something which made them draw back again. She then, much to Antonia's perturbation, released her hold on Harley and went away with Geoffrey toward the refreshment rooms.

"Oh, I do beg your pardon!" Antonia said, suddenly conscious that she had missed a step and very nearly tripped up Lord Molyneux, who insisted that it was his own fault entirely.

Antonia laughed. "Nonsense! You are too kind, sir, to lie for my sake. I was not attending the steps as I ought."

His lordship assured her that he understood perfectly and turned his conversational talents to coaxing Miss Fairfax's enchanting smile back to her lips, which by the end of the waltz he had accomplished easily.

"My felicitations, ma'am," he said. "You may now boast of having danced the waltz at Almack's. Let us recover from the agitation with some lemonade and a little—I have no doubt, stale—bread and butter."

They entered the refreshment room just as Mr Chatham-Hill was handing Isabel a cup of lemonade. Imogen Curtiz and Lord Alvanley had converged over a cup of tea, and Lord Geoffrey could be seen glowering on the scene from behind a pillar. He did not look to Antonia to be contemplating erupting into it again, however, particularly not after the arrival of Miss Cloris Beecham, looking ravishing in a yellow gown trimmed with white rosettes and pearls—and wearing *two* pearl earbobs, Antonia observed thankfully.

"*Dear* Antonia!" exclaimed this vision, kissing that lady on both cheeks and remarking how lovely she looked, a compliment which Miss Fairfax naturally returned before introducing Clory to Lord Molyneux.

"How do you do?" Miss Beecham said demurely, but interrupted herself before his lordship had finished his bow. "Oh, listen! They are striking up that Austrian tune that is all the rage. Do you waltz, my lord? But of course you do!"

Being thus prodded, Lord Molyneux had little option but to solicit Miss Beecham's hand for the dance and went away with her much in the style of a lamb being led to the slaughter. Antonia was not left to play gooseberry for very long, however, several gentlemen having discovered an ardent desire in themselves to partner the elder Miss Fairfax, so that for some time it was difficult to say whether the elder Antonia or the younger Isabel enjoyed more opportunities to take the floor. Antonia found herself regretting her promise to Imogen not to interfere when it became apparent that Isabel was favouring gentlemen—however unappealing otherwise—of large fortune. This must have struck other observers as only natural, however, for they only nodded sagely and wondered why Maria Sefton should have all the credit for having sponsored the two beauties.

Then, shortly before eleven o'clock, a discreet but palpable flurry, like a summer breeze over a meadow, spread over the room. Antonia was startled to see a young lady standing near her raise a trembling hand to her girlish bodice as she stared wide-eyed at the door. Turning her head,

Antonia saw standing there, as if he had only been waiting for someone to notice him, England's greatest living poet—or devil or clown, according to one's taste—George Gordon Noel, Lord Byron.

Whichever of his personalities was the true one, even Antonia could not deny his fascination. His dark, brooding eyes and scornful mouth, the painful deformity of his foot, his whole attitude of weary disdain, were in their own way all quite beautiful. Antonia distrusted perfection in any human being, and Byron's spectacular faults suited his flamboyant legend far more than did his perfect profile. They made him, at the same time that he was being idolised, a little more human.

He was instantly surrounded by women who claimed acquaintance and presumed upon it outrageously. Byron said little and looked pained, as if such adulation still made his head ache—even if, since the morning in 1812 when he "awoke to find himself famous," it had ceased spinning.

Standing quite still among the butterflies, Byron looked around him and nodded recognition to a few acquaintances. Antonia saw Kedrington raise a quizzical eyebrow to him, and Byron shrug lightly in return. Lord Alvanley, waiting beside Antonia to lead her onto the floor, offered to introduce her to the poet, but she declined to join the throng surrounding him, preferring, she said, to observe the spectacle from afar. Soon after, however, in the movement of the dance, she inadvertently jostled Byron as he attempted to pass near her. Alvanley offered a careless apology, but Byron disregarded him. Antonia, whose initial detachment had become tempered with a flash of understanding for Byron's peculiar vulnerability, gave him a warm smile when he bowed wordlessly to her. Barely minutes later, having stayed only long enough to turn everyone else's conversation to the subject of himself, Byron departed.

"Did you see that?" Angus Wilmot remarked unnecessarily when the door had closed on the poet and a fresh buzz of gossip had broken out. Antonia, who had discovered Angus somewhat at a loss beside the punchbowl, feared it would be a time yet before the boy ceased to emulate fashion's idols and discovered a style of his own. She hoped Kedrington would be patient with him.

"I should not take Lord Byron too much to heart," she said kindly to Angus. "He is a world unto himself, you know, and scarcely to be taken as the norm—or even the ideal."

"Yes, I understand that," Angus said, adding feelingly, "But still—I wonder how he does it?"

He seemed inclined to expand on this, but the sight of Lord Kedrington and Miss Coverley coming toward him at that moment sufficed to staunch any further confidences and, indeed, to drive Angus to retreat in disorder to the card rooms. Kedrington did not fail to notice this manoeuvre, and his silence on the matter told Antonia much of how he thought about it.

"Did you see Byron?" Miss Coverley repeated, only slightly less breathlessly than Angus. "I wonder that he troubled to come at all, only seconds before the doors were closed. . . . It's a great pity that Lady Caro wasn't here after all. . . . "

Kedrington raised a hand to interrupt her. "I beg you, Aunt, spare me any more of that lady. I have little patience with such public hysterics as Caroline would have felt it incumbent upon her to perform tonight, and I am weary of the subject. Miss Fairfax, I came to ask you to dance and to distract my mind from such unpleasantries. You see—they even play another waltz for us."

"I cannot engage to distract you from thoughts of other ladies, my lord, but I shall be happy to dance with you."

He held his hands out to her. She took them, making some jest about her dancing lessons, and he replied in kind. But a moment later she could not remember what they had said and was aware only of the pressure of his gloved hand at her waist, guiding her. She felt for the first time a certain uneasiness with him, but she could no more account for it than she could disregard the unexpected warmth she felt wherever he touched her or when she felt his breath close to her face. The warmth spread through her with the beat of the music and she felt it reach her cheeks. She hoped he would think it was only the exertion that made her redden so.

"That is very becoming," he said after a moment, of her coiffure. She thought he spoke rather quickly, as if his breath came irregularly, like hers. She schooled her thanks to be graceful but distant, so that he was moved to try another tack.

"I chanced upon your sister and Mrs Curtiz this morning," he told her. "They were coming out of Westminster Abbey."

"Yes."

"You were not with them," he persisted.

She had to smile at that, and lifted twinkling eyes to his. "I have seen the abbey before, sir. It cannot have changed so very much in the interval. Why should I go again?"

"To see how you would like to be married in it."

The sparkle faded again. "What nonsense."

"I agree. Affected, too. St George's Hanover Square it must be."

Antonia sighed. "My lord, 'I could find it in my heart to marry thee purely to be rid of thee.' "

"Brava!" he said, but did not pursue the subject, instead allowing the motion of the waltz to bind them together a little longer. When it ended at last, Antonia detached herself gently from his hold, but he kept her arm loosely on his, saying, "There is Miss Beecham giving me a reproachful look for having deceived her that I could not find my way to King Street without her assistance. I see that I shall be obliged to exercise the utmost tact when next she accosts—that is, when next I speak with her. Do me the kindness to escort me to those two chairs there by the wall, so that we may escape her for a moment. I expect it will be permissible for us to sit down briefly, both of us having made more than our share of polite conversation this evening."

When she made no response, he enquired, "You are not amused by Almack's, Miss Fairfax?"

She looked at him, but her smile was hesitant. "To the contrary, I find myself vastly entertained. But it *is* a little tiring, as if one had entered a race after not having so much as sat a horse for a long time."

"You lack a little practice only."

She considered this in silence. He was right, of course. She would soon be her untiring self again and dance until dawn. If she did not have Isabel to concern herself with . . . But she did *not* in fact need to concern herself with her niece. Isabel was doing very well on her own, and between Cloris Beecham and Imogen Curtiz she had all the advice and chaperonage she required, so that Antonia might well forget her notions of duty and enjoy herself, particularly now that Charles was there to indulge her in any entertainment she might fancy. She did not understand why she did not feel her freedom as she ought.

The viscount tried again to initiate a little small talk by thanking her for being civil to his heir. Unfortunately, this reminded her that she had

118

intended to drop a little hint to him about Angus. She remarked that she thought Mr Wilmot might profit from the viscount's attention more than from her own.

"It seems to me that he is continually clamouring for my attention. I wonder if it would improve his soul to have the means by which he indulges in lemon-yellow waistcoats cut off?"

"Have you the power to do so?"

"He receives an allowance from me, yes."

"So that you accept responsibility for him, putting him in your financial debt, but consider your duty finished there? Why do you not free him to follow your example instead of merely attempting unsuccessfully to ape your style?"

"Do you suggest I should abet him in *successfully* aping my style?"

"If you truly wish him to follow in your footsteps, yes!"

"I am visited by the suspicion," he remarked dryly, "that you are attempting to burden me with more of my family's concerns than I care to shoulder, with the sole object of forcing me to set those of *your* family aside."

"Oh, no, my lord. I am certain your shoulders are broad enough to support both."

"Vixen. I have a good mind to take myself to the country on a repairing lease and leave the lot of you to fend for yourselves."

"No," she said. "Don't do that."

He searched her face. "What's happened to you, my heart? You are most decidedly not your usual delightful self this evening."

Forced to the counterattack, she replied lightly, "How ungallant of you, my lord! Surely your instructive aunts must have told you never to say to a lady that she is in any but her best looks. If I am a little tired this evening, it is only . . . no, it is nothing of significance."

"Nevertheless, something is cutting up your peace. Will you not tell me what it is, so that I may try to remedy it?"

"Oh, no! I am certain there is nothing gentlemen detest more than a female sighing all over them in melancholy. I am not often so blue-devilled, I assure you, and I shall come about quickly enough!"

He did not pursue the subject, but made up his mind not to let so much time go by before he saw her again. She seemed almost to have forgotten what had passed between them already—did she really think she had to explain to him that she was normally the sunniest, most delightful of companions? That if anything disturbed her, it must be something of significance, even if she did not recognise it as readily as he, who knew her better than she realised? For the first time, he regretted the obligations he had taken on for friends who had once meant so much to him but whose claims now only distracted him from spending every waking thought and moment on Antonia Fairfax. He had taken them on, and he would have to see them through, but his heart was no longer in them.

= 11 =

"It won't do," pronounced Mrs Curtiz of a huge gilded pierglass that had been brought down from the attic.

"A pair, even four, would be suitable, but one alone will only draw attention to itself rather than to what it is intended to reflect."

"I very much fear you are right," Antonia said with a sigh. She had become enamoured of the idea of hanging mirrors on opposite walls of the ballroom to reflect the light from the chandeliers, but those which already hung there were insufficient to this purpose. Regretfully, she said, "Take it away, please," and two strong footmen picked it up between them and carried it out.

A number of other servants were busy in the ballroom, dusting, polishing champagne glasses, and moving furniture to and fro. The several cut-glass chandeliers had been lowered to the floor and, under Belding's autocratic direction, were being cleaned meticulously, for the first time since Charles had purchased the house, of the accumulated wax of past functions. Antonia, carefully treading her way among them, was treated to Belding's opinion of the housekeeping habits of the previous tenants, and the general despoiling tendencies of persons who let houses for a temporary period and have no care for them.

"Have we any coloured candles?" Antonia asked, cutting off this restrained but heartfelt flow.

"They may be obtained, miss. What colour would you wish?"

"Pink."

"An excellent notion," Imogen said, coming up at that moment with a cracked vase in her hand. "Do you think this can be mended?"

"Yes, I expect so. Belding will know where to send it. We mustn't use it in here, however. Someone is certain to notice the fault."

Charles appeared in the doorway just then, and Antonia, handing the vase back to Mrs Curtiz, approached him to apologise for the turmoil.

"No, no! I am delighted to see it," he said, looking at Antonia and not at the ballroom at all. "My poor abode will look as fine as Carleton House before you are finished."

"It is a very fine room to begin with," Antonia assured him, flushing a little under his intent gaze. "You must know we are very grateful for the use of it—"

"Yes. Well! I trust you will not tire yourself with all this work, my dear," he said, interrupting her. She had long since learned that Charles had no wish to hear such expressions of gratitude from her, but she attempted to voice them nonetheless. "I have asked the housekeeper to have some refreshment for you in the morning room in half an hour," he went on. "I shan't join you, I'm afraid. I am on my way to the city. Have you any errands I may execute for you?"

"Thank you, I think not."

He accepted this compliantly and said he would therefore remove himself from underfoot. She saw him to the door and, as she was watching him get into the hackney he had called for, it came to her yet again that she was behaving as if this were her own home rather than Charles's. Naturally, she must be grateful to him for making her feel at ease there and for instructing his servants to treat her as if she were its mistress. Nevertheless, she could not help a pang of guilt that this was so—even some apprehension, as if her life had been taken out of her control and was being led inexorably toward some predestined end.

Since Charles's arrival on the scene, Antonia had passed a large part of every day in his house supervising the arrangements for the ball. The responsibility for the refreshments had been happily taken over by a willing Mrs Driscoll, but that lady was obliged nevertheless to come to Antonia for an opinion on whether they ought to serve coffee at supper, or only lemonade, and on the number of cakes to be baked, and whether to include cold lobster, in which case they would have to offer two or three kinds of sauce to go with it. Belding was set in charge of arranging the tables in the supper room and the card tables in some of the smaller rooms, as well as the chairs to be set up in the ballroom to accommodate chaperones and those who did not care to dance. Antonia, although she made few changes, was not satisfied until she had inspected everything herself.

Isabel presented herself at regular intervals to enquire plaintively if please, was there not something she might do to help, upon which her aunt would send her off on some small but time-consuming errand, having long since despaired of persuading Isabel that her proper concern was only for her gown and her dancing partners.

Fortunately, Antonia had a willing advocate in the redoubtable Miss Beecham. While Isabel was torn between her natural shyness and a deeper, very feminine longing to be the belle of the season, Cloris unashamedly fostered the latter ambition. Isabel had contrived to wear each of the gowns she had brought with her only once before Cloris took her off—with a push from Antonia—to Franchon's for new ones. Cloris saw immediately that it would be useless to attempt to detach Isabel from the ball gown made for her by her dearest Miss Jensen, but she did succeed in persuading her that a lace overskirt would set the white satin off to perfection, with the result that Isabel's subsequent inspirations regarding the composition of her costume caused it to be completed at the very last minute—and then only because Imogen, finding Isabel working at it late into the night, snatched away her needle and thread and spectacles and locked the gown in her own room, where, she said, she would finish it herself.

Lady Sefton had been generous enough to call once again, bringing with her the formidable Mrs Drummond-Burrell, another of the patronesses of Almack's, who was sufficiently impressed with Isabel to go away and tell several of her cronies that the little Fairfax was remarkably taking, as well as pretty, and that she possessed a truly remarkable talent with that heathenish instrument—a balalaika, that was it. Yes, Mrs Drummond-Burrell had heard with her own ears what a charming sound could be coaxed out of it by a talented musician. This opinion—deriving in large part from Isabel's particularly enquiring of her guest what piece *she* would like to hear, and then knowing how to play it—went far to make Isabel's ball something of an Event.

Charles had been all along cheerful, eager to help, and expert in obtaining many of the items necessary to the success of the venture. He encouraged Antonia to avail herself of his house, his carriages, his servants, and any other thing she might require. Since Mrs Curtiz and even Isabel had no hesitation in taking instant advantage of this generosity, Antonia's scruples against doing so began to appear unreasonable, even to herself.

The difficulty seemed to be that now Charles was part of her life again, she could no longer conjure up the romantic memories which had been all she had of him when they were apart. Now the sheer physical presence of him overwhelmed her, and fragile memories faded and died. She was forced to confront the Charles that was now—strong, vital, and continually at her side.

She could not put these vague feelings into words, but neither could she have confided them to anyone, recognising them as foolish and sentimental and all the other things she professed to despise. In any case, Isabel was very little at home to talk to, and even Imogen had found other things to do. She at least had no scruples about ringing for one of Charles's footmen to accompany her in Charles's carriage to Berry Brothers, where she would choose teas to replenish her supply, leaving Antonia at home, counting Charles's spoons and thinking hard.

It was Mrs Curtiz who later conceived the happy notion of holding the dinner party which was to precede the ball in Mount Street. Antonia seized on this idea, pointing out to Charles that although his dining room was, like his ballroom, much larger than the Fairfaxes', their own was more than sufficient to accommodate the small party invited to dinner, and still to maintain the atmosphere of comfortable intimacy which Antonia preferred. She immediately sat down in her own library to write to the dozen persons who would compose the dinner party, informing them of the change of plan, and felt much better for it. After she had sealed the last letter, she called for her own carriage for an outing, during which she discovered at Messrs Swan and Edgar's new establishment in the Regent's Street that ribbon trim was now all the crack. She purchased a quantity of this in a shade of rose that exactly matched her favourite sarsenet gown, and returned home feeling very feminine and frivolous.

Philip Kenyon at last made an appearance six days before the Great Event, walking in at Cavendish Square as if he had only gone out to fetch a newspaper. He found Antonia discussing the musical programme for the ball with Charles.

"You had best delegate that task to Isabel, my dear," said the elder Mr

Kenyon, depositing his cane in the umbrella stand. "Charles has no more notion of what would be suitable than I have."

"Uncle Philip!"

"Father! How do you come here? Why did you not send word when you would arrive?"

"My dear boy," his patient parent explained, as he received Antonia's welcoming kiss, "why should I send word when I am here to tell you myself that I am here? How do you all find yourselves? Your arrangements are proceeding at a goodly pace, I see, just as it should be."

"We might have guessed," Antonia complained, "that you would wait until the work had all been delegated to others before making yourself available."

"My dear, I am not in the least available! If you have any notion of finding me something to do, I shall speedily make myself absent again."

Antonia laughed and said he was shameless, but asked Charles why he did not send for some refreshment for the weary traveller, which role Mr Kenyon readily fell into, supporting himself on her arm as they made their way into the drawing room. There Antonia reassured him that he would occupy a supervisory position only in regard to the forthcoming festivities, and entertained him with an account of all that had occurred since last they met.

"You will be astounded, I daresay, at the size of our guest list, but people have been most kind to us, and we simply could not leave anyone out."

"I would not be at all astounded," Mr Kenyon told her, "so you need not enumerate your guests to me. Indeed, let us take a rest from all this planning, which has already fatigued me beyond measure. I shall be glad of a cup of tea. Where is Imogen, by the way?"

"She has ventured into Saint James's for reinforcements. She must have guessed you would come today, Uncle Philip."

Mr Kenyon considered this intelligence and then announced that he had errands to run himself, and that there was no time like the present to accomplish them. This was so far from Mr Kenyon's usual philosophy that Antonia could not resist teasing him about it and asking if he had some grand new project in view.

"I do, if you must know. I shall tell you all about it—but not now, for I must call on our friend Mr Quigley, who has been making a nuisance of himself with his letters about . . . well, never mind that! Shall we take supper together tonight?"

Charles told him that they had planned to attend the theatre at Drury Lane that evening to see the renowned Edmund Kean as Richard III, and Antonia immediately invited Mr Kenyon along, saying it was just the sort of sociable outing he would enjoy, if he did not mind that they would not set out until nine o'clock.

"Quite *de bonne heure,* my dear," he told her, after ascertaining that he would be given his dinner beforehand and not be obliged to go hungry during the performance.

They were absorbed in arranging the details of this engagement when Imogen Curtiz appeared, walking into the room as if she had not been informed of their visitor's presence—which must have been the case, for she came to an abrupt halt when she saw him. Antonia had never seen quite so startled an expression on her friend's normally unrevealing countenance.

"Good heavens! Philip!"

Mr Kenyon rose quickly and moved to take her hand and raise it to his lips. As his eyes left hers, Imogen reverted to her customary composure, but Antonia had a notion that her caustic greeting was inspired by other than usual emotions.

"One never knows when to expect you, Philip," she said. "Perhaps we ought to just give you a key, so that you may let yourself in and out as you please."

Showing her to a chair and resuming his own, Mr Kenyon replied blandly that he did in fact have a key to this house, but that if she were offering him *carte blanche* at Mount Street, he would not refuse it.

Imogen maintained her equanimity, but Antonia was nearly betrayed into astonished laughter. She glanced at Charles, but he appeared to notice nothing out of the ordinary and, indeed, had risen to ring for the tea his father had earlier expressed a wish for. But he did hesitate for a moment when Mrs Curtiz addressed him.

"Charles, were you not on the point of going somewhere?"

"Ah, well . . . yes, I was."

"Excellent. Why do you not take Antonia with you? I daresay she would enjoy a drive."

Ever obedient, even to unexplainable whims, Charles bade his father and Mrs Curtiz farewell and offered his arm to Antonia. As he closed the door behind them, however, she said, "*Were* you going somewhere, Charles?"

He looked at her as if he did not comprehend the question, then smiled and admitted that if he were, his destination had gone quite out of his head.

"Yes, I was decidedly taken aback myself. We should not be so surprised, I suppose—and we may perhaps be reading too much into the incident—but it did seem to you, did it not, that we have been got rid of like a pair of unwanted visiting relations?"

"We were, indeed. Well, since there is no help for it, shall we take a drive? Not long enough, of course, to give rise to too much speculation in the household about my father's sudden business here!"

Antonia agreed and sent a maid for her bonnet and shawl. "I should prefer to walk, however. Would you be good enough to escort me back to Mount Street, Charles?"

"It will be my pleasure."

They had not gone more than a few steps on their way, however, before Antonia perceived that walking had not been such a happy notion after all. It was a bright, sunny day and all of London, it seemed, was abroad in it. A number of ladies—and worse, gentlemen—of her acquaintance waved at her from their carriages, and courtesy obliged her to return their greetings. Although he was unacquainted with the majority of these persons, Charles nodded his head graciously at them just the same, gratified for Antonia's sake—he told her—that she was so warmly acknowledged by members of, apparently, only the highest ton.

"I fear I do not understand you, Charles. I'm certain I have told you that Isabel has received any number of such callers."

"Ah, yes, but—you will forgive me, my dear—but they were calling on Isabel, were they not? It has not been clear to me until now that you have attracted such callers for your own sake, which indicates that your—perhaps I should even say *our*—past indiscretions have been forgiven us. You must have noticed that I have been reluctant to accompany you in public, but this has been solely for fear of reminding the world of our last appearance together. Now I confess that it gratifies me wonderfully to see that my scruples were groundless."

Antonia had been about to make the same observation to him, rather more forcefully. She had had the uneasy suspicion that he was about to congratulate her on her rehabilitation into Society, but then his disarming assumption of the blame in the case had stopped her. Then, too, had her own efforts not been to effect this very change in her status? She held her tongue, therefore, and, finding it difficult to address any other subject with aplomb, said nothing at all else. Charles's steps slowed to a stroll, and although she attempted to hurry him along it was several minutes before they arrived at Mount Street.

"May I come in for a moment?" he asked her, since she made no move to invite him to do so. As she could offer no plausible excuse to refuse, she agreed, and they entered the empty house. No footman was about—nearly all the servants being employed in decorative duties in Cavendish Square—so Charles removed his own hat when Antonia showed him into the gold drawing room. She seated herself opposite him and, suddenly attacked by nerves, embarked on a voluble conversation as uncharacteristic as her previous reticence had been. It was Charles who this time replied only in monosyllables as she chattered on, until at last he cut her short by rising suddenly and facing her.

"Antonia!"

Something urgent in his low voice compelled her to be still and listen to him, but for a few minutes he remained silent, too, his brow knit.

"Yes, Charles?" she prompted him.

"Antonia—"

She folded her hands in her lap and gazed at him expectantly. She could imagine what he was about to say, but although she was coward enough almost to wish it not said at all, she could not help but be moved by the emotion which seemed so foreign to him, but which was now so touchingly close to the surface. At last, he took a deep breath and plunged into the heart of the matter.

"Antonia, you may have wondered—not that I expected you to give me more than a passing thought—but you may perhaps have thought it odd or uncivil in me not to have written more—no, not that, for I have several times addressed you most improperly by letter—but at the least come to see you during these past years, particularly in view of our former . . . attachment."

"Not at all," she assured him gently. "Indeed, I was both astonished and grateful—considering my unforgiveable behaviour at the time—to find you had not forgotten me, buried in the country as I have been. You have had so many more important matters to occupy you—"

"No, no, not more important! At least, only in that they served to distract me during that period when I could not allow myself to think of you—of us—very often. As for your, ah . . . impulsiveness, I had long since forgiven what could only be put down to a young girl's romantic fancies. I knew that, with maturity, you, too, would see those fancies for what they were. But while Carey was away from home, and you were Isabel's guardian and solely responsible for the management of your brother's estate, I could not presume to impose myself upon you."

"That could never be the case, Charles. You must know that."

"Well, yes—I did know it. I knew that you would never think badly of me, but the fact is that I thought badly of myself. With time for reflexion, I came to see that I must be able to offer you more than a mouldering pile of a house and neglected lands, more than just—myself!"

"Charles—"

"No, let me finish. I might not have the courage after a moment's hesitation. You deserve so much more than I could have offered you six years ago, Antonia. You, with your beauty and kind heart, deserve to have all of London at your feet, to command every luxury, every attention. Oh, not just such extravagances as Cloris Beecham talks of constantly, but a way of life that puts you at its centre, as is only just, and provides you with everything not just for your physical comfort, but for your happiness as well. I could not ask you even four years ago, when Anthony died, to choose between what I could offer you then, and your duty to Wyckham and to Isabel. I know what your choice must have been."

Antonia was more than willing to disclaim any desire for fame and fortune, but she could not be certain that she would not have made this last choice precisely as he said. She was silent.

"I shall never be truly worthy of you, Antonia, but now that my circumstances are so much improved, I must, as they say, seize the initiative. I shall speak to Carey as soon as he comes home, which must be any day now. I have no doubt you will have more flattering offers—indeed, you must already have had more than one, but . . . "

He paused for a moment, and then seized her hands and finished, a little breathlessly, "Antonia, if devotion and a desire above all else to please you carry any weight, these I can offer you. Will you take my poor self along with them?"

"Oh, Charles, how can you be so . . . idiotish!" she said, her voice failing her and giving way to a tremulous laugh as she thought, for no reason at all, of how much less heartfelt Charles's words sounded beside those Lord Kedrington had uttered in jest. "Indeed, it is not very becoming in you to claim to hold yourself in so little esteem, and then to offer yourself to me as the best bargain I shall be able to make!"

He looked stricken and, realising that, unlike Kedrington, Charles might take this literally, she hastened to reassure him. "Now you *are* being absurd, Charles! As if I should ever believe you unworthy! I have always held you in esteem and—no, that is not the case at all. I adored you as a child, loved you as a girl, and now . . . oh, Charles, I hope you will not think me entirely idiotish to say I am afraid to say yes to you now simply because I cannot imagine a higher state of happiness with you than I have already known?"

He hesitated, not unnaturally puzzled, until she smiled and clasped the hand that still held hers more tightly, as if in reassurance. He took the hint.

"Am I to understand that you wish a little more time to consider my offer?"

"Yes!" she replied eagerly. "I mean, it is only that . . . that I must be quite certain I can truly make you happy."

He smiled, contented. "How can I refuse you, my dear? But will you—that is, how shall I know when to appeal to you once more?"

"Dearest Charles, I assure you that I shall not force you to repeat all the pretty speeches you have made me today. I know how difficult they must have been for you. I shall make my feelings known to you as soon as I am easy in my own mind about what they are."

He appeared to consider this and find it satisfactory. Then at last, he did exactly as he ought and took her in his arms.

Afterward Antonia could not, for all her efforts, recall precisely what it was that had made her hesitate to accept Charles's offer. And it was very little time before she forgot her hesitation entirely and told him what he wanted to hear.

They were to dine in Mount Street before the theatre that evening, and Charles went away only long enough to collect his father and change into his evening clothes. This gave Antonia, too, only enough time to search out her most becoming gown and to have Esmé arrange her hair with Charles's latest bunch of lilies-of-the-valley in it. Any doubts that may have lingered in the back of her mind were dispelled temporarily by her natural feminine pleasure in being adored, so that when they set forth for Drury Lane later that evening, Antonia was in high good looks and Charles glowed with pride at having her at his side.

The production was an excellent one, and by the first interval, Antonia was entranced, forgetting that it was not at all the thing to take more interest in what was happening on the stage than in the activities of the persons in neighbouring boxes.

"Do you know," she said to Charles, "I have never believed that Gloucester could have been as black as Shakespeare painted him, but Mr Kean has quite convinced me that he was. When he said, 'I am determined to prove a villain,' I quite trembled for the safety of the realm!"

Charles agreed. "One would not have thought a man of such mean stature and unprepossessing countenance could project such horror. It is undoubtedly a triumph."

He continued in this vein for some moments, and Antonia found herself, since little further was required of her in the way of conversation, glancing abstractedly around the theatre. It was then she saw that a box across from them which had been empty when the curtain rose was now occupied. She recognised Miss Hester Coverley, Octavian Gary—and Viscount Kedrington, who appeared not to have noticed her at all, for all that they had not encountered one another for more than a week. Then, with an inexplicable chilling sensation in the region of her heart, Antonia looked at the young woman with whom the viscount was absorbed in conversation.

She was somewhat younger than Antonia, with a slightly foreign look, masses of black ringlets, and the clear, delicate complexion of one who has been sheltered all her life from both the natural elements and the ravages of the Beau Monde. It occurred to Antonia that this must be the mysterious lady whom Kedrington had been disinclined to acknowledge in Hyde Park—this time without her veil. She could now be seen to be rather too dark of complexion and short of stature to be considered a beauty. It was, rather, the adoring expression in the wide green eyes and the glowing smile on the full mouth which seemed never to open in speech—so intent was she on what her companion was saying—that made her beautiful.

Antonia remembered in a rush, if for no particular reason, all the foolish things she had ever said to Kedrington—all the bantering words which had never seemed less clever than they did now in comparison to his present companion's serene, silent adoration—and suddenly the evening seemed not so delightful after all. Antonia turned her eyes away from the viscount's box and did not look that way again.

During the next act, she concentrated her attention on the stage, but her mind failed to take in what was happening on it. When the curtain was rung down for the second interval, Imogen expressed a desire for a breath of air, rose from her seat, and left through the draperies separating them from the corridor, pulling Philip along behind her.

Charles resumed his discourse, but shortly interrupted himself to ask Antonia if she cared for any refreshment.

"You are looking a little pale, my dear," he said. "Perhaps it is less stuffy outside after all. Shall we take a stroll?"

Antonia's eyes darted across the theatre to discover Lord Kedrington's box temporarily deserted, and she said quickly, "No, thank you, Charles! I had as lief remain here with you. That is . . . " She smiled and laid her hand gently over his. "Sometimes it is much more restful to sit quietly with someone one is fond of than to rush about attempting to be pleasant to the whole world, is it not?"

Charles made no reply but to return her smile and lift her hand to his lips. She studied his face for a moment, looking for something she could not define—or perhaps for something she feared to find. It was, happily, not there.

"Charles . . . "

She did not know why she hesitated. He was looking at her intently, but hopefully; not wanting to force her to continue, yet obviously eager to hear what was on her mind. She tried to marshal her thoughts, and out of the recesses of her memory at last succeeded in extracting a clear image. This was her Charles, she reminded herself, her knight in shining armour, the only man she had ever expected to love. And here he was beside her—if anything, more certain than ever that he wanted her for his wife, yet willing to let her decide his fate.

She smiled up at him and said, simply, "I have decided that I shall be very happy to marry you, Charles."

He pressed her hands tightly in his own and might even have demonstrated his gratitude in a more forceful, if less characteristic, fashion, had not Imogen and Philip returned just then to their box, full of amusing gossip about the other playgoers they had encountered in the rotunda. Antonia's laughter and the high colour in her cheeks thus seemed natural to them, even if their source was not what they might have thought. Charles, too, schooled his smiles to suit his father's *bon-mots,* but when the lights dimmed again, he reached surreptitiously for Antonia's hand and held it until the last of the House of York had been laid to rest, only then releasing it, reluctantly, to applaud the performance neither he nor Antonia had paid very much heed to for some time.

On the other side of the theatre, Viscount Kedrington's attention was not on Shakespeare, either. In fact, he had to suppress an urge to call Charles Kenyon out by donning the mask of an impartial observer and telling himself that while Antonia Fairfax has lost none of her beauty, it had undergone a change. Where once she had shone with the beauty of a loved and loving woman—not unlike Barbara's at this moment—she now glistened with the polished perfection of a much-admired object. He might have hazarded a guess as to how Kenyon had achieved this transformation in her, but he was at the same time fearful of finding it out for certain.

— 12 —

ISABEL SAT VERY still, her hands clasped tightly together in the folds of her petticoat, while Esme dressed her hair with a light touch and a constant flow of chatter meant to prohibit any reply from Isabel but a half nod of her head.

" . . . Cook says there will be lobster patties and champagne at supper, miss, but I think she was only funning—about the lobsters, I mean, for I'm sure I never heard of such a thing, and of course Cook wouldn't let me taste one. . . . Mr Charles gave Ludlow half a crown this morning for polishing up the railings so nice, and now Ludlow is puffing himself up something terrible and ordering the stableboys to look smart tonight when they take care of the ladies' and gentlemen's carriages, if they know what's good for them. . . . Rachel says Mrs Curtiz is going to wear a new dress from India—all gold, she says it is. . . . Am I hurting you, miss?"

"Oh, no," Isabel said mechanically.

Esme proclaimed herself satisfied with her handiwork and invited Miss Isabel to admire in the looking glass the intricate knot at the crown of her head, ringed with Charles's pink roses, and the carefully curled tendrils of fair hair which framed her face. Mrs Curtiz knocked at the door just at that moment and entered bearing a cup of chamomile tea—"Wonderfully soothing for the nerves, my love"—and was invited to give her opinion.

"Very clever," said that lady, who did not have to be asked twice for her views. "But just a little severe, don't you think, Isabel?"

Esme looked offended. "It's just that I have fastened the pins securely, ma'am, so they don't come out with the dancing!"

"To be sure. But I wonder if perhaps a little, ah . . . artistic disorder might be more becoming?"

"I'm sure I know what suits miss and what doesn't, ma'am!"

"Oh, do stop!" Isabel exclaimed. "Both of you—do be dears and stop fussing so! You will be obliged to do some little adjustments after I have put on my gown, Esme, and we may settle the matter of my coiffure then. Imogen, I do think I need a cup of tea after all, so if you will only allow me to drink it while it is still hot . . . "

Already regretting her impulsive words, Isabel looked imploringly up at the two ladies, who were at once all solicitude and declared they knew precisely how she felt, and if she would only lie down for five minutes and close her eyes, she would be herself again in no more time than— whereupon Isabel burst into tears, and both Mrs Curtiz and Esme were instantly silenced from the shock.

Isabel had been awake since six o'clock that morning and had spent most of her day running to and fro in a storm of energy which alarmed Antonia, who could not help wondering if something other than ordinary anticipatory nerves were troubling her usually imperturbable niece. Isabel, however, would not be drawn into any conversational subject more intimate than the hour at which their earliest guests might be expected. Antonia had set her to rearranging yet again the flowers in the dining room and fetching things that no one needed. As soon as possible, she had sent Isabel to be bathed, powdered, and dressed, with a strict injunction to Esme not to allow her to become overexcited. But it was a hopeless demand, for Isabel continued to prick herself with pins, lose her spectacles, put her petticoat on back-to-front, and tear her stocking, until Esme stamped her foot and ordered her to sit still or she would never be able to finish her toilette—which precipitated her tears as she sobbed into Mrs Curtiz's gold silk *saree.* "Oh, Imogen, can't we call it off?" Fortunately, her old friend knew how little Isabel liked to be the centre of attention, and knew also how to divert her from her vivid mental picture of herself all alone in the midst of a brilliantly lighted ballroom, and so said simply that they could not, because all of her friends were looking forward to it.

Isabel's sobs lessened and finally stopped, and when Imogen suggested that she might, without inconveniencing anyone, take a short nap, Isabel sighed wearily and stumbled toward her bed. When Esme came to wake her half an hour later, she had quite forgotten her earlier agitation and ran to her mirror in search of confirmation of what had, after all, been happy dreams. Then, before she knew where the time had flown, she was

135

standing before the glass in her white satin ball dress, with the blond lace overskirt Cloris had insisted on and the decorative knots of pink ribbon that had been her own inspiration. Around her throat was a pearl necklace of her mother's, and on her slim hand a gold ring her father had purchased for this occasion when Isabel was a baby.

"Esme! Do you hear a carriage?"

The little maid ran to the window and looked out. "Yes, miss! It's Lord Kedrington's, I believe. Oh yes, I see his crest on the side—oh, how grand he looks!"

Isabel's hands flew to her cheeks. She ran to the door, but stopped, uncertain. She ought to wait, to make an entrance when everyone had arrived—but no! It would be rude not to be there to greet them. And oh! It was only Lord Kedrington, after all!

Propelled by this obscure assurance, she glanced once more into her mirror while Esme quickly straightened the hem of her skirt for the fifth time, then snatched up her fan and fairly flew down the stairs.

His lordship was in the process of handing his hat and silk-lined cape to Belding, when out of the corner of his eye he caught a flash of white, followed by a breathless "Oh!" and the sweet smell of soap mingled with the faint fragrance of the roses Isabel wore, as she came forward to shake his hand and confide ingenuously, "I am in *such* a quiver!"

"Nonsense," said his lordship, which curt reassurance went further toward sustaining Isabel's spirits than any number of fulsome compliments would have done. She was then able to receive Clory and her brother and the Worthings—who arrived in the viscount's wake—with charming ease, and Kedrington, suppressing a smile at Isabel's expense, was able to attend to her aunt instead.

Antonia had descended the stairs some moments before, and now stood quietly to one side to allow attention to be focused on Isabel. The viscount's gaze flickered approvingly over her blue-embroidered white gown, the sapphires around her throat, and the lilies-of-the-valley in her hair, but she seemed not in the least discomfited by his intent scrutiny. In fact, she scarcely seemed to see him, so he approached her to enforce his presence upon her.

"My lord!" she exclaimed, with a bright smile that seemed to him overly brittle. "What a stranger you have become! We feared you had deserted us."

"Indeed? But when I called twice previously, only to discover you had all repaired to Mr Kenyon's house to paint dance cards or some such thing, I thought I would be considerably *de trop.*"

Antonia raised her brows quizzically. He realised that he had trod too heavily on his first step, but before he could retreat, she said in her gracious but impersonal hostess's voice, "If Isabel has not thanked you for your flowers, by the way, I must do so. She adored them."

In a fit of magnanimity, so that Antonia would not be obliged to choose among competing offerings, Kedrington had sent a large bouquet of unwearable but very lovely white camellias, which now reposed in a bowl set in the hall for all to see as they entered. He could see that his gesture had been wasted, however, and it piqued him unreasonably to see what were no doubt Charles Kenyon's lilies in her hair.

"She flies her colours in her cheeks," he said, after a pause, of Isabel.

"Who has a better right, tonight?"

The viscount sighed feelingly. "Ah, to be young again, and able to blush at happiness!"

"I don't believe you ever did any such thing."

"I confess I have no recollection of it myself, but my mother assured me it was so. The occasion, I believe, was my sixth birthday, when my tutor presented me with a catapult, which I had—secretly, I supposed—wanted for months. Up to then Mr Widdington had figured in my mind as a model of rectitude and respectability. I never thought he had it in him. Ah, here is my Aunt Hester."

Miss Coverley, in a pale blue gown adorned with rows of lace and ribbons, had at that moment entered on the arm of Mr Angus Wilmot, resplendent in lilac satin breeches, a *roquelaure* of the same remarkable shade thrown over his slender shoulders, and an expression of *ennui,* which he rapidly shed when he caught sight of Kedrington. Miss Coverley glanced all around her, and her bright eyes fairly danced at the sight of Isabel, who curtseyed prettily to her and made her welcome.

"Oh, my dear, how pretty you look! How thrilling for you . . . your first ball! Why, I remember—"

Since Miss Coverley looked about to succumb tearfully to the emotion of the moment, the viscount interrupted to warn Isabel that his aunt was the belle of every ball she attended, and every other damsel must look to her laurels when one of the celebrated Coverley Girls was about. This outrageous piece of flattery Miss Coverley countered with an admonition to her nephew not to "pitch his gammon" at her and a scolding tap of her fan on the hand he reached out to clasp hers.

The hall filled quickly now with new arrivals, who bubbled over with talk and laughter, and flowed easily into the drawing room on the tide of pleasantries and an undercurrent of curiosity as persons who had just met allowed their first impressions of one another to become firmly fixed in their minds, as first impressions generally are. Miss Coverley mentally matched the single persons present up to their most likely companions with her usual acuity—but kept the final tally to herself. Miss Cloris Beecham, in a bright green gown that was excessively becoming in spite of its effrontery, decided with satisfaction that she would receive her proper share of attention this evening, then thought no more about it. Mrs Sophie Worthing contemplated Mrs Imogen Curtiz's Indian *saree* with a mingling of envy and distrust, while the look Mr Oliver Beecham directed to Mr Angus Wilmot's costume was one of unalloyed disgust. He had not, however, been privileged to witness the funereal fashion of the month before, nor the no less inappropriate yellow at Almack's; Lord Kedrington, who had, winced, but accepted the change as a step in the right direction.

It was time to go in to dinner, and the first course was over before Antonia realised that the seating arrangements had gone somewhat awry and that Lord Kedrington was seated precisely opposite Charles Kenyon, who was engaging him in ominously earnest conversation. But with the second course, she was relieved to discover—via her Uncle Philip, who sat next to her and repeated every word he overheard—that their talk had revolved around the best manner of carving game birds, so that when the little party prepared to remove to Cavendish Square, Antonia could at least assume an appearance of being as much at ease as any other member of the group.

The Kenyons' was tonight the most brilliantly lighted house on the square. The curtains covering the long windows of the ballroom had been drawn back, and the light of hundreds of candles flickered across the view as servants saw to last-minute arrangements. The front door stood open, and a red carpet led to it from the pavement.

Belding had succeeded in unearthing a set of eight matching mirrors, smaller than the late-lamented pierglass, but in their total effect equally dazzling. Isabel gasped with delight when she entered the ballroom on her godpapa's arm, and she danced around the room exclaiming over and over that it looked like a fairyland, until Mrs Curtiz reminded her that she ought to be at the door to greet her other guests, the first of whose carriages were already to be heard in the square.

Antonia accompanied Isabel to the door, her hostess's smile fixed in place, but as her smile grew brighter and her greetings to their guests more gracefully expressed, she became conscious of a corresponding sensation of disassociation from her surroundings. It was as if the better part of her mind were elsewhere—but where? Why not at this place to which all her efforts for months had been directed, which ought to have made her as happy as all these faces she greeted without remembering seconds later to whom they belonged?

Indeed, she ought to feel a sense of achievement at having arrived at this occasion. Isabel was about to be satisfactorily launched into the ton, so that hereafter her aunt need only sit back and admire the results. Her own future with Charles was on its way to being settled, which ought to relieve her mind of that long-standing question as well. But somehow she did not feel deserving of any of the credit for the glow on Isabel's face, and she was not enjoying that sense of having come safely home to rest which she had expected on accepting Charles's proposal. She could not ascribe a cause to these dissatisfactions, and it was this uncertainty which, no doubt, accounted for her oddly jangled nerves.

But she was too practised in the art of social deception to let her uneasiness appear on her own countenance, and she said nothing to anyone to indicate that she was not in her usual spirits. Instead, she forced herself, once she felt able to leave her post at the door and join the throng in the ballroom, to concentrate on the scene before her rather than on her own chaotic thoughts. And as it came once again into focus, she could find no immediate fault with it.

Ideally, of course, there would have been only Handsome Young Men invited to the ball, of whom Isabel could have her choice of a different one for each dance; for herself, there would have been an amiable friend or two with whom to converse while watching Isabel dazzle her young men. However, Handsome Young Men generally came attached to relations of various persuasions, who had also to be invited. There must also be young ladies—with their chaperones—in comparison with whom

Isabel would shine like the evening star. It was furthermore useful to have present one or two persons of influence who would observe Isabel's triumph and spread the word of it among the ton, in the event that Isabel did not encounter a young man to her liking and would therefore be in need of a fresh supply. Their guest list was thus composed not solely of intimate friends, but included a large number of persons with whom Antonia was barely acquainted, and even some whom she positively disliked, and it was further flawed by the various relationships, antagonisms, even flirtations established long before tonight.

Isabel, having been led out first by Lord Kedrington, was now dancing the cotillion with Octavian Gary, exchanging earnest conversation with him between the steps and causing Lady Jersey to observe in a carrying aside to Maria Sefton that she was "a sweet child; a little too intelligent, but one cannot hold that against her."

Oh the whole, indeed, Lady Jersey was well pleased. She proclaimed Isabel's modesty and grace to be such as to assure—when her ladyship should have pointed it out to all her friends—her social success. She was less certain of Antonia Fairfax, who had an obstinate bent to her and would not thank anyone for presuming to advise her. Lady Jersey shrugged and pointed out to Lady Sefton, who knew it well enough, that Kedrington was likewise older than seven and might be trusted to manage his own affairs.

Kedrington, watching his lady-love dance with Charles Kenyon, was less certain of this fact. He could see plainly that Antonia was not so carefree tonight as she ought to have been. Nevertheless, the look she gave her partner was such to cause Kedrington to avert his eyes. When the music came to an end and Charles moved toward one of the windows giving onto the garden, Kedrington, out of a burst of curiosity—or self-destructiveness—followed. Shortly thereafter he found himself enjoying a very good cigar and tolerating for its sake Charles Kenyon's account of the difficulties through which he had come by it.

"None was happier than I to see this war end, my lord, I assure you! It is iniquitous that England should be deprived of her life's blood, her trade, by a tyrant with no consideration for the welfare of the nations he overruns!"

"Yes, it is inconvenient," Kedrington agreed.

"You were aware, my lord, I am certain, of the poor quality of many of the goods with which we have had to make do in recent years." The viscount, having had to do without any sort of goods at all for much of the same period, blew smoke rings and said nothing. "My man Jenkins," Charles went on, as if to a prospective client, "has a low opinion of Spanish wines, for example, but naturally, it has been very difficult until now to obtain anything else without a great deal of risk. I have lost several runners off Brittany—although the loss was not entirely mine, as others were also involved in the enterprise."

"You mean," interrupted Kedrington, who had little patience with genteel ambiguities, "that this Jenkins is a smuggler."

Charles smiled deprecatingly and conceded, "Some may describe him so. You and I know the truth of it. Also, the point is academic now, is it not? The hostilities ended at last, the Ogre confined to his much-reduced island empire, and our own island empire free to pursue her destiny. Commerce of all kind will flourish with the deprived nations of the Continent, and our destiny will flower with theirs."

Kedrington put out the cigar which had suddenly become distasteful to him, and said, "Shall we go in?"

They returned to the warm ballroom, and Kedrington was once again obliged to watch from outside the charmed circle of Antonia's awareness as she smiled dazzlingly up at Charles, who, carried away by ardent feelings, kissed her hand and sat down beside her on a sofa between two potted palms.

Meanwhile, Isabel, having stood up for half a dozen dances without a rest, observed the gentlemen's return from the garden and declared that she, too, desired a breath of fresh air. Her partner of the moment was Lord Geoffrey Dane, who was not unexpectedly eager to oblige. He was soon able to persuade Miss Isabel to sit down on one of Charles's marble garden benches, where she fanned herself languidly and attempted to engage Geoffrey in small talk. But Geoffrey, whose beautiful brown eyes had not strayed from Isabel's face during the entire set, replied to her questions in monosyllables, concentrating his attention instead on her hand, which he clasped in his own despite Isabel's attempts to extricate it. Regretting too late her determination to give Lord Geoffrey an opportunity to declare himself, which he took as license open to abuse, she glanced over her shoulder in a desperate appeal for aid. Fortunately, just at that moment, a hand came to rest on Geoffrey's blue-clad shoulder.

Geoffrey jumped. Isabel, half-hidden in the shadows, exclaimed under her breath, "Oh, thank goodness!"

"How dare you, sir!" demanded Lord Geoffrey, rising to his two inches of height above Octavian and clenching his fists menacingly.

"How dare I what?" Octavian enquired mildly, bringing Geoffrey back to earth with a thud. "I saw you sitting here—in full view of the French windows, I might add—and wished merely to say good evening to you. I beg your pardon if I have inadvertently interrupted an . . . ah, a private conversation."

"You have done nothing of the sort," Isabel said, rising and smoothing her skirts. "Geoffrey, I believe you said a moment ago that you would go to the ends of the earth for me. I wonder if you would be so good, just for now, as to go only as far as the door."

Mr Gary looked admiringly at Isabel, who with flushed cheeks but a raised chin and a determined set to her pretty mouth, appeared after all quite capable of despatching her own affairs. However, as soon as Geoffrey, recognising the futility of any attempt to bully either the lady or the gentleman, had taken himself away, all of Isabel's efforts at self-control did not suffice to keep large tears from welling up and rolling quietly down her cheeks. A moment later, she was again sitting on the cold marble bench, dabbing her eyes with Octavian's handkerchief as he, in big-brotherly fashion, did his best to comfort her. After a moment, it occurred to him that Isabel was trying to tell him something. He shifted slightly, so that she could look up. The sight of her lovely, tear-filled blue eyes nearly overset his carefully neutral sympathy, but he managed to enquire, in a nearly steady voice, "What's the matter, love?"

"Oh, Octavian, I am so wicked!"

He smiled at that, to keep from laughing aloud. "Nonsense! What can you possibly have done to merit such an accusation, even from yourself?"

"I—I *encouraged* Geoffrey! I knew all along that I could not hold any affection for him, but because he is heir to a fortune, you see—"

"Isabel Fairfax, are you telling me you are a *fortune hunter?*"

"Yes!" she said, taking him quite literally. "That is precisely what I am and—and worse, I am a *tease!*"

Clearly, that was the worst she could say of herself, so Octavian forbore to tease her in return, encouraging her to pour out the whole story of her determination to contract a brilliant alliance—which she did at some length—and then explaining very carefully that Geoffrey was no innocent and brought anything that happened to him on himself.

"You are in no way to blame if he deceived himself into believing you to be in love with him."

"Oh, I don't think he believed that," Isabel said, in something more like her usual practical spirit. She folded Octavian's handkerchief neatly and said, as she put it in her reticule, that she would return it to him when it had been laundered. Octavian, however, was not to be returned to reality so quickly.

"Is there no one you would *like* to be in love with?" he asked softly.

She did not look up at that, but a telltale blush spread over her face, visible to Octavian even in the half light of the garden. He leaned a little closer and whispered something in her ear. She looked up and smiled. He drew a deep breath and asked softly, "Shall we go back inside now?"

Isabel nodded gratefully and allowed Octavian to escort her, now much recovered, into the ballroom, where they stepped naturally into the waltz that was being played just then, and whirled away across the room in each other's arms.

Antonia, too, was dancing again, her mood somewhat lightened by having conversed with Charles as they danced. She felt less detached now, more needed. And she felt wanted again, something she had missed when her confidants had seemed to be drifting away from her. She caught Charles's eye again, and he smiled at her. He had made it plain to her that he would endeavour not to monopolise her time and thus cause undue comment among the other guests. Antonia had thought this sweetly overscrupulous of him, but still a touching measure of his regard for her and her reputation.

She had taken to the floor this time with her Uncle Philip, a partnership prompted by the glum look on Mr Kenyon's face as he watched Imogen Curtiz and Lord Alvanley enjoying a comfortable chat in front of one of the mirrors lining the ballroom. Antonia had dropped a sympathetic kiss on his cheek and pointed out that if they were to glance into the mirror, they would see him scowling at them. Mr Kenyon morosely assured her that they were far too cosy to take any notice of him. Antonia choked back a smile and, to divert him from his melancholy mood, asked him to take the floor with her.

This exercise seemed to give him courage, and at the end of the set he escorted Antonia firmly over to the mirror in question, where they discovered Viscount Kedrington to have usurped Lord Alvanley's place and to be sharing Mrs Curtiz's amusement at the activities of several of the other guests.

"Oh, look!" Imogen exclaimed. "How diverting! Cloris has at last run Charles to earth, after stalking him all evening. I wish we may hear what they are saying."

Antonia scowled, as much at Imogen's inelegant metaphor as Cloris's behaviour—but watching Charles, she had to smile at his predicament.

Charles, who had been excessively pleased with himself that everything seemed to be going so well, was, until all hope of escape had passed, blissfully unaware of his peril. Of course, he thought, it was impossible for everyone not to like little Isabel, and he ought to be pleased solely for her sake, but he would be less than honest if he did not acknowledge that he was pleased for himself as well. Such a splendid gathering! It was then that he had smiled benevolently at Miss Beecham, who was watching him from over her partner's shoulder. Cloris had winked at him, but whirled quickly out of sight in the last measure of the dance, so that she was unaware of the comical look of astonishment that had crossed Charles's face.

"Do you not dance, Mr Kenyon?" she had asked, boldly approaching him a moment later.

"I fear I am an indifferent dancer, Miss Beecham," he replied.

"How *clever* of you to say so!" was Miss Beecham's unexpected rejoinder. "I myself simply refuse to learn things at which I will never be more than mediocre. A reputation for honesty, I find, is *much* more valuable than a clumsy talent at watercolouring or playing the harpsichord—such *genteel* accomplishments, are they not?—and how much easier to say, 'No, I do not play' than to struggle through *The Creation,* which I never admired. Do *you* admire Haydn, Mr Kenyon?"

Mr Kenyon replied warily that he did not, causing Miss Beecham to burst into laughter. Fortunately, Mr Chatham-Hill and Oliver Beecham arrived at that moment in response to Cloris's request, made an hour earlier, for a glass of punch. Taking advantage of this diversion, Charles made his excuses and escaped into one of the card rooms, where he found Lady Sefton and the Worthings engaged in a round of three-handed whist. They immediately captured him to make a fourth and, to the detriment of their mutual chaperoning duties, he accepted and descended, still somewhat shaken by his encounter with Miss Beecham, into the chair they indicated to him.

In the meanwhile, Antonia found herself deserted by her Uncle Philip and Mrs Curtiz, but not by Lord Kedrington, whom she had already refused a dance and with whom she was making less than brilliant conversation in the hope that he would become discouraged and leave her before she said something indiscreet—an all-too-likely result of any exchange with him. She might have known he would not take the hint.

"I met your niece and Octavian yesterday in Gunter's," he said, "where they were sampling the fruit ices under the guise of deciding upon refreshments for the ball, and she told me it was your notion. About a separate dinner party, that is."

"No, strictly speaking, it was Imogen's idea."

"In any case, it was an excellent plan. Mrs Curtiz seems inadvertently to have hit upon a novel new entertainment, which my Aunt Hester has named a *roundabout,* if you please."

"Whatever are you talking about?"

He laughed. "You know, it is all very well to talk of giving yourself up to a life of dissipated pleasures, but I must tell you that you will be much more convincing if you are able to recognise them when they present themselves. Surely you are aware that half the season's aspirants to fashion have been going about wearing only one ear ornament since you—unintentionally, as you say—did so, and I am certain that tomorrow they will all be wearing lilies in their hair and giving roundabouts."

"What nonsense!"

"Agreed. But you may as well take the credit, for denying it will be of no use to you—or to your niece's career."

She looked up at him through narrowed eyes. "Do not imagine, my lord, that by clothing every piece of advice you wish to give me in Isabel's name you will make it any the more acceptable to me."

He was not at all put out by her severity. "But you are at least taking my advice to heart, however unwillingly."

When that coaxed a reluctant smile out of her, he was emboldened to pursue his advantage. "If you will forgive another observation, my heart, you are beginning to think before you speak. It is too bad."

"I'm sure I don't know what you mean," she said coolly, if somewhat repetitiously.

"You once told me that you always act on your scruples—and on your whims."

He thought she remembered the occasion, but she did not say so. "Can you repeat every foolish thing I ever said to you, my lord? I shall have to be on my guard."

"I remember every word, but precisely to keep you *off* your guard, which is a most unattractive position for you."

"I should call it, rather, behaving like the lady I am purported to be."

"Who is practising London manners now, Miss Fairfax?"

She did not pretend to have forgotten that, but gave him a fulminating look and, in her most scrupulously precise accents, begged him to forgive her if she attended to her other guests now. He made no attempt to stop her as she rose and moved gracefully, if with some effort to achieve that grace, away. Fortunately, Miss Coverley was sending eager signals from across the room, so Antonia made her way in that direction, to be swept away on Miss Coverley's excitedly breathless prose.

"Oh, my dear—there you are! My, what a whirl it is! My head fairly spins! All the young people look so handsome tonight, all dancing ... Oh look, there is your niece dancing again with Mr Gary! What a pretty pair they make. Kedrington is quite right, you know—it would be a pity if that did not come off."

Antonia frowned, conscious once again that she was not being confided in, that events were happening without her being aware of them.

"Oh, please do not be offended, my dear. I am an interfering old lady who delights in watching the progress of a promising *affaire,* but I assure you neither my dear Duncan nor I would dream of trying to influence either *parti,* and we are both perfectly aware of Mr Gary's position. Oh, yes, all the Garys are as poor as church mice. ... One of them is. A pastor, that is to say. Now is it Arthur or Alfred? Well, no matter. ... There is some money in the family, of course, in Octavian's uncle's estate, and it will go to Neil one day. That is, if Neil's stubbornness does not prove stronger than Junius's, who will doubtless cut Neil off without a penny if he marries his Popish sweetheart to spite him. Not that there is much hope of his getting around her father, either. ... Oh, my dear, you must not let me ramble on so, of matters in which you can have no interest!

Look, there is Mr Kenyon, who keeps looking your way—I am certain he will ask you to dance if only I were to step aside and allow him to do so. . . ."

And so the dances went on—the lively mazurkas, the dashing *écossaises,* the waltzes. But before long, supper was being served in the long room that faced the ballroom from the upper level, which began to fill with guests taking a respite from the dancing. Although the evening was far from over, it seemed now to take a turn to a more intimate mood, so that when the second supper was served at two o'clock, the remaining guests felt so at ease with one another that it was a kind of family party which gathered in the long room.

Philip Kenyon put his feet up on a sofa and ate peas with a spoon and an elegant air which made Cloris Beecham laugh and encourage him to other absurdities. Miss Coverley had dug a needle and thread out of her reticule and was mending Oliver Beecham's glove and shaking her head over the carelessness of young men with their belongings. Oliver squirmed loose as soon as he was able, and Hester turned her admonitions on her nephew, who, she informed Antonia, had been as mischievous a child as she had ever known.

"His tutor once gave him a catapult, you know. He was only six at the time—Duncan was, I mean, not Mr Widdington, and—"

The viscount interrupted. "I have already regaled Miss Fairfax with that tale, Aunt. You will have to come up with something new."

Charles and Mrs Curtiz, in an unusually congenial unity, drank tea together. Octavian Gary stood in a corner, watching Isabel with a quiet smile and a warm look that would not have pleased Charles had he observed it. Antonia was watching Isabel, who was pretending to read a newspaper clipping Harley Chatham-Hill had given her concerning the entry of the new Duke of Wellington into Toulouse. She looked up when Oliver Beecham, taking no interest in Toulouse, recalled that there was to be a balloon ascent the next Sunday in front of Burlington House and suggested that Isabel might like to see it.

"Oh, yes!" she exclaimed. "That is, if Antonia says I may."

Antonia suggested that Isabel's friends might like to make a party of it, and since no one wanted to be left out, they all agreed to the plan with enthusiasm and immediately began to think of other, even more enjoyable things they might do together. The conversation once again became very animated, and Philip Kenyon, as if to disassociate himself from such exhausting talk, put a cushion over his head and sank further into the sofa. Miss Coverley, who was able to sense the end of a party five minutes before anyone else did, suggested to Angus that they take their leave and went to say good night to Isabel.

Isabel impulsively threw her arms around Hester and thanked her for coming, then shook hands with Angus. She went around the room tearfully hugging everyone indiscriminately and exclaiming what a good time she had had after all, as each of her guests in turn laughed indulgently and shook their heads at her affecting behaviour. Then, conscious for the first time that evening of being the centre of attention, Isabel burst into fresh, happy tears and ran out of the room.

"Well!" said Cloris Beecham in her forthright manner. "I could not have made a better exit myself."

=== 13 ===

As HE WAS walking down Picadilly not many days later, in the direction of his club, Viscount Kedrington found his attention diverted by the sight of another man walking toward him on the opposite side of the street. He was a young man, who wore a curly-brimmed beaver hat and clothing which was both fashionable and fitting, but somewhat inappropriate, as if he had been accustomed to some other sort of covering. He looked, indeed, very much as Kedrington had felt in the first weeks after his return from Spain. Suddenly he knew who the young man was. He gave a low, almost inaudible whistle.

The young man spun around quickly, looking for the source of the unexpected sound. He saw the viscount, stopped, stared, and ejaculated, "Oh, my God—Lobo!" He ran across the street, disregarding a tilbury that nearly knocked him down, flung an arm around Kedrington's shoulders, and pumped his hand vigourously up and down.

"Lord, fancy running into you here! Never thought I'd live to see it—not that I'd have recognised you, rigged up like that! Bang up to the mark, ain't you?"

Kedrington stepped back to appraise his young friend and remarked that he, too, appeared to have contracted a severe case of à-la-modality, upon which Carey Fairfax threw back his head and laughed. While he recovered his composure, Kedrington examined him with a newly critical eye and thought that his relationship to Antonia Fairfax showed most strongly in his delicately shaped but resolute mouth. His nose was fine and straight, like Antonia's, but his eyes, presumably a legacy from their father, were not blue but a lively hazel, topped by straight brows set neatly in a square face. His hair was a rich brown which owed its sheen to exuberant good health and exercise rather than to the application of

Russian Oil. He was, in fact, an extremely handsome young man, but Kedrington was not about to indulge his vanity by telling him so.

"How did you get away?" the viscount enquired, rather. "Shoot yourself?"

Carey stepped back and eyed him guardedly. "How did you know I'd been shot?"

"Sapskull! No tailor worth his chalk would expend that much care on a coat only to stuff one shoulder fuller than the other with wadding. You have a bandage under there, haven't you?"

"And I thought I'd humbugged everyone! I might have known I'd never pass *your* inspection—not that I expected to be obliged to!"

"When did it happen? Toulouse? You must have been in the thick of it there."

"No such good fortune!" The lieutenant looked down at his boots and hesitated, much as a small boy ashamed of himself, not for playing a prank, but for being caught at it, might hang his head. "Dash it, Lobo—it was a hunting accident! Near Paris. Six years in Spain with nary a scratch, and then some damn-fool cit who don't know one end of a gun from t'other peppers me in mistake for a fox! For the Lord's sake, Duncan, don't tell anyone the truth—I'd never hear the end of it!"

"How did you keep it from Neil?"

"I couldn't! He was with me at the time. Carried me to the sawbones, laughing all the way, curse him." The lieutenant paused momentarily, then enquired offhandedly, "Heard from Neil lately?"

Kedrington smiled and replied only, "Bab's here."

"Is she! What, in town? Where—"

"She's living in rooms in Half Moon Street, but she's becoming restless with the wait. I took her out to the theatre the other night, and she was absurdly grateful—but I don't want her identity generally known just yet."

"Well, it's as well you warned me," said his incensed friend, "or I might have babbled it all over town!"

"I meant, muttonhead, that we can't stand here in the street talking about it. Where are you going? Come along with me to Watier's. How long have you been in town, by the way? Where are you stopping?"

"*Posada* in the City—The Sergeant, it's called. Apt, eh? But I've not been here three days. Just long enough to get this rig made and ferret out a couple of friends of mine from Harrow to lead me around. Can't get used to all this civilisation. I never had a leave in all those years, you know, and one forgets how to behave."

He looked around him wonderingly as he spoke, staring at a yellow-bodied curricle that passed. "Been wandering around gawking like any rustic. Must get home, though. Haven't written, 'cause I wanted to surprise m'family. In Leicestershire, you know."

Kedrington let this piece of gratuitous information pass. "I suspect the surprise will be yours, *amigo*. Your family is here, in London."

"What?"

The viscount had taken the lieutenant's good arm and begun to propel him gently down the street, but at this the younger man stopped and stared at him again. "How d'you know that? What are they doing here?"

"Isabel's coming-out ball took place a week ago. Were you not informed?"

"Haven't seen a letter in months; things were all at sixes and sevens there for a while, what with half the troops being packed off to America. Stayed out of Bordeaux myself and ended up in Paris instead—conquering hero and all. But never mind that! You didn't tell me you knew my family."

"If you had been clever enough to look me up when you got to town, you gudgeon, I would have told you I did." They had by this time reached the august portals of Watier's Club, and the viscount invited his young friend to come in and take some refreshment. "Augustus can scare up a proper meal even at this time of day, if you like. You're looking a bit peckish."

The lieutenant agreed cheerfully. "*You* ain't!" he said as they went inside. "How much do you ride now, Duncan?"

Kedrington grinned ruefully. "Nearly fourteen stone!"

"Ay, I thought as much," said the lieutenant, wagging his head knowingly. "It's all this high living."

It was some hours later when, having temporarily exhausted their reminiscences, the two gentlemen emerged again into Saint James's. The viscount reminded Lieutenant Fairfax once again that it behooved him to make all haste to Mount Street to inform the ladies there of his arrival, and to be certain that he would do so, Kedrington guided him as far as his own home in Brook Street, where he had his curricle brought around to convey his friend to his destination in comfort.

"Dash it, Lobo, I could *walk* there in five minutes!"

"Must I remind you again that you are no longer in Spain? Do try to remember that you were bred, and presumably still are under that vulgar exterior, a gentleman. And don't call me Lobo in front of your family."

"Oh, all right! But if you must put me in that rig, come along with me to the city first. I'll pay my shot and move out of that hole. Besides, I've got some gee-gaws for the girls in my pack."

Kedrington raised his eyebrows. "You amaze me! But I'm delighted to see you are not lost to all sense of familial duty—even if it took you deuced long to dredge up that much. How are you fixed for money, by the way?"

Carey boasted of a tidy sum in prize money, only to hear himself lectured by the viscount for not sending some of it home before now. When the lieutenant protested that Antonia had never asked for anything— had in fact insisted that they were in no need whatever—Kedrington believed him, but a thoughtful look descended on him for the remainder of their errand.

Then, having settled with the landlord of The Sergeant and thrown Carey's various portmanteaux, sabretaches, and dirty boots—which Kedrington offered to throw overboard again—into the viscount's curricle, they were soon on their way across the city again. The lieutenant's patience grew shorter with the distance between him and his family, and when they turned into Mount Street at last, he was almost standing up in the curricle in his excitement.

"I can't believe they're really here! Which house is it, Duncan? Do you realize how long it's been since I saw them? *Dios!*"

"Sit down, you young idiot! We're almost there."

Carey resumed his seat, but then began to run his hand over his face and hair, and examined his fingernails critically. "Lord, I must look like a *gitano!* Ought I to have shaved again, do you think? I had a clean uniform I could have worn, though it don't fit right on account of my shoulder. Look, you'll explain to them it's nothing to get in a quake about, won't you? You know how females are—even if they are my family! Why are we stopping?"

Kedrington smiled. "Because you're home, lieutenant."

Carey looked up at the house, momentarily riveted to his perch, but when he saw Baskcomb come up to take care of the horses, he leapt over the side and, considerably to the groom's bewilderment, ran up and threw his arms around him.

"Baskcomb! You here, too?"

"Why, it's Mr Carey!" Baskcomb cried, when he had his balance and his wits back. He shook Carey's hand warmly and said, "Welcome home, sir!"

"Thank you, Baskcomb! Is everyone at home? Never mind, I'll go and see for myself!"

He bounded up the front steps and had his hand on the knocker when the door was opened and Belding's impassive countenance confronted him. The butler was subjected to the same treatment Baskcomb had just received and was left standing, overcome, in the hall as Carey dashed into the drawing room and collided with Isabel, who ran to him and flung herself ecstatically into his arms, exclaiming over and over, "Carey! Carey! Carey!"

The Fairfaxes, the Kenyons, and Mrs Curtiz had been on the point of sitting down to a quiet family dinner when Esmé, who had not yet broken herself of the habit of running to the window whenever a carriage stopped in the street, announced breathlessly that Viscount Kedrington was calling and—this in a tone of disbelief—that he had Mr Carey with him! Antonia, on hearing the viscount's name, had half-risen to go and smooth her hair, but then hesitated, torn between conflicting emotions. Sisterly affection won out when she saw her brother, however, and turned her dignified welcome quickly into radiant laughter and kisses and an impish twinkle in her eyes as she teased Carey about the length of his chestnut curls and his sunburnt complexion and—oh, how *grown-up* he looked!

Kedrington, forgotten for the moment, entered the house in time to hear her and was stopped on the threshold by the realisation that he had not heard her laugh just so since the day they met. When had she lost that happy spontaneity he had first admired in her? And why had he let it go?

But this was scarcely the time to ponder this unsettling idea, much less act on it. The room filled with people, who surrounded Carey. Even the servants hovered in doorways, the newer ones from curiosity, the older ones waiting their turns to greet the head of the family. Philip Kenyon murmured, "My boy, my boy!" and clapped Carey on the shoulder, making him wince. Isabel remarked this instantly, and her blue eyes widened in dismay.

"Uncle Carey! What's the matter? Are you hurt? You are, you are! You've been wounded!"

The lieutenant was immediately escorted to a couch and made to sit down, while Isabel held his hand and interrogated him closely. Mrs Curtiz went off to brew him a cup of tea, and Esmé, imagining that he looked faint, remembered that burnt feathers were wonderfully revivifying.

"Stop!" Carey roared lustily, calling them back. "It's nothing, I tell you! It's nearly healed anyway! All of you just stay where I can look at you. Isabel, stop kissing my hand. Imogen, you're looking very well. Just as I remember. Uncle Philip, too—pretty stout, are you? And . . . ah, Charles, isn't it? I'm glad to see you, too."

Carey shook off the restraining arms and rose to shake hands with Charles, who tactfully refrained from making a speech, except to remind everyone that they ought to let Carey go upstairs and refresh himself before they sat down again to their interrupted dinner. This served to set Mrs Curtiz off again to have a room prepared. As the servants melted away from the doors and back to their duties, the Kenyons and Isabel, still clutching Carey's hand, followed him out amid a shower of questions about his adventures.

Antonia turned to Kedrington, who was still standing among Carey's belongings in the hall.

"I beg your pardon. We ought to have thanked you long since for bringing Carey home."

He bowed, a little stiffly. "No thanks are due to me. I happened upon him quite by chance, and as he was unaware of your presence here, I took it upon myself to inform him of it. That is all."

Adopting her manner to his, she replied courteously, but less warmly—it seemed to him—than was usual to her. "Nevertheless," she said, "we thank you. But tell me about Carey's wound. Is it—"

He stopped her. "It is not in the least serious! It is only because he received it recently that it troubles him a trifle. I assure you, within a few weeks it will have healed with no need of solicitude on your part."

"In other words, you are telling me not to fuss over him. Very well, I shall not do so. He has never thanked us for such behaviour in any case—not since he fell out of a tree when he was a child."

"Ah, the famous oak, I collect?"

That made her smile at last. "Half a dozen times, at least! Carey has not your agility."

"But he has a great many more admirable virtues which I lack." She frowned, and he recalled that he was supposed to have met Carey only that day. "One of which is a sense of time and place! I am intruding on your reunion. I must go."

"Oh, do stay to dinner. It is no trouble to lay an extra place."

"Thank you, no. It will be even less trouble *not* to lay an extra place, and I prefer to be known as a man who does not press his advantage. Good day."

He departed abruptly, but Antonia had no chance to puzzle over his behaviour before Charles came to inform her that dinner was served at last.

"Has he gone? Very well-mannered of him, I will own. Your brother is eager to talk with you, my dear. Will you come in?"

Charles placed a gentle but possessive hand on her arm, and Antonia turned away, conscious for the first time that more than a door had come between her and Kedrington. She wondered why it disturbed her so to think that their friendship might not be adaptable to her changed circumstances.

She and Charles had agreed to keep their betrothal between themselves for the present, in part because Charles felt obliged to apply formally to Carey for her hand. Antonia thought this a great piece of nonsense, but for her part, she had no wish to draw attention away from Isabel on the eve of her ball, and so she had agreed to keep their secret. The days before the ball had flown, however, in a flurry of activity. Charles escorted the two Fairfaxes to Park Lane to view Lord Elgin's celebrated marbles; he carried Antonia's parcels home from a shopping expedition, in spite of her admonition that fashionable gentlemen never did so and of Miss Cloris Beecham's quizzical look when she chanced to see him doing it; and he purchased a delicate amethyst pendant on a gold chain, which Isabel had admired in a shop window, and presented it to her as a "coming-out present."

Then, with Carey's unexpected reappearance, life became even more frenetic, and Antonia had no leisure to brood over anything weightier on her mind than her feathered bonnet. Lieutenant Fairfax was silent only when he slept, which was infrequently. His energy was boundless, and when he was not proposing an expedition to any form of entertainment that took his fancy, from the Equestrian Display at Astley's Royal Amphitheatre to the pantomime at Sadler's Wells, he passed his time with his Harrovian friends at Manton's Shooting Gallery or at Tattersall's, inspecting carriage horses with a knowing eye and the thought that, now he was fixed in town for a spell, it might be well to look into making a few purchases.

Carey was able to find entertainment in everything he did, but no less amusing to him were the personal tangles that everyone had managed to get themselves into when he was not there to steer them clear of such coils. The first of these was forced upon his notice by the sight of Octavian Gary, standing beside a pillar at a ridotto given by Lady Sefton and, unaware of being observed, watching Isabel dance with Harley Chatham-Hill. Isabel moved her head to show off her new filigree earrings and, with an animated expression, to tell her partner that Carey had brought them back from Spain for her. Octavian smiled.

"Octavian—dear friend!" Carey gushed, startling his newest dear friend, whom he then dragged around to the other side of the pillar. "Why didn't you tell me! Why didn't *she* tell me, *por Dios!*"

"Tell you what?" Octavian asked warily.

"Why, that you're nutty on Isabel, of course! Or don't she know? Admittedly, she can't see what's right under her nose without her spectacles, but . . . you ain't suffering from a deep and unrequited passion, are you?"

"How did you find out?" returned Octavian, disregarding Carey's interpretation of his state of mind.

"Well, there's a cork-brained question, when you're standing here— there, anyway—looking at her like she was some kind of vision."

"She is," Octavian told him, unable to suppress his smile.

"Delusion, more like!" Carey retorted. But he looked around the pillar again and conceded, "Well, she's a taking little thing, I suppose. But look here, Octavian—it's true, ain't it?" Octavian nodded. "Then why ain't you engaged? We could at least end this farce of her having to finish out the season—for all the world as if she was a race horse! Why ain't you at least dancing with her, instead of Chatham-Hill—that's the second time, incidentally."

Octavian explained. "Harley is merely a . . . ah, a diversionary tactic.

Have I that right? Harley is a safe friend, and an obliging one, who serves both to fend off gentlemen Isabel has no wish to encourage and to keep me informed of her well-being without my being seen to pay her undue attentions."

"Why shouldn't you pay her attentions?"

"It appears that Mr Charles Kenyon disapproves of me—I have no prospects and, worse, in Mr Kenyon's eyes, no ambition—and that Miss Fairfax therefore disapproves of me equally. At any rate, that is the reason Isabel believes is behind my being less welcome in Mount Street lately than heretofore. Also, she holds out hope—Isabel does, I mean—that her aunt will eventually find Lord Kedrington's attractions superior to Mr Kenyon's, but she insists that Miss Fairfax be allowed to see this for herself."

"Well," Carey remarked caustically, "you're being mighty obliging to Tonia, I must say! I'm in her black books myself these days for having called Charles a tuppenny nabob. I didn't know I'd set up her bristles quite so fiercely, but I can't say a word about him now—nor about Kedrington, either, for then she just looks bored and says she's sure what he does is no business of hers. She ain't exactly the one to depend on for . . . well, never mind that. I'm here now. I'm head of the family, by God, and I can give you my permission to get leg-shackled, if that's what you want."

Octavian shook his head. "No, I'm afraid you're another reason we must be patient. How could your sister help but think we were only waiting for you to return—not to mention my taking advantage of your being my brother's best friend—to, er, outflank her?"

"Well, we'll just have to bring her around of her own account."

"How?"

Carey looked thoughtful. "Well, I don't know exactly. But something will present itself; it's bound to."

But before he could even begin his campaign, it received a setback early one morning which sent Carey storming into his sister's room.

"I've been waiting hours for you to get up, Tonia!" he complained with only slight exaggeration. "Charles came around—before I'd even had my breakfast, *fijate!*—to tell me you . . . Tonia, you've never *accepted* him!"

"But, darling, I don't understand. He said he would talk to you about our plans."

"He did. Came to ask my permission to pay his addresses, for all the world as if I were your guardian. Fustian! I told him I had nothing to say about it, that you were old enough to make your own decisions. *Dios,* I believed it, too! And then he tells me he sort of hoped I'd say that, because you'd already said yes. Tonia, I thought you'd *learned* your lesson!"

Antonia stiffened. "Well, I don't know why you should think any such thing! Charles is a good, kind man who . . . who wants nothing more than to make me happy. Besides, I—I love him."

"Well, if that's true, there's no more to be said. It just goes to show how you can bamboozle some people." Carey turned to go, but, reluctant to give in so easily, asked, "What about Kedrington, Tonia? Didn't you— maybe you didn't, I don't know, but Isabel says he was—well, that he had a *tendre* for you, as they say."

He quickly regretted having said this, for Antonia replied acidly, "I daresay he will speedily find solace elsewhere. Indeed, I was under the impression that he has already done so."

"What? You don't mean Bab? Hang it, Tonia, that's only—oh, hang it!" He stopped, remembering that he had no leave to tell her or anyone else the truth of the matter just yet. "Look, Tonia, I didn't mean to rip up at you like that. It's just that it was a . . . a surprise, that's all. If you really want Charles . . . " He stepped nearer to her and gave her a kiss and an embarrassed hug, saying, "I only want you to be happy, too, Tonia."

She smiled tearfully. "I know you do, darling. And I will be, I promise."

Carey frankly doubted this, but at a temporary loss as to what he could do about it, he refrained from expressing himself more forcefully. Instead, he tracked Kedrington down in one of the less frequented corners of Watier's to put the matter to him.

The viscount had arrived an hour earlier and found his favourite parlour deserted, except for a pair of elegantly shod and hosed legs emerging from a wing chair facing the window. A second glance at the right boot informed Kedrington of the identity of the solitary gentleman, but by then he had advanced too far into the room to be able to retreat unobserved.

"Get out, whoever you are!" growled the occupant of the chair. A white hand reached out to pick up a glass of brandy that rested on a side table.

"Devilish good humour you're in this afternoon, George," Kedrington replied affably, arranging himself in the window seat opposite Lord Byron.

"Oh, it's you, is it? I might have guessed. You move like a damned Turk."

"Like a damned Spaniard," Kedrington corrected him. He glanced at the brandy glass, and Byron, intercepting the look, scowled.

"Is there any more of that?" the viscount asked with a smoothness that did not deceive the poet, but which served at least to erase the scowl.

"In the bookcase," he said, waving a languid hand in that direction. Kedrington rose to find a glass, examined the label on the bottle with satisfaction, and sat down again. There was a long silence while Kedrington looked out of the window at the traffic in the street below, and Byron settled deeper into his chair. He closed his eyes, and an expression of rare serenity suffused his handsome countenance. After a moment, however, he bestirred himself and opened one lazy eye.

"Haven't seen you for some time, Duncan. Have I?"

"No."

Byron chuckled. "That's what I like about you, you know. No wasted words, no wasted motion. Pity in a way. You have the makings of a better romantic hero than I could ever devise. Why this reluctance to take advantage of your reputation?"

"I could not hope to compete with you, my dear George."

"You're not doing so badly," Byron observed. "Who was the sunny beauty I met at Almack's? What's her name—Fairford? Anxious mothers of dumpy daughters are reportedly eyeing her with some disfavour."

"Fairfax. I was not aware that you had been presented."

"I had not—strictly speaking."

"Then I wonder you remember her amongst the multitude."

"I couldn't forget," Byron replied with a twisted smile. "She was the only one who was civil to me—and no more. Alvanley talks of the two of you in one breath. Claims your only obstacle on the path to the altar is some wealthy cit with a prior claim, but William credits the beauty with more taste than that."

It was Kedrington's turn to scowl. "Alvanley talks too much."

"Probably. But it's the only fun he has, poor fellow."

Kedrington laughed and deprecated Byron's lack of tact. "You're a dubious sort of friend, George, especially to those of us who still have some conscience left."

"But I make a dependable enemy. No one has ever been able to sully that reputation."

A double-breasted blue coat appeared in the doorway at that moment, and a soft voice said, "Ah, Kedwington! I beg your pardon—I was looking for Yarmouth."

"Not here!" Byron snarled.

"No matter," the voice assured him. Entering fully into the room, Lord Petersham was revealed in a pair of baggy cossack-style pantaloons which, like the rest of his odd costume, hung unusually well from his slender frame. "Wanted to see you, too, Kedwington."

Petersham pulled a chair up to Kedrington, disregarding Byron's withering look, and said he believed the viscount to be acquainted with a certain Mrs Curtiz.

"George Bewwy tells me she has an Assam blend that is unique. You must intwoduce me to her, my dear fellow."

Byron snorted, but Lord Alvanley, coming into the room at that moment and overhearing, said, "I'll do it! Anything to get into that house. What's the matter with you, George? A touch of dyspepsia, or have you been reading the reviews of your latest opus?"

"Who invited you in here, Alvanley?"

"Why, no one," replied his lordship, unperturbed. "The door was open, so I walked in. The door is still open, you may observe, and as I passed Kedrington's protégé Fairfax downstairs, I expect your peace will shortly be cut up by a still ruder intrusion. Best take yourself over to the Alfred, dear boy, and join the bishops. Short of mummies, there's no more peaceful company to be found anywhere."

Byron rose awkwardly, snatching at a book which his movement jolted off the side table. Kedrington caught it as it fell and handed it to him. Their eyes met briefly and Kedrington said in a low voice, "The door is open at Brook Street, too, George."

"Oh, Rogers will let me in," Byron said, indifferently, "and he lives just down the street. I can stumble that far."

He went out and could be heard stomping down the stairs, but Alvanley and Petersham, accustomed to these displays of petulance, had already forgotten him and were discussing snuff boxes. Lord Petersham had one for every day of the year as well as for all kinds of weather, but when Alvanley described a carved lacquered box on display at Rundell and Bridge's, he admitted he had not seen it and insisted upon doing so at once. Both gentlemen bid Kedrington good day and departed, leaving the viscount in the solitary state coveted by Byron. He smiled, knowing he would not enjoy it any longer than George had, and wondered what was keeping Carey.

He was shortly to be informed, when the lieutenant burst into the room with little ceremony and no formal greeting. He sat down in Byron's chair and threw one leg over the side.

"I just met Alvanley in the hall, and he invited me to join his party for macao tonight. Obligin' of him, ain't it?"

"I don't remember your being a gamester."

"Oh, I ain't, generally. Too slow by half—much prefer a good mill—but couldn't turn Alvanley down. I collect the stakes are pretty high here? I haven't played much since I've been back. I've heard about a hell in Pickering Place, though—do you know it?"

"I do. And since you have seen fit to abandon your native soil for six years, I shall excuse your having mentioned it, on the condition that you do not do so again."

"Oh—right! I ain't to go there, then. Well, it don't signify. I've got more to do than time to do it in, anyway. Will you come with me to Jackson's Saloon next week?"

"Not I. Gentleman Jackson considers my fighting methods only half-civilised at best. Recruit my secretary instead. How, by the way, is your grave wound, received in the service of king and country?"

"Much improved, thank you. I shall be able to take the bandage off next week, and the stiffness will pass off quick enough with a little exercise."

Carey had discovered the brandy and, having refilled Kedrington's glass, consumed his own portion with a singular lack of finesse that made the viscount wince.

"That isn't *vino tinto,* you know."

Carey laughed. "You talk like Antonia. She's convinced they don't use forks in Spain and quotes my table manners as proof."

"God grant her patience! I wouldn't want you at *my* table night after night."

"Oh, Tonia don't mind. The Nabob, now, is another thing. You can tell he's itching to lecture me on my lack of social graces, but he don't dare to do it in front of her."

Kedrington had no doubt that the lieutenant referred to the estimable Mr Charles Kenyon, and assumed an indifference he did not feel. "You dine in Cavendish Square, then?"

"Lord, no! Been there, of course—*Dios!* You never saw such a museum. I'm afraid to put down my hat. But he's at our place three nights out of four. I've no objection to Uncle Philip—he's a good old sort—but Charlie treats the girls and the house like they're his own, forever giving orders to the servants and such."

Carey glanced meaningfully at Kedrington, but there was no indication on the viscount's face of his feelings. Hard-put to keep all the secrets entrusted to him, Carey tried another tack. "In a way, I suppose it may be a good thing that he's practically living in Antonia's pocket."

"Indeed?"

"Well, she can't really take him seriously, can she? I mean, the more I see of him, the less I look forward to the next time! Tonia's far more intelligent than I am. It don't make sense that she should like having him around *all* the time."

"Sense doesn't have a great deal to do with it," Kedrington said dryly.

"You mean, because she thinks she's in love with him? Well, she'll see soon enough that she ain't, and when she does, you can just step in and waltz her away."

"How elegantly you express yourself, Lieutenant. I shall do no such thing."

Carey eyed his friend judiciously. "On the other hand, if she's going to be stubborn about it, I might find somebody to kidnap her, and you'd have to rescue her. Charles hates a scandal—took him years to get over the last one—and if I didn't tell you about it beforehand, you could act with a clean conscience!"

"*You* will do no such thing! Wherever do you get these hare-brained notions?"

"What's the matter with it?"

Kedrington got up and walked over to the window. Throwing it open, he took a deep breath, relaxed slightly, and remarked that it looked like showering in the night. Carey, who for once was not to be led from the

162

subject at hand, said bluntly, "Well, Lobo, you're going to have to do *something!*"

Kedrington turned to look at him. "What *can* I do?"

"You can start by telling her about Spain—about us and Neil and . . . all that."

Kedrington shook his head. "No. Neil's story isn't mine to give yet. And if Antonia takes me, it will have to be on my present and future merits. I'm no hero to her, however much I'd like to be, and I won't try to make myself out to be one by telling her tales out of the past."

"Well, then," Carey said, practically, "you're just going to have to out-Charles Charles."

The viscount, whose attempts at circumspect behaviour had done less to raise him in Miss Fairfax's esteem than to cause him a great deal of personal frustration, now felt himself come to such a pass that the idea of imitating Charles Kenyon was almost palatable. He had no intention of "living in Antonia's pocket," as Carey had described Charles's behaviour; despite all evidence to the contrary, Kedrington could not believe that such conduct would long meet with her favour. However, he thought that he could, without appearing importunate, at least call more frequently in Mount Street than he had done in the last fortnight. And now that the business of those weeks was on a fair way to resolving itself, he might perhaps turn his efforts on a friend's behalf to his own purpose. Yes, he could do that. Neil would not object.

"Are you engaged for dinner?" he asked Carey.

"No. I was hoping you'd invite me. But if you're concerned that I'll spill sauce on your table linen . . . "

Kedrington stood up. "We'll go to Stephen's Hotel. They cater to the military manner there—which is to say, they are not overly fastidious."

"Oh, right!"

The lieutenant, ever agreeable, got up and, having been reminded by nothing in particular of a rabbit hunt he and Lobo had shared near Badajoz, began to indulge in reminiscence, which lasted through five courses of an excellent dinner and well into a bottle of port in the comfort of Kedrington's library. When Octavian Gary, intrigued by the unusual noises emanating from the normally funereal nocturnal atmosphere of his employer's library, came in to investigate, the talk became even more firmly rooted in the past. Mr Gary's normally somber expression was alight with amusement at the tales of his brother Neil told by his comrade-in-arms, and Carey was far from reluctant to provide him with colourfully embroidered details of their adventures, on and off the field of combat.

Kedrington, a tolerant smile flickering behind his grey eyes and occasionally spreading to his lips, listened to Octavian's attempts to inject a few words into Carey's monologue. The lieutenant barely finished with one subject before sailing off on another, but Octavian, like everyone who crossed Carey's path, seemed charmed into tolerance by his friendly, open manner.

Kedrington had long ago observed that Carey had not the imagination to be devious or deceptive, but was blessed with a natural buoyancy of spirit. He rarely showed anger or strong feeling, merely liking some things or disliking others (Kedrington remembered his glowing descriptions of the country around Wyckham as well as his diatribes against Spanish cooking). He had come home prepared to pick up where he had left off, expecting to find everything the same—as indeed for him it was. He had the kind of good looks that would still be boyish at forty, and the sort of nature that would take whatever happened in stride. Kedrington envied him his resilience.

— 14 —

THE RETURN TO England at the end of June of the Duke of Wellington
set off a fresh burst of celebrations. Crowds of people from all over the
land came to gawk at all the "high mightinesses" visiting in London, who
pretended to deplore the vulgar behaviour of the masses but made only
half-hearted attempts to escape their scrutiny. Tsar Alexander and King
Frederick of Prussia arrived in town on the same day—but by different
routes. At Ascot, Prince William let the champagne go to his head, and
the Princess Charlotte, seizing on the excuse, immediately informed him
and everyone else that their engagement was at an end. The very popular
Prussian, Marshal Prince von Blücher, gazed at the splendour around
him and remarked what a fine capital London would be to sack. At a
masque in Burlington House, Lord Byron scowled from within a monk's
cowl at the antics of his feminine admirers.

His Grace of Wellington took the adulation showered on him more
calmly, riding about London in a plain blue coat and accompanied by a
single groom. He feigned deafness to the cheers and declined even to bow
to the crowds at a military review held in Hyde Park on a particularly fine
day at the end of June. His duchess, Kitty, a pale figure in an inappropriately
girlish muslin gown, sat stiffly in her open carriage and stared straight
ahead of her, assuming an indifference as noble as her husband's.

"The truth is," Octavian Gary informed Isabel Fairfax when Kitty had
passed by them, "that she is extremely short-sighted and generally keeps
her nose in a book, lest she fail to recognise some acquaintance. She is
foolish, for no one could possibly mind if she wore her spectacles in
public, could one?"

The review was over, but many spectators had remained to watch the
units make their way out of the park. The last notes of the band had died,

but the clop-clop of hooves and the jingle of accoutrements carried on the melody. The sun glinted on the Life Guards' new black-and-brass cuirasses, which the Prince Regent had designed expressly to impress the tsar. The colour guard went by, banners drooping a little in the heat, but the barefooted children running alongside still had energy to spare.

Isabel looked after them with a smile, but at Octavian's words, she turned her head toward him suddenly, then blushed and turned away again, her poke bonnet screening her face. She said, hesitantly, "Any lady would do the same!" Then she laughed tremulously. "We are very vain, you know, we females."

"But you are not just any female, Isabel," Octavian said, leaning closer to whisper the words. Isabel turned her head away even more and began to examine with great interest the bark of the tree beside which they stood. Octavian laughed. "You little goose! You can't see it well enough to tell if it's a tree or the side of a house."

Isabel looked up at him, tears that would have flowed freely at such words from anyone else hovering in astonishment on her lashes.

"Lovely little goose," Octavian said tenderly and put his hand under her chin to prevent her turning away again. "Who knows that I love her and would never do anything to make her cry — only to tease a smile from her."

Isabel nodded and, to be sure he did not mistake her meaning, whispered as loudly as she dared, "I love you too."

Octavian ran his finger along her forehead and tucked a loose strand of silvery hair back into her bonnet. "Then, as you will one day be obliged to honour and obey me as well, you may begin by wearing your spectacles when you need them, instead of hiding them in your reticule or your muff or your sewing basket whenever someone approaches you. Will you do that, goose?"

Isabel nodded again, then giggled, and, plucking up her courage, asked, "How did you know?" Octavian looked mysterious for a moment, teasing her, then confessed, "Carey told me."

"Oh! How wicked of him!" Isabel became suddenly indignant. "Isn't that just like him!"

"What have I done now?" demanded this reprobate, coming toward them just at that moment. Not waiting for a catalogue of his sins, however, he said, "I don't know how you two contrive always to find a

166

corner to yourselves. Lord, I was near trampled over there! Did you see the Guards? Didn't they look fine? Kedrington's here—saw him talking to Duoro a minute ago. Thick as thieves, those two are. Listen, Octavian, there's to be fireworks tonight and a demonstration of Congreve's rockets. You won't want to miss that. You, too, Isabel. It's capital fun!"

"What, being deafened by a machine that's as likely to throw rockets at us as to hit the target?"

"Oh, you don't want to believe everything you hear! Clory's coming, and Oliver, too—I ain't seen Harley yet. I don't suppose Charles will approve, though, so we'll have to count Tonia out. No, wait; we'll ask Uncle Philip—he'll talk her around! Let's find him."

Propelled by this superior force, Isabel and Octavian made their way back to the Round Pond, where they had last seen their supposed chaperones. Miss Coverley had disappeared, but Philip Kenyon was exactly as they had left him, stretched out in a camp chair, his feet up on another, watching a tall blonde lady on the other side of the pond through a pair of field glasses. Harley Chatham-Hill sat beside him, finding more entertainment in watching Mr Kenyon than in admiring the lady. He began to whistle, but stopped abruptly when he saw Isabel and stood up to greet her. Philip looked up first to see who it was before half-rising and then sinking gratefully back into his chair when Isabel motioned him to do so.

"Where is Miss Coverley, Uncle Philip?" she asked when Carey had taken Harley aside to explain the theory of rocket propulsion to him.

"She went off with the Beecham girl to look for a misplaced governess. The Beecham's governess, it was. Seems she came with one this morning and lost her." Mr Kenyon shook his head sadly. "Careless of her."

Isabel giggled, struck by the vision of Cloris beating the shrubbery of Hyde Park for the errant Miss Blaine. Octavian informed Mr Kenyon, since Carey had been diverted from his purpose, of the treat in store for them that evening, and asked if he thought Miss Fairfax would care to accompany them.

"Shouldn't think so. Heard Charles say something about their being engaged with the Worthings for the ballet—depressing company if you ask me. He creaks when he bows, and she looks everyone over as if they'd just been offered her at a bargain. Not the sort of outing I'd care for myself, but then, they didn't invite me! Am I invited to the fireworks?"

Isabel assured him that he was, so that by the time Carey recalled his errand, the matter was settled. Mr Kenyon dusted off one of his chairs with his handkerchief and relinquished it to Isabel. Harley bought ices for everyone from a passing vendor. Octavian sat on the grass beside Isabel's chair, and Carey, having taken off his coat and waistcoat, lay on his back next to Octavian. A few moments passed, during which no one spoke, and only the distant patter of hooves on the road and the muted cries of children broke the silence of the sunny afternoon. Presently, however, a thought occurred to Carey and he sat up, demanding his Uncle Philip's attention.

"Hmmm? What?' '" Mr Kenyon stirred somnolently and removed his handkerchief from over his eyes.

"It's about Tonia and Charles, Uncle Phil! Been thinking. . . . Here we are lying about on our backs doing nothing"—Isabel objected that she for one was sitting up quite properly—"doing nothing while they set off on a sure course to ruining their lives, not to mention Octavian and Izzy's, who can't get married until Tonia comes to her senses, and—well, what's to be done, eh?"

"Don't ask me," Mr Kenyon said unhelpfully. "I'm not responsible for the follies of the world."

Mr Chatham-Hill, not wishing to intrude on these family matters, wandered down to the edge of the pond to finish his ice. Mr Kenyon's eyes followed him enviously, but being pressed by Carey, he ventured to suggest that the objects of his concern were both adults and presumably knew their own minds.

"No, they ain't and they don't! Tonia don't, anyway. She's made Charles fall in love with her because she was once in love with him, and she's too stubborn to break her word to him now, even if she sees her mistake."

"Why, that's right!" Isabel said, turning to Carey. "We've been looking at this always from our point of view. We never stopped to think why Antonia *did* accept Charles. She loved him once, I'm sure of that, but I think you're right that she may be beginning to regret it. But how can she cry off? She would never deliberately hurt Charles."

"If she marries him," Carey pointed out, "they'll both be hurt."

Octavian smiled wryly. "Hearts mend, Lord Kedrington told me once. I know he didn't believe it, though."

There was a moment's silence at the mention of the name no one had wanted to speak until now but which was on everyone's mind. At last, Carey said, with feeling, "I wish he'd elope with her! That would solve everything."

"He'd have to abduct her," Mr Kenyon said, following Carey's pronouns as best he could. "She wouldn't consent to an elopement. On the other hand, I don't suppose she'd take kindly to being abducted either."

"If there were some way to make Charles believe they'd run away together, he'd have to cry off," Isabel said hopefully, but Carey stood up and began to pace the ground, complaining that he hadn't heard so many silly plots since the last time he attended the pantomime. His companions were momentarily distracted from concocting further schemes, however, by the reappearance of Cloris Beecham, followed by Miss Coverley.

"Well!" said Miss Beecham, torn between exasperation and admiration. "You will never guess what she's gone and done!"

No one saw any reason to doubt her, or to indulge in idle conjecture when it was apparent that Cloris was about to enlighten them on Miss Blaine's presumably dire fate. Octavian stood up to turn Harley's vacant chair around for Miss Coverley, who thanked him and fluttered down into it. Everyone stared expectantly at Cloris.

"She has *compromised* herself!" she announced breathlessly.

"Good God!" Octavian exclaimed. "With whom?"

"How?" Carey asked, more to the point. Clory gave him a scornful look.

"With that weedy little clerk from Hatchard's!" she said. "Apparently she was so taken with him, and so fearful that he did not return her regard, that she *accosted* him in the street and pleaded with him to rescue her from her unhappy existence—although what she's had to be unhappy about, I'll never understand. But he seemed to, and was so affected by her pleas that he began to weep in the street."

She paused, reflected for a moment, and sighed. "I don't know why I'm working myself into such a state! I never thought Frances had it in her, but I ought to be pleased to see she had *some* gumption after all. I'm sure I wish them both very happy. Why are you looking so oddly, Carey?"

Carey, who had not attended the last part of Clory's speech, was tracking down some elusive idea of his own. Startled off the trail, he said, "Eh? Oh, right! I think I may have a solution!"

Cloris could not imagine why he should think Miss Blaine's situation any longer soluble, but those who had been present during the previous discussion now turned to gaze at Carey, while—judging from his fierce concentration—he laboured to formulate his plan in words.

"Izzy, did you say Charles would cry off if he thought Tonia had . . . ah, compromised herself with Kedrington?"

"I don't know," Isabel replied doubtfully. "It is not customarily the gentleman who ends an engagement, but he does care a great deal for maintaining a correct appearance—"

"He cares excessively!" complained Charles's parent.

"But if he cares enough for Antonia, I rather think him capable of overlooking appearances."

"But if we—and I think we may depend on Lobo—dash it, I mean Kedrington—to see to it—that is, if there is sufficient substance behind the appearances, even Charles may be discouraged from behaving nobly."

Miss Coverley, never one to let scruples about intruding in personal matters deter her, had up to this point said nothing, but had listened intently to the highly interesting conversation going on around her. No one had remarked her uncharacteristic silence until suddenly she broke it by saying, "You will naturally be obliged to remove Mr Kenyon temporarily from the scene—oh, I beg your pardon, sir, I did not mean you, but your son, Mr Charles Kenyon."

Philip's and every other pair of eyes turned to Miss Coverley. Octavian, who knew the lady best, smiled and said, "Miss Hester, if I am not mistaken, you are hatching a plot of your own!"

Hester's eyes widened. "Oh, my dear boy, I never descend to *plots*—so melodramatic! I do not know how you think such a thing. However . . . "

"Yes?" prompted Isabel and Carey in unison.

Gratified by their eager interest, Miss Coverley proceeded to tell them her idea. It was apparent that she had been thinking it over for some time, for it sprang full-grown into the light of day, leaving Carey chuckling, Isabel bemused but hopeful, and Mr Kenyon lost in admiration. Everyone agreed that it was not too soon to set the plot—the plan, that was to say—*en train,* and they all went away to do so.

Miss Coverley had, in fact, already taken the first action in the campaign. Having discovered by means known only to herself that an announcement from Mount Street was to be expected any day—and that it did not concern the younger Miss Fairfax—she had invited herself to supper at

Brook Street the night before, in the course of which she contrived to mention the matter, offhandedly but at the same time in the light of an accomplished fact. She did not wait to see the effect of this revelation on her nephew, but had she done so she would have been gratified indeed — for when she had gone, the viscount had stared at the closed door for a moment, then got up to fetch a bottle of brandy. He did not trouble to decant it, but loosened his neckcloth, opened the window with one hand, sat down facing it, and poured himself a generous glass.

Long experience and a not inconsiderable talent for dissemblance hid from all but the keenest eye that Kedrington was not in the best of humours the next morning. But Wellington, calling him over as the troops were assembling for the review, took one look and said, "Hard night, eh?"

Kedrington shrugged and enquired how His Grace did this morning. Wellington snorted contemptuously.

"As well as may be expected! Better when this nonsense is over with. Devilish weather, too. We'd all be better off indoors and out of the sun."

Since only Kedrington was privileged, and accustomed, to hear the duke's salty under-the-breath comments, made at the same time that he was doffing his hat and smiling benignly at various ladies, no one took offence to them. Marshal Prince von Blücher, by contrast enjoying himself very much, soon joined the duke's party, and as they made to pass in front of the rigid, stiffly groomed troops, Wellington called back to Kedrington, "Don't leave! Have a word with you by and by."

So it was that, having become unofficially attached to the duke's entourage, Kedrington was unable to do more than bow in passing to the Fairfaxes before following the duke out of the park toward Apsley House, the Wellesley family mansion, which the new duke had recently purchased from his brother Richard.

Meanwhile, happily unaware that her future was no longer in her hands, Antonia was enjoying a leisurely drive along Rotten Row, with Imogen Curtiz seated beside her and Charles Kenyon riding alongside the carriage. Their progress was halted with increasing frequency when acquaintances of one or the other lady hailed them and approached to exchange a few words. A number of Carey's military cronies, splendid in their dress uniforms, raised their shakos to them. Charles bristled defensively at each fresh assault, until Lord Alvanley appeared, looked him up and down, and suggested that he might accompany the ladies himself for a time, if Charles cared to take a canter.

"That is a most fine and excellent horse you sit upon, *mon cher* Charles, but she is very young and a little—how shall we say?—skittish, I think. Is she not?"

Charles was not eager to concede any inability to handle any horse in his stables, but by a stroke of good luck, he just then espied a business acquaintance riding past in the opposite direction and, making his excuses, he rode off to catch him up. Lord Alvanley told the ladies he was thinking of travelling to Paris, now that half the world seemed to be doing so—the other half having descended upon London.

"I have already promised Miss Coverley to bring her a bonnet back, and I insist upon your both telling me what I may bring for you ladies. Imogen—a shawl, I think? There is a delightful shop on the Rue de la Paix, as I recall—"

"If you mean Estelle's," advised a cheerful voice coming up to them at that moment, "stay away from it! Costs you the earth, and for what? The next week your lady has a new fan and forgets all about you!"

"Good lord!" Alvanley protested, seeing that the owner of the voice, one Lieutenant Fitzroy, was followed by a number of his comrades-in-arms, "England has been invaded after all!"

Antonia only laughed, but Imogen encouraged the officers shamelessly, roundly informing the lieutenant that he was a hardened flirt and that she would be sure to tell every mama in town to keep her daughter under lock and key while he was about.

"'Pon my soul, ma'am!" the handsome young officer objected, "we have spent long, bleak years fighting in the Peninsula! Would you deny us the enjoyment of our first contact with civilisation in all that time?"

"Certainly—if that enjoyment consists of seducing defenceless ladies."

"In that case, ma'am," said the unabashed lieutenant, drawing his horse closer to Imogen's side of the carriage, "I will devote myself to a lady more worthy of my attentions!"

Antonia could not help but be refreshed by this mass infusion of high spirits, so that when Charles found his way back to them shortly after, he found his betrothed in high good humour, a circumstance which ought to have pleased him. However, since she was at that moment indulging in a light flirtation with an officer—somewhat older than his fellows, with a handsome black moustache and a languid charm which Charles could not be expected to appreciate—he received her lively greeting less than graciously.

Charles was introduced all around, but Lieutenant Fitzroy, quick to spot a damping influence, shortly excused himself, and even Antonia's moustachioed cavalier lingered only long enough to receive an invitation to call later in Mount Street before following the others out of the park.

It was not until they arrived home, however, that Antonia detected more than the usual reserve in Charles's manner. Remembering that he was never at his best in sultry weather, she invited him into the house for a glass of lemonade and, while they were waiting for it, unthinkingly treated him to a colourful description of Hester Coverley's behaviour at the review earlier in the day.

"Imagine how in her element she was with all those scores—nay, hundreds!—of young men in uniform parading in front of her! It was excessively diverting. I only wish you had been present when—Charles, I wish you would sit down. I shall have an ache in my neck if I must talk to you from this position."

Charles, who had been pacing up and down in front of her, stopped and said, "What? Oh, yes. I beg your pardon." He sat down beside her on the sofa and, taking her hand, impulsively raised it to his lips.

Unfortunately, this promising overture was interrupted by the arrival of Belding with the lemonade, and after the momentary suspension of conversation, Charles lapsed once again into a pensive mood. Antonia smiled and attempted to cajole him into a happier frame of mind by asking if he did not find Lord Alvanley amusing.

"I think he must be, if Mrs Curtiz finds him so."

Antonia laughed. "I fear Imogen's judgement is not to be relied on in this case, any more than Miss Coverley's, on the subject of—and particularly in the presence of—handsome young officers."

Charles turned suddenly to gaze at her, then took both her hands in a firm grip.

"Why, Charles!"

"Forgive me! I do not mean to be . . . unfeeling, or—heaven forbid!—interfering! But it is not Imogen's or Miss Coverley's behaviour which concerns me."

Antonia smiled at him gently. "Are you cross because I flirted with

Major Burton? I assure you, there was nothing in it, and the major knows there was not. It was only a pleasant pastime for us both."

"I do not remember you to be so inclined to frivolous pursuits, Antonia."

Resentful, she pulled her hands away. "Then you do not remember me very well, Charles. I have always been addicted to laughter and kind people, and will continue to be so."

She knew as she spoke the words that she did so only to contradict him, but her awareness of this only roused her further. "If I choose to flirt with attractive men who pay me attentions, I shall do so, Charles."

"I do not dictate your behaviour, Antonia. I only fear that . . . that you are not sufficiently discriminating in your acquaintance. Lord Kedrington, for example"—Antonia's eyes narrowed dangerously, but Charles did not perceive the warning in them—"while I was happy to find him more gentlemanly than I had supposed—"

"Oh, yes," Antonia said dryly. "He has excellent manners, when he chooses to use them."

"He is also, as I observed this morning, very much in the confidence of our great hero, His Grace of Wellington, which circumstance alone must raise him in anyone's esteem. One must, certainly, take care to cultivate the acquaintance of the more distinguished members of society, both for the natural pleasure one of sensibility must take in conversation with educated persons and for the influence such persons may have and be inclined to exert to further one's own small enterprises. Nevertheless, it is not necessary to attach oneself too closely to those whose . . . ah, personal history and habits may be, ah . . . questionable."

Antonia, surprised to find herself bristling with indignation on the viscount's behalf, brought herself sufficiently under control to avoid saying aloud that she thought Lord Kedrington would not for a moment tolerate such boot-licking as Charles seemed to consider normal social behaviour, and enquired instead what it was about the viscount which Charles found so questionable.

"I am not very well acquainted with his lordship," Charles conceded, "but there have been rumours connecting him with spies and contrabandists and other, ah . . . unsavoury persons during the war. Then, too, his family history is not perhaps the most . . . irreproachable. That is—I hesitate to mention this to you, Antonia, but there were also rumours that his father, the previous viscount, engaged in clandestine . . . ah, *amours* with . . . various females."

"Oh, the rumours are quite true, I can assure you!" she replied deliberately. "That is, if you had any scruples about repeating them. I have it myself on the best authority. But as Desmond's *affaires* were, as you call them, clandestine, and therefore not generally brought to public notice, I fail to see what bearing they can possibly have on your—on *our* relations with the present viscount."

"Do you condone such behaviour?"

"I neither condone nor condemn. I merely acknowledge its existence. My point, Charles, is that we may not, in all justice, condemn the son for the father's indiscretions."

"But the potential must be there, do you not think? And the viscount's having been out of the country all those years—"

"Do you imagine he has smuggled in a foreign code of behaviour, as you have your wines and laces? Absurd, Charles!"

She stood up abruptly, clasping her hands together in her skirt in an effort to calm herself. Charles was obliged also to rise.

"I see no connexion between my situation and the viscount's."

"No, certainly there is none!" Antonia exclaimed, suddenly deflated and eager to leave this subject of conversation. "I beg your pardon, Charles! I should not be so outspoken." She sat down again, and Charles obediently followed suit.

"Pray, do not mention it! I feel certain you are not yourself today, my dear. Such volatility is not in your nature, I know, and while I have always admired your determination in defending what you believe is right, I wonder if your judgement at this moment is not somewhat clouded by the excitement of the life you have lately been leading."

Antonia seized upon this. "Oh, yes! I think that must be the reason for my ill manners. Indeed, Charles, you must not think you are about to marry the kind of woman who indulges in megrims and fits of hysterics at the least provocation! It is only . . . Charles, do you think we might go home for a little while? Not now, of course, but after we are married? I think I shall be much better, if only I have that to look forward to."

"Yes, certainly, my dear. That would be the very thing to bring you to yourself again. Carey has mentioned to me his intention of posting up to Wyckham one day soon to settle himself in there—to make his bivouac, as he calls it—and I do not doubt he will be happy to make rooms ready for you to visit, as well."

"Yes, I'm sure he will. But Charles, have you no intent to open Windeshiem? I had expected that we would live there, at least part of the year."

"But, my dear—surely you are aware that Windeshiem has been up for sale for some months? In fact, my father tells me that he is on the point of signing the final papers at any time now. It is a pity, of course, to lose a valuable piece of property in the country—not to mention a house large enough to entertain in during the winter—but my father, as you know, has no head for business and has no other income left but what Windeshiem produces. Happily, I have been able to persuade him to let me invest the proceeds of the sale to his advantage. He has not told me the name of the buyer, nor the precise sum settled upon, but I must leave at least that much to his discretion."

Antonia's heart had sunk with a sickening plunge during this speech. "Charles—you do not mean we are not to live in Leicestershire at all?"

"Why, no!" he said with some surprise. "We shall live at Cavendish Square. Naturally, you will be free to visit Wyckham whenever you so desire, but my life is here now, with my business—Antonia, are you quite well? You look markedly pale, my dear."

Indeed, another distasteful thought had come to her to make her feel quite ill. "Charles," she ventured, "if your father could not . . . that is, how has Isabel's season in fact been paid for?"

Charles looked uneasy, but chose honesty as the most expedient policy in this case. "It has been my honour, and pleasure, to do this little favour for Isabel," he said.

Antonia—who had been telling herself that she should have guessed this long since; should have foreseen, too, that she could never expect Charles to change his life to suit her fancy—nevertheless found she could not accept these truths with any sort of equanimity, and ran from the room. A moment later, she had thrown herself on her bed and was indulging in the floods of tears she had a moment before promised Charles she was in no way subject to.

— 15 —

"WEBSTER, IS THE carriage in use?"

Webster stared at his employer for a full minute before comprehending the import of this ordinarily innocuous query. He was assisted in reaching an understanding, however, by the sight of Mrs Julia Wilmot buttoning her gloves, and by the undeniable fact that she was wearing a bonnet. Stammering a little, he ventured the information that Miss Coverley had taken the carriage out earlier that morning and had not yet returned.

"I am certain, madam, that if I had only known—"

"Very well, I shall have to take a hack. Kindly call one for me, Webster, and do not stand about gaping."

Webster did as he was told, knowing better than to ask questions—but they would be raised, he also knew, by anyone who saw Mrs Wilmot that day. He did not know that her unprecedented action had in fact been prompted by her mentioning to Kedrington that she thought she would ask Miss Fairfax to tea, and his reply that he would be out of town that day. As Julia had not mentioned any particular date, she was somewhat taken aback, but since Kedrington rapidly made his escape, she could only enquire of Hester instead what ailed the tiresome boy. She did not for a moment believe Hester's suggestion that Kedrington must be suffering from a headache—an obvious fabrication which only served to whet her curiosity more—and she demanded a full explanation. Hester compromised by delicately recounting a partial history of Kedrington's attraction to Antonia Fairfax, but when Julia threatened first to take the shameless girl to task for leading Kedrington on in that fashion, and then to box the clumsy gentleman's ears for bungling the affair, Hester was moved to reveal the whole story.

Thus it was that Antonia discovered Julia Wilmot seated precisely in the center of the gold drawing room of the house on Mount Street, both hands resting on the handle of her parasol—which she held balanced on its tip on the floor in front of her—and both eyes directed at the door by which Antonia entered.

Well aware of the singularity of Julia's venturing outside Coverley House, Antonia had received the announcement of her visit with astonishment and was not a little apprehensive to hear what had brought her out. She made haste to the drawing room in order not to keep Julia waiting, drew a long breath, and opened the door.

"It is very good of you to call, Mrs Wilmot," she said, advancing toward Julia with her hand outstretched.

"Yes, it is," Julia agreed, ignoring the hand. Antonia withdrew it. "I nearly caused Webster a fit of apoplexy by doing so."

This tart reply was so absurdly like what Kedrington would have said in the circumstances that Antonia could not help but smile, and since her visitor declined to shake hands, Antonia bent to kiss her dry cheek instead. Julia seemed to approve of this liberty, and a little of the starch went out of her. She watched Antonia carefully as she sat down in another chair and rather deliberately spread her lavender skirts neatly around her and folded her hands primly in her lap.

"May I offer you some refreshment, ma'am?"

"Thank you, I never take spirits."

Antonia was tempted to offer a glass of milk but confined herself to asking, "How am I deserving of the pleasure of your call, ma'am?"

Julia was silent for a moment, gazing thoughtfully at Antonia. "My nephew . . . ," she began uncertainly, and stopped. Her gaze shifted to the bowl of yellow roses on the mantel.

"Kedrington is a hopeless romantic," she remarked, apropos of nothing. "You wouldn't think so to listen to him, I grant you, and Lord knows where he gets it from. Not from my line. In my day, a young man ran off to foreign parts when he'd done something disgraceful at home, not from some misplaced longing for adventure. Nevertheless, he went, and I'd have thought age and experience would have cured him by now, but no. He is stubborn as well, and finally having exhausted his bent for the exotic, he must needs involve himself in other people's quixotic adventures—encouraged, unfortunately, by that flibbertigibbet Hester. You have only to mention a case of injustice or ingratitude or unrequited love to either of them, and they're off to set all to rights. Kedrington lacks only a white horse and a suit of armour to complete the farce. Not that he'd care two pins to be laughed at, but he may one day be rebuffed, and he'd find that less easy to stomach. I know I should." Julia sighed.

Antonia, against her volition feeling sympathy toward her, leaned forward to touch her hand. But Julia's mind was elsewhere; for a moment she seemed unaware of Antonia's presence or of her surroundings. Antonia sat back to await her return.

She had not entirely comprehended Julia's meaning, but her words had shed new light on a matter Antonia had deliberately locked into the dark of her mind. She had long ago observed Kedrington's indifference to the pinpricks of the workaday world and his amused acceptance of its follies. Since this attitude was the apparent if not the ultimate source of his disastrous charm, she had not hitherto looked for any other. Now she wondered how much Julia knew about her relationship with Kedrington, if she might be warning her that she could not live up to his expectations — not knowing that so far as Antonia was concerned, he could have none.

Presently, Julia came to herself and fixed her eagle stare on her hostess. "Well, madam, as you may have gathered, I do not approve of this particular streak of madness in my nephew — but there it is, and it will not be overcome as long as he remains incapable of letting the world turn without giving it a push now and then. His only hope is to marry some romantic fool as hopeless as he is, but he will not help himself as he is so eager to help others."

She paused to study Antonia's expression — which that lady schooled only by digging her nails into the hands she kept clutched in her lap. What *did* Julia want of her? Even if she did not know about Charles, why should she think, as apparently she did, that Antonia had anything to say to the matter? It was soon revealed, however, that Julia knew more than Antonia imagined.

"The fact is," Julia said, "that a certain rumour has reached my ears — no, not a rumour, for I lend no credence to those, but a piece of news which has the ring of truth. Will you tell me, please, if you are indeed engaged to be married to Mr Charles Kenyon?"

Antonia replied coolly, "I am indeed so, ma'am. May I ask how you came by the information? It is not yet generally known."

"Then you have not yet sent an announcement to the newspapers?" Julia countered, disregarding Antonia's question.

"Not as yet."

Antonia would have stopped at that, but Julia's look was compelling, and she found herself, much to her annoyance, explaining, "This was meant to be Isabel's season, not my own. I'm sure Charles and I are both too old to indulge in such nonsense in any case."

"Very commendable," Julia remarked dryly. She studied the handle of her parasol intently for a moment, then abruptly stood up and, with the air of one washing her hands of the matter, said, "Well, madam, it is your error, if you choose to make it."

Antonia flared up. "Pardon me, Mrs Wilmot, but what I choose to do, in error or not, is hardly your affair!"

Julia glanced sharply at her and changed her tack. "Are you in love with him?" she demanded.

"Our . . . our affection is of long standing."

Inexplicably, Julia unbent again, and sighed. "My dear, you are perfectly right to wish me and my meddling ways at Jericho—as my graceless grandson would say. I apologise for my manners. My only excuse is that there is someone very dear to me who does have an interest in the matter—no, do not look like that. He knows nothing of my visit here, and I have no intention of telling him of it. Understand only that my concern must be with his happiness, and I would never forgive myself if I did not seize every opportunity to do what I may to forward that happiness. However, I see that there is nothing further I need . . . I may do here. I am certain I wish you very happy, my dear. Good day."

She departed as abruptly as she had come, and Mrs Curtiz, who met her in the hall and saw her out, brought a puzzled expression into the drawing room a moment later.

"What did she want?"

"I am not perfectly sure," Antonia said, upon consideration. "She asked me if it were true that Charles and I are to be married, and wished me happy."

Mrs Curtiz raised an eyebrow at this intelligence, but made only a noncommittal response and seemed to dismiss the matter. "Is there anything you would like from Grafton House, my dear? I am just on my way there. Or would you care to accompany me?"

"Thank you, no, Imogen. I think I will stay and finish that new collar for Isabel's blue morning dress. She may want to wear it tomorrow. Did you know about this expedition to Richmond Park, by the way? Apparently it has been planned for some weeks, but I don't remember anyone mentioning it before."

"I daresay it was simply forgotten, what with one thing and another," Mrs Curtiz replied in what Antonia could not help feeling was an uncharacteristically inconsiderate way. "They've asked me to go along. It will be just Clory and Harley Chatham-Hill and Isabel and myself—oh, and Oliver as well. Quite unexceptional, you see—and more than likely supremely uninspiring."

Somewhat mollified by the notion that she would be spared the romps of a crowd of bumptious youngsters, Antonia remarked only that if Imogen were going, there would be no need for her also to play gooseberry. She repressed her initial absurdly childish feeling of having been left out of a treat and bade Imogen as cheery a good-day as she could contrive.

Really, she reflected later as she sat dutifully stitching, she could not imagine why she had become so easily overset lately by the least little thing. She and Charles had patched up their quarrel—at least, she thought they had done so, but now she came to think of it she realised that she had been the one to do the patching, overcome by a distinct feeling of guilt over her unladylike conduct in the park.

Dinner that night was a decided setback, however. Charles was in high good humour, expatiating over the boiled turnips—Antonia wondered if he had always had such pedestrian preferences in food—on the new "subterranean farms." Charles and his father were going off in the morning to inspect one of the deposits of surface coal which had reportedly been discovered under a parsonage in Kent, and Charles had waxed enthusiastic over the fortunes being made by the men who had bought up such properties during the war and developed them. He quoted output quantities and annual profits, not to mention the rents and royalties taken in by the owners of the land, who had nothing to do now but sit back and count them.

"That is how fortunes are being made now," he said, punctuating his discourse with a slice of glazed ham on a fork. "Not in farming—that is as uncertain nowadays as speculating on 'change. Wasted effort, too, when there are so many more secure ways—not just in mining either—to invest money."

"I'm sure you are not alone in thinking so, Charles," Antonia said. "But a good many modern minds are turning back to agriculture as well. Ned Fletcher says—"

"Ned's idea—pardon me, my dear—of good management is to wrest every possible penny out of the land and then to plough every one right back in again. Very conscientious of him, I don't doubt, but that leaves no room for options, no alternatives in case of—God forbid—another war, or even a drop in the price of wool."

"Ned is the first man in the county to hear of every modern improvement, every economy!"

"Yes, yes—and he practises them. But don't you see, my dear, that is like painting a corpse. You still see life on the surface, but everything underneath is decaying. Have at least a part of your land surveyed for possible mineral deposits. That's the way to ensure your keeping it."

"It isn't my land," Antonia reminded him, thanking the heavens that Carey would no more think of tearing up one of his fields in search of coal or copper than she would, but not saying so to Charles.

She looked to Carey, seeking confirmation of her faith in him, but her brother appeared not to have been attending to Charles at all—and, as sometimes in the past, not even according him the courtesy to listen before disagreeing. Rather, he had been attempting to make Isabel lose her countenance by twisting his own into a variety of absurd positions—a game they had often played when Isabel was a child. Just as Antonia glanced their way, Isabel succumbed to the giggles she had been holding in. Charles glowered at Carey without interrupting himself to point out the sin Carey seemed so blissfully unaware of, and indeed compounded by imitating perfectly Charles's glower—at which point Antonia herself choked back a laugh. Then she, too, broke into open merriment when Carey began digging into his turnips with a technique remarkably similar to shovelling aside earth to get at a seam of coal. In another minute, all three Fairfaxes had fallen into the kind of uncontrolled whoops they had been used to indulge in at Wyckham, where Anthony had been the one to feel obliged to disapprove their juvenile behaviour.

Anthony, however, had always ended by joining in the laughter. Charles did no such thing. Instead, he rose with great dignity, begged their pardons with the excuse of some pressing work to attend to, and took himself off without his sweet or his port. Antonia took him this latter to the study an hour later and found herself once again apologising and Charles once again sweeping aside her contrition and saying that there was no need whatever for an apology. How could he be offended at anything his lovely Antonia found amusement in? He kissed her gently on the forehead and suggested that she had doubtless overtired herself and would feel more like herself after a good night's rest. Antonia could not help thinking that "more like herself" was what she had felt giggling over the dinner table. It was a lowering thought.

She needn't expect them back before three days, Philip informed her on taking leave of her the next morning; they would more than likely look in on a family friend in Tunbridge Wells. Antonia could not help but feel a little relieved to hear it, for she had slept poorly after all and knew that nothing would be more likely to result from her weariness than another quarrel with Charles. She would have enjoyed a day in the country herself; London had never seemed noisier than last night, when she had been jerked from her fitful dozing regularly on every hour by the cry of the watchman. But since it was not to be granted her, she must settle for a restful day at home alone.

Even Carey had deserted her for some masculine pursuit typical of those he had plunged into on his return, apparently to make up in a few weeks the deprivations of years. Not that anyone could accuse Carey of neglecting his duty, of course. Like a fresh breeze through the house, his return had caused Antonia to wake up to what she had not realised had become a routine. Her brother's manner had not changed in six years, but he was more accustomed to discipline now, so that between sparring contests at the Fives Court, and frequent visits to the Cockpit Royal, he was quietly but effectively taking over his duties as head of the family.

On the whole, Antonia did not begrudge him his position, but she found it somewhat disconcerting in the particular. When she asked Belding to order a case of port to replenish their stock, she found that Carey had already seen to it. When Isabel went to her uncle instead of herself to seek approval of a new bonnet, Antonia could not but feel a little hurt, even though she herself now turned the household accounts over to Carey for his weekly approval. The readiness with which he despatched the tasks she had formerly assumed herself, and the skill, acquired in the army, with which he handled the household staff, met with Antonia's admiration, but she soon began to feel somewhat superfluous. She was not accustomed to being a lady of leisure.

There was also the risk she did not care to run, of coming to resent Carey for what in the end was only the natural course of events. The possibility seemed remote, but even having thought of it, Antonia felt, brought it closer. Carey, of course, could have no such fancy. He had fallen back into his old life as easily as into the huge feather bed provided for his comfort—for unlike Kedrington, he had no nostalgic preference for camp beds and, since he was waited on slavishly, little effort on his part was required to satisfy his every whim.

It only added to Antonia's feelings of uselessness that Imogen, now being squired about by Philip Kenyon and Lord Alvanley, required Antonia's company far less frequently nowadays. And Isabel, likewise caught up in a social whirl, scarcely was able to spare even the few moments of her customary early-morning visit to Antonia's bedroom. Isabel could scarcely be faulted for this—her aunt would have been the last to deny her her new friends—but Antonia missed their talks and the small moments together of their quieter days at Wyckham. She could not, moreover, help feeling herself something of a failure with regard to Isabel. She had urged her niece to come to London, against Isabel's inclination, hoping that she would enjoy her season as any pretty young girl should, only to have Isabel conduct it in her own quiet, competent way, with no help whatever from her much-distracted aunt, and to have her, as a result, grow further away than ever.

This left only Charles to whom Antonia's interests were paramount, a situation which ought to have been wholly satisfying. Yet Charles had, unintentionally no doubt, turned things around so that Antonia felt it was up to her to look after Charles's interests, particularly in the face of the gentle but general disapproval of her acceptance of his proposal. It was doubtless selfish of her to wish to be cosseted herself, and now and again assured of her worth, and treated like a treasured prize won after long, hard combat. But Charles was no hero, as she had once imagined him, no Galahad. She told herself that he was more than that; he was the comfortable life she had always taken for granted and that had been so nearly torn from her. Charles would make her comfortable for the rest of her days. She would always know what to expect from him; there would be no upheavals, no surprises. She did not understand why this comforting prospect depressed her so.

So it was that when Mrs Curtiz returned from her errand, she found Antonia brooding over Julia Wilmot's visit in a mood bordering on the megrims and certainly marked by a surplus of self-pity. Imogen appeared not to notice this, however, instead pulling off her bonnet, ringing for tea, and delivering a brisk account of her exceedingly uninteresting—in Antonia's sulky view—errand.

"I wish you would not be so hearty, Imogen," she said at last, somewhat querulously. "It is enough to give one a fit of the dismals."

"It seems to me that you are already well along in one," Mrs Curtiz observed unsympathetically. "Are you enjoying it?"

Antonia was about to wax indignant, but finally thought better of it. "Oh, dear! I shall be turning into another Maria anytime now. What a dispiriting prospect."

"I think you would best avoid any more such thoughts, my dear; indeed, this solemn cast of mind you have lately adopted does not at all become you. Can I not divert you with some more frivolous amusement?"

"But it is my very frivolity that has brought me to this pass. No one takes me seriously and, indeed, I cannot have a high opinion of myself just now either."

Sensing an imminent relapse into self-castigation, Imogen turned the subject by the simple expedient of announcing that she wished to do so.

"I forbid you absolutely to mention anything having to do with your own or anyone else's mental processes for the next twenty-four hours. No, let us say thirty-six hours, for I daresay we shall be back very late."

"Back from where?" Antonia asked, feeling a flicker of interest in this mysterious statement and eagerly fanning it.

"Vauxhall. What do you say to attending the masque there tomorrow night? We can all go—make a proper family party of it."

"Oh, that would be nice! But—Vauxhall? Oh no, I daren't. Charles would never approve."

"Pooh," said Imogen to Charles's approval. "He is not here, and will never know. Everyone will be masked, after all, so that no one will be likely to carry tales back to him, either."

Such was the state of Antonia's mind that the assurance of Charles's not knowing of her indiscretion seemed to obviate the necessity of her staying virtuously at home—and missing all the fun. And suddenly, fun seemed very important. She did not think, now she considered it, that she had truly enjoyed herself at anything for weeks.

"I shall wear that Arab costume I wore once to Wyckham and that you all enjoyed so much," Imogen went on. "I came across it in an old trunk that was sent down here in mistake for another, and it is still in wearable condition."

This effectively clinched the matter for Antonia. Forgetting Charles's opinion and her previous lamentable association with Vauxhall Gardens—forgetting everything but the fun of dressing up for a party—she asked Imogen, "What else have you got in that trunk?"

If Imogen's smile at her eagerness was a trifle smug, Antonia did not notice it. Nor did she question the mysterious appearance of Imogen's trunkful of wonders acquired in her travels and the fortuitous presence therein of a Spanish dancer's costume complete with mantilla and high-heeled shoes which fit her perfectly. So determined was she to sink herself utterly in dissipation, in fact, that when Isabel returned home and was bidding Octavian Gary a discreet farewell outside the door, Antonia opened a window and hallooed loudly for him to come in and hear all about the proposed treat, which he was immediately invited to join in. If this was to be her last fling, Antonia told herself, disregarding the amused stares directed at her, she would at least see that Isabel enjoyed herself with the escort of her choice. As for herself—why, she would be happy to share Carey with Imogen.

So saying, she pulled Isabel off to show her a perfectly elegant Chinese gown she had unearthed from Imogen's bottomless trunk. Octavian and Mrs Curtiz exchanged a speaking look.

= 16 =

By the next evening, Antonia was quite caught up in the spirit of their outing. All three ladies were soon rummaging gaily through the myriad possibilities for costumes they had to choose from. Isabel seemed uncharacteristically delighted at the notion of dressing herself up from out of a trunk and attempting to disguise her identity from even her best friends; Antonia made up her mind that, what with her crowded calendar, Isabel was sorely in need of some light diversion of this kind—which notion served to give Antonia's own childlike enthusiasm some other justification than a mere selfish thirst for frivolity.

In the end, Antonia decided that the Spanish dancing costume was best for her, despite its lamentably snug fit across the hips. The black high-heeled shoes which matched it, on the other hand, gave her extra inches that were undeniably attractive—and served to balance the width of the skirt, so that Antonia felt dashing indeed, particularly with a lovely fringed shawl flung over her shoulders and a black half mask which served to disguise her most inappropriate hair colour.

Isabel, after changing her mind a dozen times, settled on the embroidered Chinese silk gown her aunt had first chosen for her, which had a high neck and elaborate closings all the way down the front. Imogen modelled for them the identical flowing white Arab robes which she had worn to Anthony's party years before, and declared that the matching veil would be much more comfortable than the masks the others wore for the same purpose.

Octavian, dressed as a gondolier, came to call for them at ten o'clock—an hour, Carey declared, that he was rapidly becoming accustomed to and, so long as no one roused him out of bed too precipitously the next morning, one that he was willing to adopt as a permanent way of life. Carey wore

187

his uniform, but drew the line at a mask, saying that since he had never touched a razor in Spain, he would not now be recognised clean-shaven.

The merry little party crossed the river from Westminster in a scull, accompanied by a boatload of musicians to play alongside, and entered the gardens by the Water Gate. It was then a pleasant stroll, through a grove of elm and sycamore trees which sheltered the orchestra pavilion, to the most secluded of the three graceful colonnades of pavilions where boxes could be rented for the evening and dinner ordered. Mr Gary, efficient as always, had obtained a box that had a fine view of the grove, where the musicians were already playing among the twinkling lights that festooned the trees throughout the gardens.

Seated in their box, they could also observe, to their right, the beginnings of the several walks that led into the more wooded parts of the gardens. It was not until they were all seated, however, and Carey had ordered them a sample of every delicacy offered for their supper, with a magnum of champagne—"to start with"—that Antonia made note of an odd circumstance.

"There are chairs here for six people," she remarked, "but we are only five."

There was a brief pause before anyone ventured to respond to this, but then Imogen said offhandedly, "Oh, we hoped that Kedrington would be able to join us, but as it was not certain that he could, I did not think to mention it to you before."

"That is *not* why you did not mention it!" Antonia said, levelling an accusing gaze on her.

"But why else, love?" Isabel asked, all innocence. Antonia shifted her look to her niece, but could read no hidden meaning in her face. Carey gazed blandly off into the trees, not meeting his sister's eyes. Before she was able to put her suspicions into words, however, Lord Kedrington himself arrived on the scene.

For a moment, she could only stare at him. He was wearing a black biretta and black cloak, which he removed with a graceful flourish to reveal a long black-buttoned priest's soutane beneath. That the effect was considerably diminished by the spark of devilment in the viscount's eyes did not prevent Antonia from exclaiming impulsively, "So *that* rumour at least was true!"

He laughed and pulled the empty chair out to sit down, and Antonia's fascinated gaze moved from the black hair falling slightly over his high collar down to the broad, sun-bronzed hands adorned only by his signet ring.

"I trust you left off your ring when you genuinely intended to travel incognito?"

"My heart, there is nothing more incognito in Spain than a priest, ring or no."

It seemed to Antonia that the look in his lordship's grey eyes would have deceived no one into thinking him a man of pious principles, whatever he wore. She was likewise a little startled to discover that she liked him in this guise—not that Kedrington had ever been conventional, but she had come, she realised, to take him for granted as the man of fashion he had once told her he had set out to make of himself. That he had succeeded all too well in doing so was evident from her reaction to this unexpected change in him, and she caught herself remembering, too, their mild flirtation at Wyckham and even his absurd proposals. She wondered if she were still capable of coaxing one out of him.

Suddenly, she flushed and lowered her eyes. What was she thinking of? Just because Charles was not with her did not mean that she could behave in a way he had made all too clear to her he did not approve; it would be too disgraceful in her!

"Do try a slice of this lovely ham," Imogen said to her just then, transferring a piece of it to her plate with a fork, and Antonia realised that these jumbled thoughts had passed through her mind in no more time than it took for the waiter to place a large platter of artistically arranged cold meats, fruits, and sweetmeats before them. Reassured that she had not made a fool of herself, she accepted Imogen's offering and said she might try a bit of the chicken as well.

"You are eating like a trooper, lieutenant," Kedrington admonished Carey, who had helped himself to a liberal portion of everything. "Don't they feed you at home?"

"They feed me civilised portions at home," Carey said, unabashed. "This ham is sliced so thin you could inhale it."

"Which I've no doubt you will."

Carey cast him an aggrieved look, but moderated his gluttony some-what and was wholly diverted, a moment later, by the approach of

Lieutenant Fitzroy and two companions, who greeted the entire party cheerfully.

"Ho, Kedrington! Where'd you steal that unlikely get-up from?"

"I'll have you know, Fitz, that it was come by legitimately."

"Well, since you ain't been ordained so far as I know, you must have wheedled it out of the superior at the convent in Burgos—or was it the abbess on the other side of town?"

The militia thought this a great joke, but Kedrington only abjured the lieutenant to mind his tongue, if he knew how. Fitzroy proved that he did by being charmingly gallant to the ladies before taking his leave and dragging Carey away from his supper with the promise of showing him a mechanical marvel called the cascade, which purported to imitate precisely the sound and appearance of a real waterfall.

Octavian refilled everyone's champagne glass, and they settled down to listen to the music of the orchestra, which was happily distant enough to permit intimate conversation. They were not so out of the way in their box, however, that all the world did not seem to pass by, and the river of fashionable strollers—adorned in every variety of fancy dress from togas to red Indian buckskins—soon yielded up another friend in the person of Miss Hester Coverley, escorted by Lord Alvanley, who bowed low to all the ladies and took up a post near enough to Mrs Curtiz to permit a whispered conversation between them.

Miss Coverley deftly manipulated the hoop of her Marie Antoinette ball gown to assume Carey's vacant chair beside Kedrington and, temporarily forgetting the presence of others, exclaimed to him, "Duncan, dearest, I have just heard that all is on its way to being settled about Barbara! My dear, how wonderful! However did you persuade Junius to accept it?"

"Even Junius will bow to a *fait accompli,* my dear Aunt, if it is sufficiently sweetened to allow him to bend his notions of honour. But all this is of no interest to our friends here. Accept a glass of champagne, if you will, by way of celebration, but do let us reserve explanations for another time."

All this was, to the contrary, of considerable interest to Antonia, but she would have died before revealing her rampant curiosity, so she only smiled companionably at Miss Coverley and made up her mind to call on her first thing the next morning. Meanwhile, that lady embarked on her usual comprehensive summary of all the persons she had encountered in the brief stroll she had thus far enjoyed through the gardens—and whom she had had no difficulty in identifying.

"But we have not yet visited the rotunda, where I believe some new paintings have been hung since our last visit. Imogen, dear, will you not come with us to view them?"

This suggestion received Lord Alvanley's vocal endorsement, and very shortly the party in the supper box was reduced to four. It struck Antonia that this was becoming entirely too cosy, but when she glanced at Kedrington, he gave her a bland look that conveyed nothing. Conversation lagged somewhat, as Octavian and Isabel found more eloquence in each other's eyes than in mere words. Antonia attempted once or twice to introduce a subject, only to receive no assistance whatever from any of the others. Kedrington, in fact, seemed to be taking a perverse delight in disobliging her. She scowled at him and received an impish smile in return. She shrugged and sipped again at her champagne.

It was only a matter of minutes before, not at all to Antonia's astonishment, Isabel and Octavian declared that they would promenade off their supper on the Italian Walk, and deserted them with no further ado. Antonia thought that she saw Octavian slip his hand into Isabel's as soon as their backs were turned, but she found she could not find this at all improper. Indeed, she smiled after them and thought that they were much wiser than their elders, having seen from the beginning how matters would conclude between them.

Kedrington showed no signs of taking similar liberties with her hand, despite their convenient solitude, and, feeling a little giddy, she was on the point of asking why he did not, when he dampened her giddiness somewhat.

"And where is Charles when you need him?" he asked in a flippant tone which sounded nevertheless decidedly anxious.

"He and Uncle Philip went to look at a coal mine in Kent. I don't know when they will be back."

And she didn't care, she told herself sulkily. Almost as if he had read her thought, Kedrington laughed.

"In Kent, of all places! I had no notion he was interested in such things."

"Philip heard about it from a friend of his, I believe," Antonia told him, thoroughly bored by the subject now. "I must say, I shan't be sorry if it turns out there is nothing in it."

Kedrington remarked that this was often true of speculative mines, but then dropped the subject, much to Antonia's relief. She did not want to think about Charles tonight. She was not precisely sure what she preferred to think about instead, and so determined to clear her mind of all thought. Champagne bubbles were a remarkably efficient means to achieve this, she was beginning to discover.

She could not have said how much time passed in silence—indeed, she would have been hard-put to say how long they had been in the gardens at all—before Kedrington said, "Perhaps we had better see if we can find the young people. Unless you would rather view the delights of the cascade or the rotunda?"

The notion of mingling with the large crowds surrounding the many entertainments offered at Vauxhall had considerably less appeal than a quiet stroll in its wooded walks, although Antonia could not dredge up very much concern for her niece's whereabouts. Isabel, at least, could take care of herself.

"I think I would rather walk around a bit, please," she said, standing up rather too suddenly and wobbling on her high Spanish heels. Kedrington took her arm, and she noticed that her shoes brought her closer to the level of his mouth than normally, a phenomenon which struck her as filled with fascinating possibilities.

He smiled. "Yes, I think a little fresh air would be in order."

He kept her arm firmly in hand as they made their way down the long Italian Walk, one of the two wide avenues in the gardens. It was connected with the parallel Grand Walk by smaller cross-walks, which were not quite sufficiently dimly lighted that they could not see couples strolling arm-in-arm along them. After some time unbroken by conversation between them, they reached the end of the walk and were obliged either to turn to the left to reach the Grand Walk or to return the way they had come.

"What's down there?" Antonia said, pointing down a walkway to their right, the terminus of which could not be discerned in the dim light. "Let us go that way."

Kedrington hesitated momentarily but, ever obliging, guided her down the Dark Walk.

"Is this where Evelina was accosted?" she asked.

He laughed. "My heart, it is bad enough that you read the novels of Miss Fanny Burney without being able to quote their more salacious passages at will. I had not thought you so abandoned."

"I had not thought you so stuffy," she riposted. "Even Charles would have taken the hint by now."

She could have bitten her tongue before the words had passed her lips. She gasped and looked at him in acute embarrassment. But he did not look in the least disconcerted, nor did he appear to think any the worse of her for her impulsive indiscretion. Quite *unlike* Charles.

He was watching her narrowly, and her intended apology died unspoken. Instead, even more brazenly, she stepped closer to him, until the fringe of her Spanish shawl became entangled with the buttons of his soutane. She had left her mask behind in the box, she remembered now, without regret.

"I am not made of marble, Antonia," he said, a little shakily.

"I hope not."

As if of its own will, his head moved toward hers. His lips brushed her hair, then her cheek. Gently, but as if the gentleness cost him a good deal of effort, he moved his hand to her chin to hold it in place and kissed her very softly on the lips. She was conscious only of a mild astonishment that a mouth which looked so harsh and unyielding should feel so soft on her own.

But then it was gone and, with a total lack of coquetry, she opened her eyes to wonder why, and he saw the disappointment in them. It was as much as he could do not to visit Evelina's fate on her there and then, so he stepped back hurriedly, as if to thrust away the temptation. Startled, she stumbled slightly, turning her foot. The heel of her shoe snapped off and she would have fallen had Kedrington not quickly caught her and held her up.

Laughing a little and nearly as unsteady as she was, he said, "My heart, what has happened to your usual grace?"

She smiled. "I find it has succumbed to a most unusual agitation."

She thought he might kiss her again and raised her face hopefully, but instead he looked around and said with some relief, "There is a bench we may sit down on. Give me your shoe and I will see if I can mend it well enough for you to walk on."

He assisted her to the bench and lowered her gently onto it, then took her proffered shoe and examined it. From somewhere within the folds of his garment he produced a pocket knife, with which he deftly removed a nail and replaced it in a more useful position. In another moment she had put the shoe back on, but neither of them showed any inclination to be on their way. This time, her head having cleared somewhat of the treacherous influence of the wine she had so freely imbibed, she waited for him to speak.

It took a further several minutes, but at last he said, with some effort, "You may have noticed, Antonia, that I have not proposed marriage to you for some time."

"Yes, I must say, I've missed that. One becomes accustomed to the most peculiar things! Have you . . . have you the intention of resuming the practice?"

He refused to be drawn into laughter just yet. "Not if I am to meet with the same resistance."

She hesitated. "I—I do not *wish* to offer any resistance, but I cannot help but be a little wary. I very much fear I am being overly feminine and do not know my own mind, but I must be sure of not repeating my mistakes."

"Antonia, I was defeated at the start of our relationship by your roseate remembrance of your first love. Am I now to be punished because the reality did not measure up to that dream? You are unjust!"

"On, no! I did not mean it to sound like that!" She clutched his arm. "Do not be cross with me, Duncan, I beg you."

She looked at him pleadingly until he relented and smiled once more. "Miss Fairfax, are you by any chance proposing to *me?*"

She blushed and lowered her eyes. "I wish it were not true that I have been terribly foolish. I have done my best to make you unhappy. There is no way I can undo that damage."

"There is. You have unburdened your heart to me. Now make your repentence real by telling Charles the same thing—and by marrying me."

"I—"

"But only if you love me, Antonia. If you do not, all the rest is of no importance."

"Oh, but I do!" she said, and burst into tears, a circumstance for which his lordship would ordinarily have rebuked her severely, but now he found it much more to his liking to take her in his arms and comfort her, and then, when he had dried her tears, to kiss her again—not so gently nor so briefly this time.

When at last she emerged breathlessly from his embrace and looked up at him with a mixture of delight and surprise in her eyes, he laughed and said, "My heart, had I known you were subject to such violent changes of mood, I am not at all sure I would have accepted your offer! For such a reasonable man as myself, a volatile bride might not be at all the thing. I wonder if I ought to reconsider?"

"Monster!" she protested, laughing. "You are not in the least reasonable, but merely stubborn, as I admit I am myself. But do you not think we may be able to detect, and therefore to modify, that fault in each other?"

"I doubt that we shall find it necessary. I feel certain that we shall always have well-meaning friends and relations—such as my future brother-in-law!—to point them out to us. Naturally, I cannot help but be grateful for his interference thus far—for I've no doubt our meeting here tonight was of his contriving—since it has produced such an end as a good friend would wish, but I cannot feel I can tolerate much of the same in future!"

"You *are* very good friends with Carey, are you not? Did you meet in Spain? Is that it?"

"Yes, that's it."

"I wish you had told me. Or that he had."

"Again, my stubbornness was at fault. I wanted you to accept me for myself, not as a friend of your brother."

"As if I would be so easily swayed."

"Yes, I realised you could not be when you accepted Charles Kenyon in spite of everyone—and in the face of Carey's obvious dislike of him. That was stubborn of you—but courageous, too."

"It was nothing of the sort," she said flatly. "I was simply jealous of Barbara Neville."

"Bab?" He did not understand at first. "Of course! I pledged Carey to secrecy on that head as well, fool that I was. Antonia, I never had any interest whatsoever in that quarter, and Bab never had eyes for anyone but Neil Gary, Octavian's brother. They met when Neil was home on leave two years ago, but the two fathers opposed the match—Henry Neville because the Garys are poor, obscure, and not worthy to kiss the hand of his only daughter, and Constant Gary because Barbara is a Roman Catholic and because his brother Junius, who controls the pursestrings, threatened to cut Neil off. Petty objections, perhaps, and easily overcome if only the elders could have been brought to speak to one another.

"I chose to exaggerate the difficulties, as if there had been murder done or treachery committed between the families, to make the task more worth my while. But even if just cause was lacking, it took a good deal of persuasion on my part, and finally a secret marriage—last month in Dover—to break down their stubbornness. Since most of my family was ranged on old Neville's side, the, ah . . . negotiations had to be clandestine. It was always only Neil I wanted to help, and by the time he and Bab were married, it seemed as if I'd already lost you, so that I never thought telling you about it would serve any purpose."

He smiled at a memory and added, "Julia didn't think it was too late, however. She told me only yesterday that I should not give up, but I had no idea she knew anything about it and so could not share her confidence."

"Then that is why she came to see me. She was . . . reconnoitering! But I cannot imagine how she guessed—that is, I did not know myself that I would change my mind."

"She came to you?"

"Yes. I was amazed to see her, to say the least of it. But she merely asked me if it were true about Charles, and when I said it was, she wished me happy and left as suddenly as she had come. I can only suppose there was something—some hesitation—in the way I spoke which told her, before I knew it myself, that I would never marry Charles."

"Why *did* you accept him?"

"Oh, he was a . . . a child's dream come true. I had loved him as a girl and never thought that time—time apart—would be bound to change us both. I think I began to see almost immediately that it had, but I thrust the truth aside, telling myself that it didn't matter because what I admired most in Charles—strength, generosity, dependability—he still had in abundance. But I could never make a joke that he understood, or make him see that in all those years I had learned to think for myself. Nor could I accustom myself to the idea of living in London for the rest of my life, with only Christmas visits to Wyckham to renew my soul. At first, I thought *you* were so town-bred as to never leave the world you seemed so comfortable inhabiting."

"My heart, why do you suppose I bought Windeshiem—and, I might add, sent an army of servants and carpenters and glaziers there to refurbish the place?"

"You bought Windeshiem? Have you meant all along to live there?"

"No, I had hoped all along that *you* would live there! I suppose the redecorating was a desperate attempt to convince myself that it really would happen. If not, it would have been a waste of a great deal of money, for I would certainly never have set foot in the place if you had married Charles after all."

"Oh, Duncan, what *will* I tell Charles? He really believed he was being generous to give me another chance; he'll never forgive *another* disaster in Vauxhall Gardens. Indeed, I'm convinced that is why Carey chose this spot—but it is too shabby to treat Charles like this!"

"Would you go through with the wedding, then, merely to avoid behaving shabbily?"

"Don't be idiotish."

"Then tell him simply, as you've told me—well, perhaps not precisely as you told me!—that you have made a mistake. Even Charles should see that, once it is pointed out to him."

"But it's not even the first time—"

He sighed and kissed her again. "Really, my heart, I have no wish to hear any more of your past amours! If they continue to weigh so heavily on your conscience, unburden yourself to a diary—not, I beg, to me. Besides, there are unidentifiable objects falling on us while we sit under this tree. I suggest we go on, and put the waiting conspirators out of their suspense."

They rose, but Antonia had long since forgotten her loose heel, and no sooner did she put her weight on it than it broke off again.

"Oh, dear! I'm so sorry, but I'm afraid you are going to have to mend it again."

"Certainly not," he said. "I have many interests in life, but developing a skill at cobbling is not one of them. I have a better idea."

So saying, he slipped his arm under her legs and picked her up as easily as if she weighed nothing at all—which she was painfully aware was far from the case. But not daring to struggle for fear of doing him an injury, she could only laugh.

"Oh, put me down! This is too absurd."

"Not at all. Imagine the delight of our plotting friends when I carry you back like a Roman abducting a Sabine. Carey will be certain to appreciate the gesture, even if you do not."

Unfortunately, the first person they encountered as Kedrington rounded the turn into the Italian Walk was not Antonia's brother but her former betrothed—understandably, since he was unaware of his changed status, astounded to see his much admired lady in a position he could not help but recognise as compromising.

"Bother!" Kedrington said, inadequately, and came to a halt. Gently, he lowered his burden to the ground. He kept a firm grip on her for a moment, until it occurred to him that if he removed Antonia's other shoe, she could at least walk steadily, if to the ruination of her silk stockings. However, the sight of Viscount Kedrington calmly lifting Miss Fairfax's foot and removing the shoe while she balanced herself by gripping his shoulders with both hands incensed Charles even more than the initial shocking sight had done.

"Antonia!" he uttered in ominous accents.

Up until then infinitely more intrigued by watching Kedrington's ministrations to her person than in ascertaining the reason for them, Antonia had not at first even seen Charles, and now she turned her head only to say, mildly, "Oh, hullo, Charles. What are you doing here?"

Kedrington's muffled laugh was lost in Charles's wrathful "Antonia!"

"Oh, do stop saying 'Antonia' in that nonsensical way, Charles. I broke my heel, that is all. Lord Kedrington has been so kind as to . . . er, to—"

"To take her off your hands, Kenyon. I'm sure you understand."

Kedrington smiled amiably at Charles, whose powers of speech seemed to have fled, for he could only look from one to the other of them in blank astonishment. He looked oddly out of place in his well-cut but, by comparison with the colourful garb all around him, drab grey superfine coat and pantaloons. Since no one else ventured to say anything either, he at last muttered in a hoarse voice, "I will speak with you another time, Antonia," before turning abruptly and walking away down the path at a stiff, agitated gait.

There was a moment's pause before Antonia said, "Yes, but what *was* he doing here?"

Kedrington turned toward her and studied her face. "Are you still tipsy, my heart?"

She shook her head. Nothing seemed to jar loose inside it, so she said, "No, I don't think so."

"Good. Then let me remind you that you have just promised to marry me instead of Charles. Did you mean it?"

She tried to concentrate her mind on the question, to convince him that she was not being impulsive and frivolous this time. She even tried to remember a gentler Charles, one who had loved her sincerely and might even be hurt at losing her. But the present sensation of Kedrington's arms around her and the closeness of his lips to her own were too strong. The image of Charles Kenyon faded from her mind, and she smiled up at her true hero, the answer to his question alight in her eyes.

They were not at all surprised, on returning to the pavilion, to discover that the rest of their party had quite vanished, so that Kedrington was obliged to see Antonia home. It was a long time before they could bring themselves to say good night, and still longer before Antonia fell asleep that night, with the memory of Kedrington's laughter—oh, it had been so long since she had enjoyed laughing with anyone!—echoing in her ears.

She came down to breakfast the next morning, however, to find the entire family, and Octavian Gary, waiting for her. None of them appeared in the least anxious or remorseful, but they had the grace to say nothing until she smiled, then laughed, and finally told them roundly that they were entirely shameless for having deceived her so basely. At that, Isabel flung herself into her aunt's arms, saying happily, "I knew you would not be angry with us!"

There followed a merry round of hugs and thanks and apologies— mainly on Antonia's part for having reduced them to conspiracy through her foolishness. After a time, however, it occurred to her that one friend who might have been expected to be present was missing.

"Where is Clory?" she asked, having been informed by her Uncle Philip that Charles had gone off in a huff—which Philip took no share in—back to Kent after discovering that the unexpected business which had called him back to town had been a fabrication on Carey's part.

The conspirators exchanged glances, but it was a long moment before Isabel said, "Clory and Oliver have decided to take a jaunt into the countryside—to Kent, I believe."

"Kent?" Antonia said, bewildered.

Isabel nodded. Carey grinned. "Right! To Tunbridge Wells. To . . . ah, comfort Charles. Lord, I wish I could be there to see the Nabob's face when Clory catches up with him!"

Antonia stared at her brother, comprehension dawning. "Carey, how *could* you!"

"Me? What did I do? I don't even know who's going to come off worse out of this campaign—Clory or Charles!"

Everyone enjoyed a hearty laugh at this, and indulged in speculation on the effect the news would have on Clory's many beaux. This led to further hilarity when Carey imaginatively described the shattered reactions of the various mamas who had indulged hopes of Kedrington's favouring their daughters, with the result that when Antonia told Mrs Curtiz that next week would suit her nicely for the wedding, no one immediately noticed the satisfied expression which settled on Imogen's face.

"Then Isabel may be married out of Windeshiem."

Antonia smiled and nodded.

"And I may leave the details to you while Philip and I are on the Continent. We shall, of course, return in time for Isabel's wedding."

Antonia's head jerked around, and she gazed in amazement at her friend, who was calmly pouring herself another cup of tea. "Imogen—Philip—do you mean to tell me . . . no, I cannot credit it!"

"I don't know why not," Mr Kenyon said. "You've swallowed taller tales than that lately."

Antonia rose to hug Imogen and wish them both happy as well, but then she sighed and said she hoped there would be no more such agitating news that day, for she had more than enough to suffice her. But that night she joined Carey and Isabel and Mrs Curtiz in a raucous game of backgammon which, because she was too happy to think of sleep, lasted far into the night. When at last they did go up to bed, however, Antonia stopped her brother on the stairs to kiss him good night and to ask, "Carey, how did you and Duncan meet? He was not in the army, was he?"

"No, he was with a band of *guerilleros,* near Salamanca. He saved my life there, Tonia. I'd got caught on the wrong side of the Guarena, when we'd had to ford it in a hurry. My horse had been shot out from under me. But the *guerilleros* raced in between us and the French, and Lobo picked me up like I was a baby and carried me across the river on his horse."

"Then I have even more reason to be grateful to him than I knew."

"Don't tell him I told you. He has the greatest aversion to being thought a hero."

Antonia smiled. "Then you may expect to have to tell me everything you know about him yourself—for he is my hero now, too!"

If you have enjoyed this book and would like to receive details of other Walker Regency romances, please write to:

Regency Editor
Walker and Company
720 Fifth Avenue
New York, NY 10019